FRAUKE SCHEUNEMANN

Frauke Scheunemann was born in Dusseldorf in 1969. She received a doctorate in law, then completed her training at North German Broadcasting and worked as a journalist and press spokesperson. She has been writing full time since 2002, and has published a series of highly successful novels together with her sister, Wiebke Lorenz, under the collective pseudonym of "Anne Hertz." Frauke Scheunemann lives with her husband and their four children in an old parsonage in Hamburg.

SHELLEY FRISCH

Shelley Frisch holds a PhD in German Literature from Princeton University. Her many acclaimed translations include biographies of Nietzsche, Einstein, and Kafka (for which she was awarded the 2007 Modern Language Association Translation Prize). She is the author of *The Lure of the Linguistic.*

Frauke Scheunemann

*Translated from the German
by Shelley Frisch*

CORVUS

First published as Dackelblick in Germany in 2010 by Goldmann Verlag.

First published in trade paperback in Great Britain in 2012 by Corvus,
an imprint of Atlantic Books Ltd.

This paperback edition published in Great Britain in 2013 by Corvus,
an imprint of Atlantic Books Ltd.

Copyright © Frauke Scheunemann, 2010
Translation copyright © Shelley Frisch, 2012

10 9 8 7 6 5 4 3 2 1

A CIP catalogue record for this book is available
from the British Library.

Trade Paperback ISBN: 978 0 85789 314 7
Paperback ISBN: 978 0 85789 316 1
E-book ISBN: 978 0 85789 315 4

Printed and bound by CPI Group (UK) Ltd, Croydon, CR0 4YY

Corvus
An imprint of Atlantic Books Ltd
Ormond House
26–27 Boswell Street
London
WC1N 3JZ

www.corvus-books.co.uk

Anyone who has never had a dog doesn't know what it means to love and to be loved.

—ARTHUR SCHOPENHAUER

I would sooner go without a man than without Felix, my dachshund.　　　—INGRID STEEGER

I am convinced that basically dogs think humans are nuts.

—JOHN STEINBECK

chapter one

What a dive! Sure, I knew it wouldn't be the Ritz, but this accommodation is really the limit. *Beyond the pale*. Musty and dark – and filthy. I try not to focus on my surroundings, but the muck left behind by my predecessors is hard to miss. Clearly, no one's been cleaning up round here for quite some time. It's enough to make me want to howl with rage – how did I wind up in a mess like this? This morning I was in the parlour at Eschersbach Castle, and now this. So I go ahead and howl for real.

'Give it a rest – you're getting on my nerves!' comes the snide remark from off to the left, in the very next second. Right: I forgot to mention the worst part, namely my roommates. Five in all, most of them unbelievably scruffy. It's not just the way they look. These guys are dim-witted commoners, who of course view a noble guy like me as an easy mark. My family tree goes all the way back to 1723; I bet these ignoramuses can't even tell a marquess from a marrow dumpling!

My grandfather appears before me in my mind's eye. '*A von*

Eschersbach is always up at the top, no matter where he may find himself. Don't ever forget that!' he used to tell me. Oh, Grandpa, if you could see me now – I have definitely hit rock bottom. The very thought of this makes me howl even louder. Somebody's got to get me out of here!

'Come on, sweetie, calm down.' A hand reaches through the bars and ruffles the fur behind my ears. 'Soon there'll be a delicious snack, and everything will look brighter. The first day is hard on everyone.'

Hmm, that's a nice voice. I look over to find out who it belongs to. Next to the cage there's a young woman in overalls, smiling at me encouragingly. Her hand smells of ordinary tinned food, but her touch makes me feel more relaxed. I lick her fingers, and she starts to giggle.

'Oh yes, you like that taste, don't you?' she whispers to me.

Oh dear, if she only knew! Up to now, my pampered dachshund palate has tasted only the most delectable fresh offal and tripe. We were served ready-made food only when Emilia, our cook, was sick or on holiday. Just thinking about Emilia gives me a knot in my chest, and I can't help whimpering a bit. When I had to leave her this morning, she cried. God only knows how humans pull that off. For the first time in my life, I would have given anything to be able to shed a few tears too.

'You poor thing, still feeling bad?' the woman in charge of us asks sympathetically. 'Don't worry – you're so cute we're sure to find a new mistress or master for you soon. I promise!' Then she strokes my head again and pulls her hand back through the bars.

I turn round and trot over to the other corner of the cage. A ray of sunshine is casting an inviting little bright spot onto the floor, and I decide to make myself comfy. Of course I'm not the only one to get this idea. Before I can lie down, a huge black something-or-other steps right on my paws.

'Little guy, I think you'd better vamoose to the other side. This is my spot.' To add authority to his pronouncement, his final words crescendo into a hoarse growl.

What a ludicrous cur! Does he really think he can put me to flight? Me? My ancestors went hunting with the last emperor! I shake my head.

'I don't believe,' I retort with as much dignity as I can muster under these adverse circumstances, 'that this establishment takes reservations. I was here before you, so I will lie down on this spot. Kindly allow me to do so.' With these words I push Mr Something-or-Other aside and lie down quickly. He stares at me in stunned amazement. He has surely never encountered such civil resistance. I stretch out contentedly. Turns out Grandpa was right – a von Eschersbach is up even when he's down.

While I lie there musing about when something to eat might be coming along (no matter how modest the meal is sure to be), my sunny spot suddenly darkens. What's that, a cloud? I look up to see what in the world is casting this objectionable shadow – and find myself staring into the face of a rather unpleasant-looking boxer.

He shoves his nose right up to mine and gives off a whiff that really takes my breath away. 'Watch out, you conceited squirt: if you weren't new here, you'd be a dead dog. Our rules apply here, and you'd better stick to them. If my friend Bozo tells you to beat it, then ...' He moves in even closer and nips at me quick as a flash.

Ouch! A sharp pain shoots through my right ear. Help! This guy is a menace to society! I bark my head off. I reckon I've been put with a bunch of militant stray dogs perfectly prepared to resort to violence. But no matter how much I bark, no one comes, not even the young woman in the overalls.

Boxer and Bozo sneer smugly. 'Save your breath. She can't hear you now – she's over by the cats. We could do you in, and no one would come to your rescue. One more dead dog to add to the list in this joint. Who cares?'

I feel the hair on the back of my neck stand on end and a chill run down my spine. Bozo, the black mutt, plants himself in front of me once again. 'So, what was that again? When I say beat it ...'

'I beat it?' I squeak out to finish his sentence.

'Right. Ten out of ten. Good dog.'

Bozo gives my sensitive nose another hard jab with his grubby paw. I jump out of the way in fright and scurry to the other corner of the cage with my legs trembling. Two other dogs are sitting there looking bored and watching the whole thing. Death and destruction appear to be par for the course around here; at any rate, no one cares that I've just been the victim of a crime.

An old pointer moves aside when I settle down next to him. At least he's not going to be the next one to bully me. We sit side by side for a while without saying anything. Then he sidles up to me and whispers in my ear, 'You're better off not starting a fight with those two. They're really dangerous. But if you stay away from them, they usually leave you alone.'

Stay away from them? You've got to be joking. This cage is pretty small, and we're six dogs in here.

It seems that the pointer also just realized that that's out of the question; in any case, he grins at me with a twinkle in his eye and murmurs, 'Hah! Well, do the best you can. By the way, my name is Fritz.'

I don't say anything at first. Things being what they are around here, I don't have much interest in chatting. Instead I lay my head on my paws and watch Bozo and the boxer lounging on my little patch of sun. They're probably making fun of me right now. I actually really like being a dachshund, but at this moment I would much rather be an attack dog. Staffordshire bull terrier, pit bull, or some other breed that screams out *licence to kill*.

'Hey.' Fritz pokes me in the side. 'Don't be sad. The woman in charge here just told you that you're the type humans go for; somebody'll get you out of here soon. And then you'll give those two idiots over there the finger, since it's a sure thing that no one will want *them*.'

I look at Fritz and think about what he's saying. I hope he's right.

•

The next morning I feel knocked out. I hardly got any sleep last night, and when I finally drifted off for five minutes, I had terrible nightmares, about boxers and pit bulls chasing me through the cage, and about huge quantities of horrid-tasting tinned food. I wearily make my way over to Fritz, who's standing at the cage door wagging his tail.

'Morning. How come you're so wide awake and in such a great mood?' I ask him.

'Well, today's visiting day. And if someone comes along in search of a dog, I want to make a good first impression. I'm not as young as I once was, so it's more important than ever to seem active and cheerful. You'll see; humans go for that sort of thing.'

Could he be right? I don't really feel like playing the dachshund who performs on command, but I admit that the thought of settling in here for the long haul is horrifying, so I position myself next to Fritz and start wagging my tail back and forth a little halfheartedly. Do humans actually fall for a cheap trick like this? Unbelievable.

'So tell me, what's your name?' Fritz asks.

'Carl-Leopold,' I reply curtly.

'Carl-Leopold? That's a funny name for a dog.'

'I don't think so. It's a matter of ancestry.' Philistine! What would he know about lovely names? 'I'm a von Eschersbach,' I add proudly.

'Von Eschersbach? Doesn't ring any bells,' Fritz mutters and keeps wagging his tail.

I sigh. He really *is* a philistine. A nice philistine, of course, but he still is one. Just when I'm about to start filling Fritz in on the outlines of my family history, I hear a door slam in the building next to our kennel. I stand rooted to the spot. Not that the sound itself is so loud – after all, the noise level in this place is enough to make a dachshund's delicate ears fall right off. No, I'm intrigued by an indescribable aroma wafting straight towards my nose. Fritz seems to have picked up the scent as well; he's stopped that stupid tail-wagging and is now squeezing his nose through the bars.

'Do you smell that too?' I ask him.

He nods.

'Great, huh?'

'Yeah, amazing!' he agrees.

'That is the most beautiful scent I've ever smelled on a human,' I tell him.

This scent clearly belongs to a human. Dogs pick up on that right away. But what sort of human could this be, with such a good scent? Not the ordinary kind of good, like the smell of pork sausage or chocolate cookies. No, it's more like … I mull it over … yes, that's what it is: like a beautiful summer's day. A jolly summer's day. Very much like flowers, a bit like strawberries, with a hint of peppermint. Fantastic.

'We'll probably be let down the second we see the human. The silliest people always smell the best,' Fritz explains with an expert air.

'Really?' I ask. 'I've got to admit that I've never noticed any connection. I'm not a good judge of that.'

'No, it's true. I'll bet you anything.'

We train our eyes on the door, and there she is, heading our way, towards the cages, followed by the lady in the overalls. Fritz was way off the mark. For a human, she's magnificent, like an angel. She's chatting with the other woman, and laughing while she speaks. Her eyes are laughing too, which looks particularly lovely, and is pretty rare for humans. Most of the time their laughter is no more than a grimace. Which is a pity. I mean, if I could laugh, I'd bring my eyes into it; that looks a whole lot better.

'Hmm, so you're looking for a dog on the small side? And you'd prefer a puppy?'

The angel nods.

Fritz's ears droop as soon as he hears that. He knows it means that, once again, there's no mistress for him. Pointers are far from small – and Fritz hasn't been a puppy for quite some time. He lowers his head. 'Good luck!' he whispers to me, then trots off.

Of course I feel sorry for him – but maybe this is my big chance? I try out Fritz's tactic once more, wagging my tail like crazy and barking in the friendliest tone I can come up with. Sure enough, the two women head straight towards me.

'This one, for instance, is our latest addition. We just got him. He's about six months old.'

She sticks her hand through the bars, and I race to lick it. Well, if that doesn't make a good impression on her, I don't know what will. The angel bends down to me.

'Oh, what a sweetheart you are! Such a cute fellow!'

I jump up and down enthusiastically.

'Yes, he's quite adorable. A dachshund mix.'

Ouch! *Mix?* Damn, that hurt. I instantly drop the enthusiastic dog act. Not that what she's saying isn't true; it is. Miss Overalls is right. And that's the humiliating truth, in a nutshell: I am a mutt. The product of Mummy's affair with a very dashing terrier. And that's exactly why I'm here. I may be Carl-Leopold von Eschersbach, but I'm not a pedigreed dachshund with the best papers. *Absolutely unsuited for hunting – and for breeding, of course.* That's what the old lord of the castle said before he put me in a box and drove me here. Emilia cried, but she had already taken in my sister, and two dogs were certainly too much for her to handle.

I think I must have started to whimper, because now the angel sticks her hand through the cage and strokes me.

'Oh, you poor thing, what's wrong? Are you sad?'

How embarrassing! A von Eschersbach doesn't cry – and certainly not in front of such a beautiful lady! Heavens, what are things coming to?

But it turns out that this was just the right thing to do, because the angel gets up, points to me, and says, 'That's the one I want. No doubt about it. Can I take him with me right now?'

The lady in the overalls nods. 'Come in with me and we'll take care of the paperwork. He's had all his injections, and he comes from a reputable breeder. A little slip-up, you might say.'

These last words make her giggle. Which makes me want to nip at her hand, but I don't, otherwise I'd wind up staying here.

•

Twenty minutes later I'm sitting in the crate stowed on the back seat of Caroline's car. Caroline – that's the name of my angel. I found that out when the two women said goodbye. Caroline. A lovely name. Quite noble. Most likely – oh, what am I saying – of course Caroline is of noble lineage. A dog like me is sure to pick up on something like that. Caroline is certainly in a good mood. She's whistling a song, and from time to time she takes a peek in the rear-view mirror to have a look at me.

'So, sweetie, now you'll get to see your new home. I can't wait to find out how you like it.'

Nor can I! I wonder if it's as nice as Eschersbach Castle. With a big park. And lots of burrows. The car slows down, then stops. Caroline opens the door and lifts out the crate. Now the aroma of strawberries and mint is right in front of my nose, and I would love to lick Caroline from head to toe, but first I'll have to wait to get out of the swaying crate.

It grows darker all around me, and my crate begins to sway even more: Caroline is carrying me up a flight of stairs. I try to push my nose through the bars of the crate to get a first sniff of my new residence. It appears to be a place that houses several humans – and several animals. Right away I can make out at least one cat.

Now Caroline is putting down the crate, and I hear her opening a door. She pushes the crate along with her foot, then fumbles with the cover, opens it up and lifts me out gently.

'This is it! Here's where you'll be living from now on. Take a look around, little guy.'

It's so bright in the room that at first I can't see anything at all. I squint a bit and try to adjust to the light. The outlines of what seems to be a human living room gradually come into focus. In front of the window there is a big couch that looks like an ideal spot for a little dachshund to enjoy a comfy nap. Wonder if Caroline would allow that? It was strictly forbidden in the castle. Which meant, of course, that my sister and I liked nothing better than to hop up onto the couch in the parlour. It was hilarious to watch the old lord of the castle rush towards us like greased lightning in spite of his limp and try to chase us away by brandishing his cane as menacingly as he could.

I scamper over to the couch and sniff at the slipcovers. Hmm, strawberries and mint here as well. But there's something else too. Not an animal. More like a human. I dive deep into the scent. Hmm, do I have a new master as well as a mistress? It's certainly not the scent of a woman. While I'm still mulling this over, Caroline lifts me up and puts me on the couch (yippee!), and sits down next to me. I lick her hands full of glee – this woman clearly knows what dachshunds love. She laughs and pulls her hands away, then she looks at me thoughtfully.

'So, little guy, I've got everything you need: a basket, a lead, a food dish and food. There's only one thing missing…'

I shake my head; as far as I can tell, that sounded pretty complete.

'You still need a nice name.'

I squeal in surprise – I have a nice name *already*! Or did von Eschersbach just park me at the animal shelter without mentioning it? Without saying a few things about me? How cold-blooded of him!

Evidently, Caroline notices my sense of outrage, and she lifts me onto her lap; then we gaze into each other's eyes.

'Hmm, now, what could a little fellow like you be named? What do you look like?'

I try my best to act haughty and dignified. Maybe if I do that, she'll think of Carl-Leopold all by herself. To enhance my distinguished appearance, I let out two more statesmanlike barks. Come on, Caroline, put your thinking cap on!

'You're certainly no ordinary dog; you strike me as someone with real character. In some way you're much bigger on the inside than you seem from the outside.'

Yes! Exactly! She's just about to come up with it! I throw my head back majestically.

'I know! I'll name you Hercules.'

What was that? HERCULES? I'm ancient Greek instead of ancient nobility?

chapter two 🐾

Hercules! I admit that Caroline may not have the best of taste when it comes to picking names for dachshunds, and this strange new name will take some getting used to. But she does have the knack for choosing the right place to live. The house where I'll now be living seems to be almost as big as Eschersbach Castle. My hunch that Caroline comes from the finest of backgrounds appears to be correct. The neighbours don't exactly live in simple cottages either. Just behind our house is a park, though I'm not entirely sure whether it all belongs to Caroline, since it is so huge. When we take a walk there, I can't even tell where the park ends – amazing!

Not only is it big, but there are adventures to be had here. After just a couple of steps, I catch the scent of the first rabbits and squirrels. I try to start running, when a rude jolt to my neck reminds me that Caroline got me something that I'm absolutely unaccustomed to: a sort of rope that she attached to my collar. Ouch! What kind of thing is this? I turn round, put the thing in my mouth and pull at it a bit. Caroline kneels down to me.

'What's going on, Hercules; don't you like your new lead? Maybe you've never gone for a walk like this. I'm not at all sure whether a little dog like you can do this straight away – walk with a lead, I mean. But unfortunately, there are lead laws here, and I can't just let you run around.'

When I hear 'lead laws', I start chomping at the rope even more frantically. Not that I know what the term means, but it definitely sounds like something aimed at dogs.

'Tsk, tsk!' Caroline says, and pats my head gently. I let go of the lead and look at her.

'I think I'll have to buy a book about dog training. Or maybe enrol you for a few hours of obedience classes? You're the first dog I've ever owned. But yesterday I suddenly had the feeling it would be nice to have a friendly, loyal creature around me.'

OK, that business about dog training is of course absolute nonsense, and I hope Caroline realizes that herself. But the part about the friendly, loyal creature fits me to a T, as it does all von Eschersbach dachshunds. I would even go so far as to claim that we're renowned for that. *A von Eschersbach never leaves his owner. Never! Remember that, Carl-Leopold!* I hear Grandpa's words ringing in my ears. But what about if the *owner* leaves the *dachshund*? Grandpa would certainly have drawn a blank on that one too, I add grimly. Just as a bad mood comes over me, Caroline starts rustling around in her pocket and comes out with something. Hmm, not just any old thing. I know that smell! It's pork sausage. Sure enough, that's exactly what she's holding under my nose.

'Here, sweetheart. Let's begin our first lesson in taking a walk with something you'll like. I *hope* you like this.'

I grab the piece of sausage and jump up and down for joy. Caroline needs to know that this was definitely the right idea.

'You like that, don't you? Maybe we should stop the lead training for now and drop in on Daniel instead. It's time for you to meet him. At this time of day he's bound to be hard at work and might be grateful for a little change of pace.'

Too bad; I would have liked to stay in the park, even on a lead. Maybe we would have run into another dog, and I could have got the lowdown on the neighbourhood. After all, you need to know the lie of the land. But if this Daniel is so important, that's fine by me!

Caroline keeps to exactly the same route back as we took coming here, and I do my best to trot nicely behind her on the lead. Maybe I'll get another piece of sausage if I give her a sense of pedagogical accomplishment. Sure enough, she turns around to me for a second.

'Good, Hercules! You're a quick learner!' she says, to praise me, but she doesn't reach into her pocket again.

Oh well, I'm not really hungry anyway.

By this point we're back in front of our house. I wonder if this Daniel lives here too. Caroline bends down and picks me up.

'So, let's go off to the workshop!'

Workshop? Interesting word. I wonder what we'll find there. We go into the house, but unlike the last time, we don't head upstairs; we go four steps down. Then Caroline opens the door, and we're in a room that has a strong smell of wood. I snort in amazement. Do humans really keep forests inside their houses? And can it be that foxes and rabbits live here? Not that I actually see any trees. That's odd.

From one corner of the workshop-thingy I hear someone whistling. Might that be Daniel? Caroline carries me in the direction of the sound. We come into a room that has two big windows, with the warm afternoon sun streaming in. Just behind the windows there's a meadow, which looks quite pretty. In front of the windows there's a big table, and behind the table is the human with the nice loud whistle. He's holding a long thingamajig that looks like a branch with long hair. When he sees us, he sets the thing aside and stops whistling.

'Well, what have we here? Did someone get lost and wind up at our place? Or do we have a visitor?'

Caroline shakes her head. 'Neither. We have a new member of our household. May I introduce you? Hercules – Daniel. Daniel – Hercules.' Then she puts me down on the table next to the thingamajig.

'What? You bought a dachshund?'

'A dachshund mix; yes, I did.'

I can't help myself – I simply must shake my head furiously and growl in angry protest. The two of them look at me in amazement.

'Hey, what's this? Doesn't he like men?' Daniel wonders.

Caroline shrugs her shoulders and scratches me behind my

ears to calm me down. 'I hope that's not the case. At any rate, they didn't say anything about that to me at the animal shelter, and I had in mind to bring him along to the workshop during the day.'

Daniel smiles. 'Well, maybe he's a proud little fellow and doesn't like you calling his pedigree into question.'

They both laugh, and Caroline picks me up again.

Could you please tell me what's so funny about that? I may not know too many humans at this point, but one thing's for sure: these two-legged creatures are distinctly less sensitive than us dogs. They clearly have no idea what ails us. I suddenly get the uneasy feeling that living with a human like that day in and day out might not be all fun and games. But at least this Daniel is on the right track. We'll bring him up to speed!

'Can I hold him?'

'Of course!' Caroline hands me over.

Daniel has a firm but not unpleasant grip. He's just a bit taller than Caroline, and from up here I can see that his light hair curls in every direction all over his head.

'So, little guy – don't you like me?'

To make it clear that the opposite is the case, I lick Daniel's face.

'So much for the idea that he doesn't like men,' Caroline says happily. 'He's really taken to you.'

'That's a relief! If the three of us are soon going to be spending our days together, any other reaction would be a problem. A dachshund that keeps nipping at my calves would have put a spanner in the works.'

Oh, I get it. Daniel is the master who comes along with my mistress. He must be the one I was smelling upstairs in the apartment. I've often heard that humans like to pair up and then stay together as a couple for quite a long time. I always found that idea odd. But when I see the two of them, I can easily understand it. They seem so ... so at ease with each other. Almost like my grandpa with the old von Eschersbach. Those two went hunting together for fifteen years. You can't be more of a couple than that. I wonder whether Caroline and Daniel also go hunting together – or do human couples have other ways of spending time in pairs?

'Just a quick business question: did Mrs Brolin call again?' Caroline asks Daniel. 'She wanted to come in today with a cello to find out how much it's worth. She'd like to get it refurbished, if it's worth it.'

Cello. What a beautiful word. So soft, yet also kind of ... fiery. What might it be? And I wonder if it has anything to do with that thing Daniel had in his hand before. Well, I'll find out; after all, from now on I'll be around here quite a bit.

'Yes, she was here briefly and left the instrument in the shop. I put it over on your work table. But she's not in any special hurry. It's fine with her if you give her a call on Monday.'

'That's good. Quite honestly, I'd love to take the rest of the day off and show Hercules his new home and the neighbourhood. We just tried a little walk in the park, but Hercules doesn't like his new lead. Maybe I'll get in some more practice with him.'

'Go ahead; there's nothing urgent on my end either. At least nothing I can't do without you.' Daniel smiles again and hands me back to Caroline.

It's great that humans are capable of making such a variety of facial expressions. Of course it's much easier when you don't have so much hair around your eyes and nose. Just now, this Daniel looked at my Caroline as if he'd like to lick her face too. But humans don't seem to do that. At least I've never seen them doing it. And they don't jump up and down either. Isn't that weird? It feels so good to do that when you're happy.

'Daniel?'

'Yes?'

'It's OK with you that I have a dog, isn't it?'

'Sure, don't worry about it.'

'I mean – I just got the idea on the spur of the moment, and I would have preferred to ask you first. But then curiosity brought me into the animal shelter and I fell instantly in love with this little fellow.'

'He really is sweet. I can understand you wanting to take him home with you on the spot. Just look at those big brown eyes! He doesn't really look like a mixed breed. Floppy ears and short legs – and he has a rather long back as well. If you ask me, he's certainly from a genuine line of dachshunds; there are guaranteed not to be many other breeds in the mix.'

Daniel, you're my man! I feel like leaping right out of Caroline's arms into Daniel's, and licking him from top to bottom – his compliment was just what I needed. I feel as though I've instantly grown by a paw's breadth. I bark with pride.

PUPPY LOVE

'That seems to have made you really happy! Caroline, I think you're dealing with a very proud specimen here. Looks as though we'll have to go to great lengths to live up to his demands.'

The two of them laugh once more, and Caroline scratches me behind the ears again. 'Well, sweetheart, I will do my best to make you feel at home with us.'

Lying in my new little basket that night, I'm tired, but happy. We spent another hour walking in the park and practised the thing with the lead. I did Caroline the favour of walking behind her obediently, for the most part. Every once in a whole, though, when I was sure that I'd just passed a burrow, I plopped down on my rear end and growled like mad. After all, I have a reputation as a hound to defend. But a little friendly persuasion and several slices of pork sausage made me agree to a rather long walk in the park attached to that lead. We also ran into a few dogs, but I didn't feel like chatting. There'll be plenty of time for that tomorrow.

Before I fall asleep, Caroline comes back again and puts a soft blanket into my basket. She cuddles with me a little, then she whispers in my ear, 'You know, sweetheart, it's such a shame I didn't get a dog a long time ago. This really is an ideal place for a chap like you. During the day you can come to the workshop with me or roam around in our back garden. And whenever I take a break or have time off, we'll go for a walk. How does that sound?' she asks me, and now I finally – finally! – get the chance to lick her face. Caroline giggles, pets me again, and says good night.

Huh, I've really struck it lucky: a nice mistress, a nice master

– it's actually a really nice family again, just like at Eschersbach Castle. OK, there's no Emilia, and Caroline didn't get me anything like fresh tripe; to celebrate the day, she opened a tin for me at dinnertime. But that doesn't matter. If this is the bourgeois lifestyle, I can get used to it. At least things seem to be on the up and up around here, and I have yet to meet anyone who is as cold-hearted as old von Eschersbach. Yes, the happiness of ordinary folks: there's something so soothing about it. To hell with nobility. I think about that yummy pork sausage one last time, then I drift off.

chapter three 🐾

I feel like clamping my paws over my ears. Or creeping under the couch. What I am going through right now is really scaring me. A man I've never seen before has just come into our – or I suppose I should say Caroline's – apartment, and started shouting his head off the second he got here. I'm stunned. Who is this awful guy? And where's Daniel? Doesn't he want to protect his woman? Maybe I should run out and find him so he can help Caroline. Of course that would mean getting round this shouting guy, and I have to admit I'm too scared to do that. You know what I really hate about humans? They can be so horribly loud! My ears are excellent. The way I see it, people shouldn't talk so loudly or listen to earsplitting music – another thing they seem to enjoy doing. But that's neither here nor there.

This man's aggressive manner reminds me of Bozo and that boxer. He's huge, quite a bit taller than Caroline. And his hair is as jet-black as Bozo's coat. He has those same bossy moves and that same inane tone. I peg him for a commoner through and through, just like Bozo-Boxer.

The man is waving his hands around and pointing – at me! Oh no!

'What's got into you? I go on a business trip for a measly three days, and you go out and buy a dog?'

Bozo-Boxer has turned beet red. Something tells me that I'm not going to fare quite as well with him as I did with Daniel. But that doesn't matter a bit as far as I'm concerned. The main thing is that my master likes me. And I hope he gets here soon. All this yelling can surely be heard in the workshop even by human ears, which are not exactly great. Now Caroline is planting herself squarely in front of the man. She clearly wants to defend me. A grand gesture, but that's not how it should work. If anyone here needs defending, it would be my mistress, by her brave hound. There's no way around it – I have to plunge into the fray.

Just as I'm gearing up to take a bold leap straight to a sensitive spot on that guy so I can assume the perfect biting position and sink my teeth into him, the unthinkable happens: Caroline moves up to the vile man and strokes his arm.

'But honey – we did agree that a pet is a good idea. So yesterday, on the spur of the moment, I went to the animal shelter. Please – don't be angry! Hercules is so sweet!'

Honey? I hope I heard wrong. As far as I know, 'honey' is what human couples say to each other. The way the gardener always says 'honey' to Emilia, which is just fine, because those two are a couple. Could Caroline have two men? And one of them is this low-life? Still, Caroline seems to have calmed him down a bit, and he's toned down the yelling.

'You and your spur-of-the-moment ideas. Buying a dog without asking me – what a crazy thing to do!'

'Well, I thought you're away so much and we have the big back garden, and Hercules can come to the workshop with me. Daniel is OK with that.'

'Of course he's OK with that. He's quite the wimp. If you were to suggest that the two of you start parading around in garter belts at the shop tomorrow, he would say yes to that too.'

'For goodness' sake, Thomas – stop picking on Daniel all the time. He may not be a go-getter like you, but I can't imagine a better partner.'

So that's his name: Thomas. And he obviously knows Daniel. What an interesting combination. Do humans live in threes as well? Dachshunds say that way back in the dim and distant past, dogs lived together in packs. Of course several females were together with one male. If there's something like a pack of humans, maybe they do it differently. Maybe each woman needs several men. There's still quite a lot to learn for a young dog like me, that's for sure.

'No, of course you won't find a better partner,' Thomas sneers. 'There are not too many violin makers around these days. But just because your dear sweet colleague in the workshop puts up with anything from you doesn't mean I have to.'

Thomas laughs scornfully. Caroline starts crying, and it

dawns on me that Daniel and Caroline may not be a couple, or at least not a romantic couple. Instead, for some crazy reason, Caroline seems to be Thomas's wife, and she just works with Daniel. I think that's how it is. How ghastly!

I'm totally confused now, and I've stopped listening to all the outrageous things Thomas is still coming out with. I'm too busy scrambling to work out how it is possible for Caroline and Thomas to be a couple. No way did Caroline pick him out on her own. How could this have happened? Do people have some higher authority that throws men and women together, kind of like a breeder? Up to now I thought that couldn't be the case; I reckoned people were creatures with free will. But when I see what's going on here, things must operate some other way. And – quite obviously – that other way doesn't work very well.

•

'Caroline, you're just kidding yourself. The thing with Thomas and you is simply not working. It never has, and it never will.'

'How do you know? Just because you're a psychologist doesn't mean you can see into the future.'

'No, not because I'm a psychologist, but because I'm your best friend Nina, and I've been watching the whole calamity for four years now.'

We're sitting in a café – well, Caroline and Nina are sitting, and I'm lying. Caroline came here with me after the fight with Thomas. A short time later, this Nina joined us, and then it got rather interesting, because Caroline and Nina have been discussing exactly what's been on my mind today, namely what is Caroline doing with Thomas? Nina clearly doesn't like Thomas either, but, unlike me, she doesn't make an issue of his unpleasant smell and loud voice. She lists all kinds of other reasons, most of which I don't really understand. But whatever – bottom line is that Nina and I come to the same conclusion: he's not for her. Caroline does her best to defend him, but Nina sticks to her guns.

'I mean, let's be honest here, Caroline: you were so desperate that you went out and bought yourself a dog. What's next?'

Hey! Is that an attack on me? I growl a bit just to be on the safe side. Caroline leans over to me.

'It's all right, Hercules. Nina doesn't mean that.'

Nina rolls her eyes. I see exactly what she's doing from my spot next to Caroline's chair. 'Yes, I do; I mean precisely what I'm saying! What you need is a man who loves you as much as you love him. A stupid dachshund like that is absolutely no substitute.'

Stupid dachshund? Does she have any idea whom she's dealing with? A mere growl will not do this time. I jump up from my spot and give Nina a good solid barking. She raises her eyebrows in surprise.

'What do you know; it really seems as though he understood me. OK, I take back that last thing. You're not a stupid dachshund. But I'm sticking to what I said before – you can't make up for that idiot Thomas. Although I admit you're quite cute.'

Well, there you are; that's better. I lie back down.

'Hercules is not a substitute for love. That has nothing to do with Thomas. I've been wanting a dog for a long time.'

'What nonsense. That was a typical sublimation.'

'Yeah, yeah, you're a psychologist, so you've got it all worked out.'

I don't know exactly what 'psychologist' means, but it seems to be something quite alarming. At any rate, Caroline has already said it to Nina a couple of times, and it sounded as though Nina was suffering from a serious illness. Kennel cough at the very least. The poor thing. It's odd, though; she looks perfectly healthy – rosy cheeks, big clear eyes. I bet she even has a nice cold nose. And she has shiny brown hair. But if it is an illness, I hope Caroline doesn't catch it and become psychological too.

'Look, just come out and say it: you're not happy with Thomas, and you never will be. Keep the dog, but split up with the guy.'

Exactly – that's what we'll do! I get up and wag my tail. Unfortunately, Caroline is not as pleased with this advice as I am, and she starts to cry.

'You don't understand me. Thomas and I – we simply belong together. I know it for a fact. Just the way we got together in the first place: it was destiny!'

So that was it: destiny. A mysterious word. Is that the higher authority that brings humans together? And if so, how could destiny be so off the mark? I try to picture destiny in person. Maybe it's like the old von Eschersbach. Stern. Scary. Somewhat self-righteous. Of course, if destiny is anything like von

Eschersbach, it really could get something wrong. After all, the old guy made a huge mistake in his judgement of yours truly, otherwise he wouldn't have taken me to the animal shelter.

Suddenly I lose interest in the conversation between Nina and Caroline. My thoughts are back at the castle: with Mummy, my sister Charlotte and Emilia. I wonder how they're doing? For the first time in these past three exciting days, I feel a strange longing for them. Does everyone in my family miss me? Or aren't they even mentioning me any more? I wonder whether Charlotte can sleep well without me lying next to her in the basket. Oh, Charlotte, will I ever see you again?

'Hey, Hercules, what's wrong with you? Don't you feel well?'

I seem to have started howling. At any rate, Caroline and Nina have stopped talking, and Caroline has lifted me onto her lap. When I look at her face, I'm astonished to find that her eyes are all red. It doesn't take much to make humans cry, but evidently it takes a toll on them. I quickly lick her hands to show her that everything's OK, but Caroline still looks worried.

'Hmm, I wonder what's up with him.'

Nina shrugs her shoulders. 'Maybe he's not so happy with Thomas either! After all, Thomas would love nothing better than to kick him out.'

Woof! What was that? Thomas wants to kick me out? Am I going to wind up back in the animal shelter tomorrow? With Bozo and that boxer?

•

When we get home, I'm still quite upset. I'm wondering whether Caroline will really take me back. That would be terrible. I suppose there's no way round the fact that I have to get into Thomas's good books. I decide to show myself to best dachshund advantage the next time I see him. That goes against the grain, because a von Eschersbach does not grovel. Then again, my last act of civil disobedience was not exactly a rousing success, and it ended, as we all know, with a painful bite to my ear.

But Thomas doesn't appear to be at home right now; in any case, Caroline isn't calling his name. She just puts her handbag down for a second and rummages around for her apartment key.

'Let's stop by the workshop again, Hercules.' Then she opens the door. 'Come, sweetie!'

I'd like nothing better! I'm delighted to be seeing Daniel again, and I run down the stairs behind Caroline with my tail wagging.

But once I'm down there I find out that while it still smells like wood, it doesn't really smell like Daniel. That's funny – where is he? While Caroline goes to one of the tables and clears it up a bit, I run off and look for Daniel. I discover that the rooms here in the workshop are arranged very much like those in Caroline's apartment: two connected rooms on one side, and a third room behind them, then a long hall, and another room in the back. In that one, there's a really strong smell of the forest – and when I peek in, I see whole stacks of wood piled up there. That's odd – what does Caroline need all this wood for? Von

Eschersbach collects bottles in his cellar, and Emilia's husband collects those colourful little paper rectangles with serrated edges, but wood? I guess there's nothing that humans *don't* collect.

'Hercules, where are you?' Caroline calls down the hall. I trot out of the room with the wood. 'Oh, what are you doing in the lumber storeroom? Smells good, doesn't it?' I lie down in front of Caroline's feet, and she pets me a little. 'Or are you looking for Daniel?'

When I hear that name, I wag my tail. Caroline needs to know that he's my idea of a nice master.

'Oh, so that's what's going on. Daniel is nice, isn't he? But it's the weekend, and we don't usually work then. I just have to do a couple of things that I haven't got round to finishing since you moved in. Then we'll take a little walk, I promise. You can look round a bit in the back garden until I'm done, OK?'

That sounds like a good plan. I haven't had any chance at all to inspect the garden. In fact, other than the apartment and the workshop, I still know nothing whatsoever about the house, and I'm looking forward to exploring it bit by bit. Caroline goes up to one of the windows in the second room and opens it, and now I notice that from there, two steps take you straight into the garden. I race up the stairs and the next thing I know, I'm sitting in the grass. It's wonderful – how that tickles my belly! The sun is shining on the tip of my nose, and it makes me sneeze.

Caroline laughs. 'So, have a good time – I'll leave the door open, and you can come in any time you get bored.'

Don't worry, Caroline; that is guaranteed not to happen! I trot off and sniff the giant tree towards the side of the house. Hmm, interesting. Obviously, no dog has been here for quite some time, because there is nothing marked on this trunk. I lift my leg to make up for lost time as quick as I can. I haven't done this very often, and never on such a wide trunk, so the whole thing looks a bit amateurish. But so what? I'll have chances galore to practise in private, until I get as good at it as the grown-up males I've been secretly watching. They're so nonchalant about the whole thing: they run past a tree and simply lift up their leg, as if it were no big deal.

I try it out again on the other side; after all, it's important to get the knack of it with both legs. It's not all that easy! Good thing no one sees me.

'Well, little guy?' comes a voice directly above me at just this moment. 'That looks pretty inept. I guess you haven't been doing it very long – ha-ha!'

Who the devil is that? I look up and see a fat black cat in the treetop. Oh no, how humiliating! Someone watching me in secret, and it had to be a cat!

'By the way, this is my back garden and my tree – so I'll ask you to refrain from peeing around here. It is revolting, and it stinks.'

With these words, the cat slowly climbs down the trunk, then stands in front of me. That is one big fat cat! I start to growl.

'What's this? Is that any way to greet someone? You dogs have the worst manners. You drop by my living room without so much as knocking, and don't even introduce yourself. Well, whatever,' the cat sighs, 'let's start again: I am Mr Beck.'

Oh, so this is a tomcat.

'I am Carl-Leopold von Eschersbach. Delighted to make your acquaintance, Mr Beck.' After all, I don't want it said by someone like this that I don't know how to behave.

The cat sniggers. '"Carl-Leopold?" That's funny; I thought I just heard Caroline calling you "Hercules". And "von Eschersbach" sounds really over the top.'

What a nerve! I'd love nothing better than to sink my teeth right into this fat critter's heels – but after dealing with the cats at the castle, I know that if I do so, a little dog like me could wind up in a great deal of pain. These creatures are really speedy and have very sharp claws. Although I'm fuming on the inside, I try to act cool.

'A fabulous lady like Caroline can call me anything she wants, but for an ordinary cat like you, I'm afraid I'll have to insist on Carl-Leopold. Incidentally, this is most certainly not your living room; it's my new garden. I must therefore ask you to stop climbing that tree, which is also now mine. You'll damage it with your claws.'

The cat's tail begins to twitch, not, unfortunately, because he's quaking with fear, but because he has broken into downright hysterical laughter.

'That's great – you're just what I needed! I was starting to get a little bored – but with a clown like you around, this will certainly turn into a very entertaining summer.'

Beck starts rolling on the ground with laughter. He is obviously having a great time. I, on the other hand, could tear the hair right out of my tail. No one takes me seriously. Little by little, Mr Beck quietens down again, gets up and shakes himself for a second.

'Now seriously, little guy – who do you think you are?'

I'm just about to reply when Beck's paw whizzes by my nose, missing it by a fraction of an inch. 'Wait a second – that was the wrong question to ask! Don't start that nobility stuff again.'

I growl. I don't want Beck to get the idea that I take insults lying down – claws or no claws.

But Beck pays no attention whatsoever, and forges ahead: 'I've been the only animal in this building for quite a long time, if you don't count that stupid parakeet up on the third floor. And just because you were brought here by Caroline, who, I admit, is quite charming, you'd better not get the idea that I'm about to budge from my territory. This *was* my back garden, this *is* my back garden, and this *will stay* my back garden from here on in! So be glad you're allowed to catch some rays of sun on your nose every now and then, and stay away from the tree. Get it?'

With these words he wheels round and clearly intends simply to leave me standing there. That is the last straw as far as I'm concerned. I take a leap forward and snap at Beck's tail. I'm actually intending to stop just short of it, the way Beck did when he swiped his paw. Unfortunately, he picks this very moment to lower the tip of his tail to just where my muzzle is aiming – and before I know it, I've bitten right into it. Ouch. That must have been a wee bit painful. Maybe even more than a bit. But it wasn't on purpose, honestly!

Beck makes a loud hissing sound and gears up for revenge. I take to my heels. Being clobbered by a cat on day two is certainly not how I would have pictured my smashing debut. Before he catches me, I take a daring leap through the open window of the workshop.

I almost land right on Caroline's feet, and she looks at me in astonishment.

'What are you up to, Hercules? Stunt flying?' She looks out of the window and sees Beck, who slams on the brakes just in the nick of time. 'Did you get into a fight with the cat?'

I feign innocence and wag my tail.

'Now really, Hercules! Mr Beck is a very nice old gentleman. Besides, his mistress always waters my flowers when I'm away. You need to behave yourself.'

How embarrassing! She knows the cat quite well. I pretend I've found something fascinating on the floor to stare at. Still, I can't help thinking that Caroline's taste in men – both human and feline – is anything but exquisite. First this unbearable Thomas, then Mr Beck – it seems downright miraculous that she took me and not Bozo from the animal shelter.

Thinking about Thomas reminds me that I simply have to make a good impression on that idiot today. I've got to make sure that the idea of taking me back to the shelter doesn't even cross his mind. Besides, one enemy in my immediate vicinity is quite enough, and I doubt that I'll need to keep sucking up to

Mr Beck. I resolve to grab the first chance I get to bond with Thomas.

A von Eschersbach doesn't shilly-shally – he seizes the moment, boldly and valiantly. And that's exactly how I'll handle it, Grandpa: boldly and valiantly.

chapter four 🐾

Sure enough, the chance to bond with Thomas comes even sooner than I expected. The very next night, I'm lying in my basket, unable to sleep. There is too much running through my mind. Thomas. The little incident with Mr Beck. The conversation between Caroline and Nina. I even have to think about Fritz, the pointer from the animal shelter. I'm tossing and turning.

Suddenly I hear a sound. It's a murmur… or maybe a whimper? I jump up, climb out of the basket, and head out of the living room and into the hall, where I can hear the sound much more clearly. It really is a whimper, and it was coming from the bedroom! Oh no – is something wrong with Caroline? The door is open a crack, so I'm able to dart in without making a sound. Unfortunately, it's quite dark, so I can't make out a thing.

There's that sound again. The whimper has now turned into a groan. But to my great relief, it is definitely Thomas who seems not to be doing so well. My first thought: Caroline's OK. My second thought: this is my big chance! The thing to do is to act boldly and valiantly. It is totally obvious that Thomas is lying in bed and writhing in pain. Caroline seems to be sleeping – or at least she doesn't appear to hear him, otherwise she'd help him, of course. So I'll make sure she wakes up and Thomas doesn't have to keep suffering. Then he'll realize what a great dog I am and how good it is that Caroline got me.

I jump into the bed with a bold and valiant leap, and land right next to the groaning Thomas. It's astonishing that she doesn't hear him, because she's practically lying right under him. I've already mentioned that humans have really bad ears. But don't worry, Thomas; you now have a new and loyal friend. He really is writhing in pain, and his face is turned downward. I give his neck a quick lick so he knows that help is on the way. He flinches. Then I start barking as loud as I can to make sure that Caroline finally wakes up.

•

The next thing I can still recall is that I'm flying right across the room and landing hard next to the door. Then all of a sudden the room lights up. Thomas – who is miraculously cured – is standing over me and looking daggers at me.

'You fucking mutt! What were you thinking? I'll get you!'

He raises his hand – is he thinking of hitting me? I try to run for cover, but where can I go? I howl in panic. Help! What is going on here?

At this moment, Caroline appears behind Thomas. So she

finally woke up from all the noise. She grabs Thomas's shoulder from behind and pulls him back.

'Don't you dare lay a hand on Hercules! He wasn't disturbing us on purpose.'

Thomas wheels round to her. 'What? That mongrel jumps into our bed, just when I was going strong, and you defend him? I'll show this stupid beast what I think of his little interlude.'

'Thomas!' Caroline calls out sharply. 'You take your hands off Hercules right now. Right now!'

She bends down to me and takes me in her arms. By this point I'm shaking like a leaf. This is simply too much for my sensitive nerves. I have no clue what's going on here: what does she mean by 'disturbing'? And what does he mean by 'going strong'? Thomas ought to be glad that at least I recognized his critical condition. Instead he actually wants to clobber me. And my behind is still hurting from the kick he gave me in the bed. I start whimpering. I have never been treated so unfairly. Compared to this psychopath, the old von Eschersbach is charity personified.

'You poor thing, you're trembling all over!' Caroline gives me a hug and nestles her face in my neck. 'Don't worry; I'm here with you. I'll take good care of you.'

Thomas sneers. 'Are you for real, Caroline? Do you have some kind of erotic relationship with that dog? You don't seem to care one bit that we were interrupted. You were probably even glad. At least you don't have to tell me you have a headache this time.'

Hold on: Thomas is groaning, and Caroline has a headache? Interrupted from doing what? No matter how hard I try, I can't seem to make head nor tail of what's going on. The only thing I know for sure is that my attempt to smooth things over with Thomas like a good little dachshund has gone horribly wrong. And I don't even know why. I wonder whether they'll let me take my new dog bone to the animal shelter. Not that it matters; Bozo and Boxer would probably grab it away from me in no time.

I spend the rest of the night in my basket. Although I'm dead tired, there's no way I can get any sleep after this whole disaster. Every once in a while, I raise an ear and listen in the darkness. All is quiet. But even if I were to hear a sound again, wild horses couldn't drag me back into a room with Thomas in it.

•

The sun is shining through the workshop windows, and several inviting spots are forming on the old wooden floor and calling out to me: *Come over here, Carl-Leopold, lie down on me and take a little rest!* This invitation is just what I need. I still haven't got over what happened last night. I waver only on whether I should pick out a spot in Caroline's part of the room or lie down next to the table where Daniel's working right now.

I finally lie down next to Daniel. I feel pretty pathetic, and I'm scared that Caroline could hold everything that happened against me. Not that she's said anything to that effect, but it's a bit unpleasant for me, because I clearly messed up big-time.

Even after giving the matter quite a bit of thought, I still don't know what I did wrong, but I hate the fact that Caroline had to defend me to Thomas once again.

'So, how was the weekend? How's life with your new dog?' Daniel asks Caroline.

I fold my ears and bury my nose between my front paws. I don't want to hear the story that's bound to follow.

'Great! Thomas is really happy about the little guy too. Well, you know how much he loves animals.'

Huh? Was it something I ate this morning? I am obviously hallucinating.

'Really? Nope, I didn't know that he's so keen on animals. So much the better! The two of them should get along splendidly. They can go hiking together or do survival training or whatever it is that a real tough guy does with his dog.'

Have I got it wrong, or am I detecting a touch of irony in what Daniel's saying? As a dog, I have a hard time working out how to tell when humans do that irony thing – they often use the same words to mean something completely different. I still have a clear memory of how von Eschersbach first said 'Good dog, great idea!' when I jumped onto the parlour sofa with wet paws, but then reached back with his walking stick and hit me on my hind legs. It took me two hours to calm down. Mummy had to explain to me that humans often say the opposite of what they mean to highlight the fact that they don't mean it at all. Crazy, right? There must be a couple of very impractical and unnecessary convolutions in people's brains. Probably walking upright makes them hold their heads too high up in the air. It's easy to see that that's not good for the brain.

I also have to wonder what would make Caroline tell a story like that. Why doesn't she want to admit that our life together has got off to a disastrous start? Could a love of animals be something that raises the value of a human male? The way aggressive hunting skills, keen vigilance and great fortitude are the marks of an outstanding hunting dog? I know quite a bit about outstanding hunting dogs: Mummy made the finals of the national championship three times. The shelves in Eschersbach Castle are groaning under the weight of her trophies, and she never got a score lower than 'Excellent 1' (popularly known as 'E1'). So if a love of animals is one of the criteria, and Caroline is intent on demonstrating that Thomas is a candidate for E1, her story makes sense, of course. But on the other hand, even a little dog like me sees right away that Thomas wouldn't get more than a 'Satisfactory', even if he does love animals – which I doubt.

But back to the subject of irony: I honestly hope that Daniel did not mean what he said literally. For me, the combination of the words *Thomas, alone* and *survival training* yields associations that differ considerably from those of a great friendship between man and dog. I can easily picture Thomas sending me over a cliff into a very deep chasm or tying me to a tree in a deserted forest and just going off without me. In that case, I'm better off in an animal shelter. Maybe I can set up a canine group home with Fritz, who, unfortunately, is still sure to be there, and we can get our own little kennel. It could even be right next to a bunch of cats, for all I care.

'Listen, Daniel, you don't have to make fun of it. I really think that Hercules and Thomas will get to be good friends.'

Oh, thank God! It *is* irony. No dangerous solo expeditions with Thomas.

'I'm not making fun of it. I just doubt that your dear sweet Thomas is going to be jogging through the park with a sweet little guy like Hercules any time soon. That clashes far too much with his well-cultivated image as a tough guy.'

'What do you have against Thomas, anyway?'

'Nothing at all. I just wonder sometimes what he has against me.'

Caroline laughs out loud. Sounds pretty fake.

'Oh, please – Thomas has nothing whatsoever against you. Just the opposite – he thinks you're very nice.'

Caroline's voice, which is always so warm, now has a hollow undertone. I wonder whether Daniel hears it too. He sighs.

'Sure he does.'

'It's just that the two of you are pretty different from each other. But you could be friends anyway.'

Daniel doesn't say anything in reply; he just lets out a deep breath. It's fairly obvious that he doesn't want to discuss this with Caroline. Too bad – I would have liked to find out more about his opinion of Thomas. Maybe he could be my ally. That'd be nice; turns out I could really use a friend in this house.

•

Around noon, Caroline and I pop into the apartment for a bit so she can give me my meal. She actually did buy a book about dogs – I saw it lying on the living room couch – and maybe the first thing she read was the chapter about healthy food. In any case, she's now moved on from tinned food. On our walk this morning, she got me some fresh offal. When she cooked it, a delicious aroma spread throughout the apartment. Yummy! A very pleasing development.

'So, sweetie, this has to cool down a little, then you'll get it. Let's wait another five minutes. I have to make a phone call anyway, then I'll give it to you.'

She puts my bowl of offal into the refrigerator and goes into the room next to the living room. I stand around and try to decide where I should go, then I head into the hall. While I ponder what to do until lunchtime, I see that the bedroom door is open again. For the past two days, I've been making a big detour around this room, but now my curiosity prevails. Maybe I'll find something there that would explain what really happened that terrible night. Not that I know what that might be, but at least I'd like to have a look around again in the light of day. From the other corner of the apartment I hear Caroline talking to that black piece of plastic. From everything I've now picked up about humans in general and women in particular, that is a sure sign that she is completely preoccupied for the time being. The same thing always happened with Emilia. You could swipe the most wonderful stuff from the kitchen while she was on the phone.

I cautiously poke my muzzle through the crack in the door. Sure enough, the coast is clear. Before you know it, I'm in. At first glance it is certainly unexciting. But it's the second glance that's said to make things interesting, or, should I say, the second, intense *sniff* that a canine brings to bear. So I decide to subject everything here to a thorough sniff test.

I start with the bed. The usual: the right side smells like Caroline, and the left more like Thomas. Well, of course; what was I expecting? That's how the two of them sleep. Just when I am about to hop down again, I notice the hint of another smell, not directly on the bedclothes, but under them, on the mattress. I move the bedding aside so I can get a deeper sniff. Strange. Caroline's side has her usual fantastic Caroline smell, and Thomas's side smells as unpleasant as the rest of him, so there are no surprises there, but there's a third smell in this bed. It's … hmm … I'm not sure … somehow … is it or isn't it? … It's really hard to say! So my nose begins to move slowly and methodically over the whole bed one more time.

Just then, the bedroom door is pushed wide open. 'Hercules, shame on you! What are you doing in our bed again?'

Caroline is standing in front of me and wagging her index finger at me disapprovingly. I look down at the floor in shame. How can I explain to her what exactly I'm looking for, when I don't even know myself? All I know is that I've just discovered something very strange.

'Dogs don't belong in the bed, Hercules. You have a very comfortable basket, and you will kindly stay there when you want to sleep. You can sit on the couch with me, but you're not allowed in the bed. Thomas was really angry with you, and I promised him that I'd train you a little better. I want you two to be friends. And that's not helping!'

Now Caroline looks really sad. That's a bummer. I fold my ears and hop down from the bed. This idea of investigating the bedroom was dumb, and I'm none the wiser for it.

'Don't look so sad. A sweet dog like you just has to learn things now and again. Come, your meal should be just about ready.'

Nuff said! I race to the kitchen. Caroline takes the bowl out of the refrigerator, gives it a stir, and sets it down in front of my nose. Hmm, yummy. With such a nice big portion of offal, the greatest of worries are soon forgotten.

•

Back in the workshop I get in an hour of sleep. Daniel made me a second basket out of an old box and a pillow – that guy really thinks of everything. Then all of a sudden I wake up. I get the feeling that someone is torturing Mr Beck. In any case, really horrendous noises are resounding in my ears. So high and shrill; a wretched whining. I jump out of the box and run towards the racket. There, in one of the front rooms, Caroline is standing and holding something on her arm. But it's not Mr Beck; it's one of those little wooden cases that seem to be lying around everywhere in the workshop. They look weird. They come in all different sizes. They don't have corners; instead, they're round, and look as though someone glued two circles together. And they have a long neck, which is where Caroline is now beating away at it with a hairy stick. I suppose I should say that she's stroking away at it – and it seems to be hurting the case, because whenever she does it, it makes a terrible noise.

Egad – it makes the blood run cold in your veins! I can't help it – I start howling, hesitantly at first, and then I really let go. Caroline puts the case down, and Daniel comes running into the room. He sees me howling my heart out one last time, then he bursts out laughing.

'Oh, jeez, don't tell me that Hercules doesn't like music! Well, then, you've come to just the right place!'

Music? Are you saying that's music? You can't mean that! I know music from Eschersbach Castle. In the parlour, there was not only my favourite sofa, but also a thing called a piano. Von Eschersbach played on it every once in a while, and although it wasn't something I would have chosen personally either, it wasn't nearly as bad as what I just heard. And when I was allowed to go shopping with Emilia, the car played music. Of course it was way too loud, but otherwise actually quite nice, with a clear rhythm and really fast. But this was just absolutely awful. And so piercing. Never in a million years was that music. I shake my head vigorously.

Caroline and Daniel exchange baffled glances.

'Maybe the notes are too high for him. Get the cello; perhaps he'll like that better than the violin.'

Daniel goes off and comes back with one of the bigger cases.

Ah! This is the thing with that beautiful name. Well, I hope it sounds half as nice as the name. Daniel sits down on a chair and tucks the cello between his legs. He also takes the stick in his hand, then moves it back and forth slowly. Sure enough, noises start coming out of that as well, and they really sound much better. I grunt contentedly and lie down in front of Daniel, my head on my front paws.

'OK, Hercules is not a violin guy, but he doesn't seem to have anything against music in general,' Caroline concludes. 'So he'll just have to take a little walk in the garden when we tune the violins. Too bad; the violin is such a great instrument.'

'Who knows how that sounds to dogs' ears? He probably hears some high-pitched tones that we don't. There are those dog whistles that we can't even hear, but dogs do.'

'Hey, did you pinch my dog book when I wasn't looking?'

'No, but we always had a dog at home. Quite a few terriers, and once we even had a dachshund. So you can call me an expert.'

'Good to know. I will certainly bombard you with technical questions very soon. But now I have to get back to work. So, Hercules, if you know what's best for your ears, you're better off in the garden.'

That's fine; it means I can practise peeing.

chapter five

The garden is peaceful and quiet. I peer around to make sure I don't have any uninvited observers this time, then I head for the big tree and raise my leg. OK – here we go! It's working better already. That stupid Beck can shove it. Besides, it's not his garden – it's mine. After all, it goes out from Caroline's workshop, so Beck is nothing more than a visitor. Naturally, he's welcome to come here; a von Eschersbach is always a paragon of refined hospitality. But if this stupid tomcat thinks I'm going to do his bidding just because he's been living here longer, he's sadly mistaken. I will not back down. A von Eschersbach never backs down.

I try it a few more times, switching between my left and right legs, but eventually I get bored. It's time to have a look at the other corners of the garden. Behind the tree there's a big lawn, and the sun is shining invitingly over there. Otherwise I find it quite boring. There's not a trace of rabbits or moles. Here and there a squirrel runs across the grass, or at least it smells like that. But squirrels aren't worth the effort; they jump up into trees far too fast as they run away from you. Even a daredevil like Grandpa wouldn't stand a chance.

The lawn is framed by flowerbeds to the left and right. It smells sweet and summery here, and a couple of bees are whirring from blossom to blossom, heavily laden with pollen. I sniff around the edge for a while, but can't discover anything interesting. Just as I'm about to turn round and head over to the front garden, I hear someone calling.

'Hercules! Hey, come on over here!'

Would that be Mr Beck? What does he want – to go another round with me? I decide not to respond.

'Come on, Hercules.'

I turn round slowly, but don't move from the spot.

'OK, fine. If it's such a big deal to you: Carl-Leopold, would you please come?'

Oh, so now he's singing a different tune. Beck seems to want something important from me. But where the devil is he? I can't see him anywhere. Not on the lawn, not in the tree – not anywhere.

'Beck, where are you? I can't see you.'

'I'm up here.'

'In the tree?'

'No, on the table.'

On the table? I don't see any table! I look around, but I'm still baffled.

'On the table that's on the lawn. Go behind the flowerbed and you'll see it!'

49

So I trot behind the left flowerbed and, sure enough, I see a big garden table, or I suppose I should say the *legs* of a table. My height doesn't make it easy to see much behind these tall plants, but that's got to be it.

'Exactly; you're in the right spot now. Jump onto the chair and you'll see me.'

What kind of guessing game is this turning into? I look around for a chair and find it right next to the table. Wow, is that high! I hope I can make it with one leap.

'Listen, Beck, I don't know if I can jump up there. That's pretty high for me. Why don't you just tell me what you want, or, even better, how about coming down to me?'

'That won't work. You'll see why in a second. So give it everything you've got and jump!'

I heave a sigh and move back three steps so I can get a running start. Then I zoom off and dive onto the chair. Did it! OK, just barely, but still. Feeling a bit smug about this accomplishment, I look around with my head raised high – and spy Mr Beck smack in the middle of the garden table. Actually, he's inside a birdcage that's smack in the middle of the garden table.

'Now do you see why I can't come?'

Beck gazes at me forlornly. I, on the other hand, have to do everything in my power not to fall off the chair laughing.

'What are you doing there? You look hilarious! A fat cat like you in such a little cage!'

'Yeah, thanks a lot for your sympathy. What am I going to

do? I had a once-in-a-lifetime chance to nab that annoying little know-it-all of a parakeet. Unfortunately, I didn't think about how the cage door opens to the inside, and I can't get it open now because my big body is blocking it.'

'Like I said: you're fat!'

Beck ignores this remark, and instead shoots me as piercing a glance as a cat can muster through the bars of a cage.

'You've got to help me, Carl-Leopold. If ol' lady Meyer sees that I snatched her bird, there'll be real trouble.'

'She can come up with that idea even if you're not sitting in the cage.'

'Yes, she can *come up* with the idea, but she can't *prove* it. My first master was a lawyer, and I'll tell you – humans think there's a world of difference between thinking and knowing.'

'Be that as it may – why should *I* help you? I ought to be happy to have you wind up in an animal shelter or wherever else. You'll finally leave me alone.'

'Hey, come on, pal – is that any way to show your solidarity with pets?'

'Solidarity with pets? I don't know; I wouldn't mind asking the parakeet about that.'

Just when I'm about to turn round, Mr Beck takes one last crack at it: 'Fine, call it what you will. But if you've ever toyed with the idea of burying the hatchet between us, now would be an extremely good time to do so. Think how useful it would be to have a friend in this house – someone who knows a hell of a lot about humans.'

All right – he's got me there. I sigh. 'Fine, then, what should I do?'

'Come up to the cage. It can be opened from the top too, but in order to do that, the knots in the cord have to be chewed through first, and I can't do that with my teeth.'

I look at what he has in mind. Sure enough, the cage has an upper door as well, which is fastened with a kind of band. The knots in this band are outside the cage and look like something I can handle.

'I think I could manage that. But we'd have to tip over the cage or else I won't be able to reach the knots.'

'Yeah, no problem. Knock the cage off the table; I'd rather have a few scrapes than keep sitting in here.'

'Well then, here goes!'

With one good shove I push the cage over the edge of the table. Needless to say, it hits the ground with a thud and lands on the side.

'Ouch!' Beck cries and gives himself a good hard shake. 'Oh well, that ought to do the trick.'

I hop from the table to the chair and back down to the ground. Then I stand next to the cage and take a careful look at the matter again. Yes, that's how it could work. The knots are just at the height of my muzzle. And my talent for chewing things to bits is renowned. I would even say I'm a legend in this field. Much to Emilia's chagrin, since it cost her a pair or two of shoes. But this ability needs to be practised somehow.

It takes me less than three minutes to get the band off, and the door opens. Luckily, it opens outward. The opening is on the small side, but Mr Beck squeezes through with all his might. It is astonishing how flexible cats are. Actually, they could be handy to have around when you want to inspect the contents of burrows, but they're probably too chicken to come face to face with a badger, so of course a parakeet is an easier target.

Beck sits down next to me, panting hard.

'Thanks, my friend.'

'Happy to oblige. But tell me this: you really finished off that poor parakeet? Yuck.'

I look at the cage. That's funny: there are hardly any feathers. All I see is a little green plastic bird lying on the bottom, all scratched up. Did Beck gobble up the parakeet complete with its skin and feathers? The very thought sends shivers down my spine. It's one thing to hunt down your prey – but eat it all up? Oh well, to each his own. But Beck is oddly quiet.

'Hey, what's going on? Cat got your tongue?'

'Well, um, how can I put this – the parakeet is still alive. I didn't eat it.'

'It's alive? You mean you were in its cage, and it's still alive? So where is it?'

'This is embarrassing to admit. It wasn't even in the cage when I chased it.'

I look at Beck wide-eyed.

'Yeah, I know what you're thinking. But here's what happened: that stupid bird wasn't in the cage. I went for a walk in the garden this morning, and when I saw the cage on the table, I thought this was my big chance. So I make a beeline for the bird-cage, grab the guy, take a bite – and wind up with that stupid plastic thing down there in my mouth. See what I mean? Ol' lady Meyer just wanted to clean the cage and that's why she put it out. The bird wasn't in there at all – just his plastic friend.'

'Huh? You did what? You seriously hunted down the plastic bird there?' I burst out laughing. 'What a joke! How could you mistake that thing for a real bird? You'd have to be as blind as a bat, ha-ha!' I roll back and forth on the lawn in pleasure.

'Well, the plastic toy does look like a real bird,' Beck argues in a huff.

'Yeah, maybe there's a vague resemblance. But it *smells* completely different!'

Beck sits there in silence. It's pretty clear that my new friend is hard hit by my gloating. OK, maybe I shouldn't push it.

'Hey, I'm sorry. I didn't mean to make fun of you. I just couldn't picture how that happened.'

Beck looks at me sadly. 'I can tell you exactly how it happened. I'm a really old tomcat who no longer has the best eyesight, and my sense of smell is even worse. That's how it happened. Of course a spring chicken like you can't picture that.'

Oh dear; he's depressed. Of course it's a pretty silly mess: climbing into a cage without any prey and not being able to get out again by himself. I try to cheer him up.

'Oh, come on, you can do lots of things I can't begin to do.'

'Yeah, like what?'

Beck stares into space dejectedly. I think for a minute – but no more than a minute, because I come up with something I really do envy him for.

'Well, you just said it yourself. You know people well. You understand them even when they're doing really strange things. I get the feeling I'll never understand them.'

I think that was just what Mr Beck was hoping to hear; now he's smiling again, and he gives me a nudge in the side.

'Right you are, little guy. I really do know people well. But I'll make you a suggestion: now that we're friends, I'll help you too. I'll help you understand people.'

chapter six 🐾

Something behind my right ear is itching horribly. It started about three days ago, and every day it gets a little worse. Unfortunately, I can't reach this spot with my tongue, and every time I scratch it with my paw, I feel a searing pain in addition to the itching. Damn. I don't want to seem like a crybaby, but it's getting really unpleasant. I decide to try rubbing myself on the door frame. It's slightly rounded, so maybe it'll work better than with my claws.

'Hercules, what are you doing?'

Caroline comes round the corner and kneels down in front of me. I keep rubbing and let out a little howl. She pulls me away from the door frame and puts me on her lap.

'Something's wrong here, little guy. Is your ear hurting?' She strokes my head, and when she gets to my right ear, I wince. 'Yes, you have a little lump there.' She touches the exact spot where it hurts, and I yowl.

'Daniel, can you come over here? I need your expert advice.

Hercules has a kind of lump on his ear, and it seems to be hurting him.'

Daniel pokes his head out of his room. 'I'll be right there; just have to finish something.'

I hope Daniel can help me, because the more I think about it, the more my ear hurts. By now the itching has almost completely given way to a continuous throbbing. I lay my muzzle on my front legs and whimper a little. It can't hurt for people to know how bad I feel.

'So, Hercules, let me have a look.'

Daniel leans over me and gently pushes my right ear forward. I whimper a little louder. Once Daniel has felt the lump, he spreads out my fur.

'Ah. That's what I thought.'

Caroline gives him a worried look. 'Is it something serious?'

Ugh. Now I'm worried too. Is my ear about to fall off? That'd be a big problem for me: not only is a good sense of hearing important for any hunting dog, but I'd also be the ugliest dachshund on the planet – no doubt about that.

Daniel shakes his head. 'No, no, don't worry. It's just a tick.'

Phew! Am I relieved! I've heard of ticks, and you can survive them. I've never had one myself, but Emilia always checked us carefully for those after we played in the castle grounds.

'Still,' Daniel continues and something about the sound of his voice makes me think the idea of the ear falling off isn't so far-fetched after all. 'Still, the whole area seems to be inflamed. The spot where the tick bit him is pretty warm and it's starting to fester. Of course we can pull out the tick with tweezers now, but I would take Hercules to the vet just to make sure.'

Oh no, please not to the vet! The very idea sends shivers down my spine, and I actually feel the hair on the back of my neck rising.

'Wow, Hercules, you can really give me the evil eye,' Daniel remarks in amusement.

I can't imagine what's so funny about that.

'Your new roommate seems to understand exactly what we're saying, and he probably wouldn't like to go to the vet at all. Look, he's stiff with fear.'

He hands me to Caroline, who takes me in her arms and strokes my head to calm me down. 'Oh, Hercules, don't you worry. A visit to the vet isn't bad at all.'

Well, with all due respect, I know better than that. Of everyone in this room, I'm the only one who's had this experience as a patient. Twice, even! The first time I let myself be fooled by that friendly-sounding baloney until this guy known as the vet suddenly lifted up a fold of my skin and stuck a needle into it. You have to picture this – a needle! Right into my sensitive skin! A vet isn't bad? It never ceases to amaze me what nonsense humans declare with deep conviction. How I wish I could speak to them at times like that!

While I struggle with the fact that the only way to express my undeniably important and relevant thoughts is by barking loudly, the doorbell rings. Caroline puts me down again and opens the door.

'Hi, everyone!'

'Hi, Nina! Gosh, I almost forgot about you. I'm afraid our plan for today is going to change somewhat.'

Nina looks disappointed. 'Oh, why? What happened?'

'Hercules got a tick, and the whole area is inflamed. I have to take him to the vet. I won't have any time later; I have too many meetings with clients.'

'That's too bad! But maybe the appointment won't take too long, and we can go out for lunch afterwards. If that's the case, I'll just come with you now. Where are we heading?'

'Huh, I haven't given that any thought yet. I didn't think I'd need a vet so soon. Do you know one, Daniel?'

Daniel mulls it over, or in any case furrows his brow, and that's usually a sure sign of mulling things over. I have to get used to looking humans in the face more often; you pick up quite a bit about the mood people are in right then. I've now learned a thing or two about how humans operate, but maybe Beck could give me a little coaching.

'Well, our old vet was top notch, but I'm not sure whether he's still practising. He was the best in the business, and famous all over town. His name was Wagner, and his surgery was just round the corner on Hellmannstrasse. Call directory enquiries.'

•

Less than half an hour later, the three of us are sitting in Dr Wagner's surgery. The von Eschersbachs' vet always came to the castle, so in that respect my visit to the vet today is a premiere of sorts. And I have to admit that if I didn't have such a bad pain in my ear, it would actually be quite interesting here. From my spot on Caroline's lap I have a perfect view of the carrier under the chair next to us, and it contains two rabbits. Amazing – I've never been so close to them. I feel a warm tingling in my nose. I would love nothing more than to hop onto the ground and have a good look at the two of them. Maybe I could chase them through the waiting room – just for fun, of course. You know: solidarity among pets and all that. Still, a little pinch in the hind legs wouldn't kill them. I notice that the pain in my ear really lets up at this thought.

I slowly glide my front paws off Caroline's lap and take a quick peek up at her to see if she's watching me. No – she's having a lively conversation with Nina about her favourite topic: Thomas. I gently slide off Caroline's lap and land right in front of the rabbit carrier. Caroline pets my head just a little, then turns back to Nina. I look around – the coast is clear, because the human in charge of the rabbits is at the reception desk talking to a young woman. So, friends, how about we play around a bit, huh?

I press my nose to the carrier. A splendid smell – I could bark for joy! But I'm better off dispensing with that, because then my plan will surely be exposed, and the fun will be over before it even starts. Instead, I try to lift up the latch that locks the little grille on one side of the carrier. The rabbits are staring at me, and they don't look happy. But that doesn't bother me, so I grab the latch with my teeth and lift it up. With a soft 'click', the grille opens out. Fantastic! It worked! I stick my head right into the carrier and try to grab the bigger of the two rabbits. It squeals in fear; clearly it has no sense of fun at all. But before I can really nab it, something incredible happens. The other rabbit shoots out as quick as lightning and bites me right in the centre of my nose. I howl loudly and pull my head out of the carrier. What a dirty trick!

The rabbits seize their chance to escape and jump right out of the carrier. I bark furiously and try to chase after them, but forget that I'm on a lead. Nina gets caught in the lead when she jumps up in fright as one of the two rabbits scurries through her legs. She stumbles, starts to stagger, and falls straight into the arms of a man in a white coat who at just that moment opens the door next to our row of seats and innocently asks the group, 'Ms Neumann with Hercules?' When I see him, a strange feeling runs through me. But I don't get round to thinking about it much more, because now the owner of the rabbits has run over to us from the reception desk, calling, 'Bobo, Snow White! My poor darlings!' and trying to give me a good solid kick. I jump out of the way and duck under the nearest chair. Caroline is now tugging frantically at my lead, and the granny diagonally across from us, who is sitting there with her old cocker spaniel, has a coughing fit from all the excitement. The man in the white coat – evidently Dr Wagner – is still holding Nina in his arms, and I'm waiting for him to drop her and start chasing after me.

But nothing of the sort happens. Instead, Dr Wagner starts

laughing out loud. A very dark, jovial laugh. A laugh that rings a bell with me. All of a sudden it feels as though I'm back at Eschersbach Castle, sitting with Charlotte on the cold tiles in the vestibule of the stables. I can almost hear the voice of the old von Eschersbach talking to the vet. Dr Wagner isn't any old vet; he's my vet! I start barking excitedly – I have no idea whether it's out of fear or joy.

'Well, little guy! I'm certainly impressed by all the havoc you've created here!'

Dr Wagner kneels down in front of the chair, under which I'm still cowering, and pats my head. Now Caroline leans over next to him, unhooks my lead, which is all knotted up, and pulls me out from under the seat.

'Oh, God, Dr Wagner, this is so incredibly embarrassing. I'm so sorry. I hope nothing happened to the rabbits.'

Huh! What a traitor! What does she care about some rabbits? She ought to be worried about me instead – first I'm stricken with that dastardly rot on my ear, then I'm brutally confronted with my past. At least Dr Wagner has his priorities straight. He shakes his head, then takes me in his arms.

'Don't worry; no need for embarrassment. This little guy can't help himself. A dachshund mix, isn't he? You surely know that dachshunds have been bred for centuries expressly to go for the throats of these very rabbits. And even the best behaved dogs can't fight three hundred years of breeding.' He pets me, and I lick his hands. 'By the way, Hercules looks familiar to me somehow. Have you been here before with him? We don't have a patient file for him yet.'

Caroline shakes her head. 'No, I'm a new dog owner. A friend recommended your practice to me.'

'Oh well, I must be mistaken, then. After all, I took over my father's practice only about a year ago, and I'm afraid I do still mix up my patients now and then.' He turns to Nina. 'I hope I didn't offend you with my little rescue manoeuvre?'

Nina lets out a very odd giggle and says in a voice that doesn't sound anything like her: 'Not at all; quite the contrary. You came just in the nick of time; thanks so much.'

'That's good. Well, then, let's have a look at Hercules. Will you come with me?'

He opens the door he just came from and with a sweep of his hand invites us inside. Caroline goes first, and Nina, who evidently doesn't want to pass up the chance to see my examination either, doesn't sit back down, but follows Caroline right in.

Dr Wagner gives the young woman at the reception desk a quick nod. 'Sinje, can you help Mr Riedler catch Bobo and Snow White? We don't want them falling victim to the next hunting dog that comes along.'

Behind the door, there's a brightly lit room with a table in the middle. Dr Wagner puts me on it and looks me over.

'So, Hercules, where does it hurt?'

'He has a tick behind his right ear, and I'm afraid the bite got inflamed,' Caroline explains.

Dr Wagner runs his hand along my ear until he comes to the lump. When he touches it, I flinch. In all the chaos out there, it actually stopped hurting, but now the throbbing has become almost unbearable again.

'You're right; it is inflamed. I'll pull out the tick now and disinfect the spot, then I'll write a prescription for an antibiotic. It's possible that the tick infected him with a few germs. I'll also give him a plastic collar so he won't be able to scratch himself there for a while.'

That's just great! Things are going to be grand for the next few days. I'll bet that Beck will collapse in laughter when he sees me with that thing.

'How about you grab Hercules's front paws and I'll put a muzzle on him? We don't want him biting one of us when I remove the tick.'

'Can I make myself useful too?' Nina asks.

If I'm not mistaken, she's trying to make a good impression on Dr Wagner. She's not usually that saccharine.

'Thanks, Ms ... uh ...'

'Bogner. Nina Bogner.'

Now that I have a muzzle on my nose, I don't have a perfect view any more, but it's good enough for me to notice that Nina is positively beaming at Dr Wagner. You can see all her teeth. I have to admit that, for a human, she has quite a nice set of teeth – though her voice now sounds more like a warble. Not so nice.

'Thanks, Ms Bogner; that's kind of you. But we'll manage.'

'Well, it's just that I'm so concerned about our little friend there. You know, I love dogs.'

Man, all that nonsense is getting on my nerves. I certainly

hope Dr Wagner will be done soon and we can go home again. Out of the corner of my eye I see that he is now holding something like tongs in his hand. He leans over me and – OUCH! I *knew* that a visit to the vet always ends in pain, and today is no exception. I'd like nothing better than to snap at Dr Wagner, but the stupid muzzle stops me from doing so.

'Hang in there, Hercules! We're almost done,' Wagner says. 'Just another few seconds and you can get back down from the table.'

He takes a little bottle with liquid and opens it, and a penetrating, pungent odour fills the room. Ugh, that smells horrid! Wagner dribbles some of that stuff onto a pad, then he dabs the spot with it. OUCH all over again! It burns like hell, and this time I'm able to break away from Caroline and jump up. I growl furiously at the two of them.

'Hercules!' Caroline scolds me. 'Dr Wagner just wants to help you. Be a good dog and lie down again!'

'That's not necessary, Ms Neumann. I'm finished. The tick is out, and I've disinfected the spot. My assistant will give you the collar and the antibiotic. Hercules needs to get the medicine for the next seven days in his food. Then everything should be just fine, and your Hercules will soon be his old self again.'

•

Ten minutes later, I'm on Caroline's lap, and the two of us are back in Nina's car. Nina is clearly in a great mood; at any rate, she's whistling a happy tune.

'What's got you in such a good mood?' Caroline asks her.

'Oh, you know, that was quite interesting. Sort of a lunch break of a very different kind. I've never been to the vet's.'

'Well, why would you? I've always had the idea that you don't much like animals. I have to be honest: your newly discovered love of dogs surprises me a bit.'

'Why? Hercules is such a sweet little guy. Next time you go to the vet's, I'd like to come along.'

'Really? Are you sure that this has nothing to do with some other sweet little guy?'

'What? I don't know what you're talking about.'

I'm with Nina on this one; I have no idea what Caroline's talking about either. What other sweet little guy? I didn't see anyone there besides me worthy of that distinction.

'Oh, come on, don't act like that. Do you really think I didn't notice the way you were drooling over him – the vet?'

Nina doesn't say anything; she just keeps on whistling.

'Come on, admit that you like him. I get that. He's good-looking, and the way he caught you right away – really old school.'

Caroline giggles. Nina still won't say anything. Human communication is baffling.

•

Once we get home, I want to head straight back to my basket, but that plan goes out of the window, because even before Caroline can open the door, Beck comes zipping past us as if by chance and whispers to me, 'We have to talk, right away!' Can't a guy get a little peace and quiet around here? On the other hand, Beck made such a big deal out of it that my curiosity prevails.

'All right then, in the garden, as soon as I can,' I say with a sigh.

Beck nods and disappears. I look up at Caroline, start to whimper, and run back and forth looking restless.

'What's wrong, Hercules? Do you have to go?'

I give a short bark and start running towards the garden.

'Hey, not so fast! I have to get to the workshop right away.'

I pause for a second, then I start whimpering again.

'All right, if it's that urgent ...'

Once I'm in the garden, I see Beck sitting under *our* tree. I plop down next to him. 'So, what's up?' I ask.

Beck draws a deep histrionic breath. 'I have made a sensational discovery.'

chapter seven 🐾

'W here? I don't see anything!'
      'Over there!'
   I stare intently at a row of houses diagonally across the street,
but for the life of me I can't make out the sensation that Beck
claims to have discovered there. OK, maybe it's because this
completely oversized plastic thing around my neck gives me a
somewhat limited view, but there's nothing I can do about that
now. Beck pants impatiently.
   'Well, then we'll just have to get closer. Come on, run over!'
   'Wait a second. I first want to find out what we're doing here,'
I hedge. Just what I needed. I can't run very well with the collar;
I keep getting stuck on something.
   Beck sighs. 'We're here to solve your big problem.'
   'Huh?' This cat is starting to get on my nerves.
   'Oh, what am I saying – it's more than a big problem; it's your
very biggest problem.'
   'My biggest problem? Just tell me that over there we're going

to find the proof that I'm pedigreed and von Eschersbach was hallucinating the whole time.'

In my mind's eye I see a pedigree certificate, as long as a roll of paper towels, issued in my name.

Beck grunts. 'Nonsense. Don't start that pedigree stuff again. Nobody cares about that. Your biggest problem is Thomas.'

'Well, yeah.'

'You did tell me that Thomas wants to get rid of you.'

'Right.'

'And what does that mean?'

'That I should behave better?'

'Wrong. It means that you have to beat him to it. *You* have to get rid of him, before *he* can send *you* back to the animal shelter.'

'I have to get rid of Thomas?' I stare at Beck in disbelief. 'How am I supposed to pull that off? Are you suggesting that I attack him and bury him in secret? I think you're overestimating me. I'm a dachshund, not an attack dog.'

Beck shakes his head. 'God, are you thick in the head! Not that way! You now have a historic opportunity to get Thomas off your back once and for all, though not, of course, if you keep standing here rooted to the spot. Come on, follow me!'

I sigh. When will this day finally start to calm down a bit?

•

Even once we get to the other side of the street, I still don't understand the reason for Beck's excitement.

'Excuse me, it's obvious that today I am simply no match for your farsightedness. What is so earth-shattering here?'

'You're standing right in front of it.'

'Huh?'

'In front of Exhibit A.'

'Exhibit A? I'm starting to get worried about you. All I see here is two cars and a fuse box. Come on; don't keep me in suspense. After my visit to the vet today, I'm pretty wiped out. If you could just get on with it and tell me what I'm doing here, I would be greatly indebted to you.'

'Of course. All you see here is two cars. I, on the other hand, see a black metallic BMW. This is the first component of a brilliant, airtight case, at the end of which Thomas will wind up being put out to pasture, and you will take his place on the couch. Let's move along to Exhibit B. Mr von Eschersbach, kindly follow me. We have to conduct a surveillance of the premises.'

Did I mention that Beck once belonged to a lawyer? One very unpleasant upshot of this time is Beck's need to introduce legal mumbo jumbo when the mood strikes him. It's tragic how much humans rub off on their animals. I wish it worked the other way round as well. If it did, the world would be a friendlier place.

'Let's go, dachshund! Up onto the fuse box!'

With one leap, Beck is up there.

'Have you gone out of your mind? How am I supposed to get up there? I can't even do that under normal circumstances – and with this thing on my neck it's completely out of the question.

So either you tell me now, right away, what all the fuss is about, or else I'm going back home.'

Beck looks offended. 'I would have expected a little more involvement on your part. After all, I'm doing this just for you. It doesn't matter a bit to me what your Thomas does with his time. But because you're a friend of mine ...'

'Hold on; what do you mean by that? What's going on with Thomas?'

Beck jumps back down from the box and lands right next to me. Cats have no trouble doing that.

'So, now for the record. This morning I was taking my usual little stroll. I always like to be on the other side of the park; I find there's better air here, more mice, quieter – you'll come to see that yourself once you've been here longer—'

'Beck,' I interrupt him impatiently, 'what about Thomas?'

'As I was coming along here, the aforementioned BMW stopped right next to me. And who got out?' Beck gives his voice an air of importance: 'Thomas!' He pauses meaningfully.

'So what? Why shouldn't he drive here? He probably works here. He drives to his office every morning.'

'Jeez, Hercules! Don't be so naïve! Even the laziest human can make the distance from our house to here in no more than five minutes on foot. This isn't the office! And it gets much better!' Now the tip of his tail starts twitching back and forth in excitement. 'Thomas then went to the entrance of this house, where we're standing right now. He opened the door and – was greeted by a young woman! She flung her arms round his neck!

In the hallway; I saw it with my own eyes!'

I shake my head. 'I don't see what's so exciting about that. These humans are constantly flinging their arms round each other's necks. Probably they're not all that able to stand on two feet, and every once in a while they have to prop themselves up on other people. Nina, for instance, today at the vet's—'

'Stop talking nonsense, you stupid dachshund!' Beck interrupts me gruffly. 'Not like that! They kissed! Do you get it? Thomas kissed another woman!'

'Why shouldn't he? I've seen that lots of times. Caroline and Nina kiss each other's faces now and then; that's just one of those human rituals.'

'With their tongues?'

'What?'

'Do they kiss each other with their tongues?'

I'm confused. Kissing with your tongue?

'You mean licking each other? I've never seen people doing that. They don't do that at all. Which is a pity.'

'But that's exactly my point!' Beck cries triumphantly. 'They *do* do it! Though not always. Only when they want to mate. And that's just what I saw. I went out of my way to slip into the hall because I suspected something like that was going on. Thomas licked this woman with his tongue, and she did it to him too. Here's what happened. First they kissed the normal way, and then they stuck their tongues in the other one's mouth. An unmistakeable sign! There's some major cheating going on here, and I've exposed it!'

That is way too complicated for a little dachshund. My ears are buzzing – both of them – and that has nothing to do with the collar. Evidently, my confusion is written all over my face, because now Mr Beck moves even closer to me and whispers conspiratorially.

'Carl-Leopold von Eschersbach, I will bring you Thomas's head on a platter. He's cheating on Caroline with another woman. As you surely know, men and women like to form couples, and once they've done that, they stay in pairs. Anything else is cheating. That is, mating with a woman or a man other than the one you belong with is cheating. And kissing the way Thomas and this other woman kissed is usually the way cheating starts. My old master, the lawyer, was an expert on this subject. Many men and women came to him when they wanted to separate from their partners because of cheating. Then we had a specialist who took pictures of these cheaters so that there would be proof. These pictures quite often showed people licking each other that way. When our clients saw the pictures, they usually cried at first – then my master helped them get rid of the cheater. So that's my plan: we show Caroline that Thomas is a cheater, then we throw him out. Brilliant, isn't it?'

Now I'm all excited too, and wag my tail back and forth like crazy.

'And you think this'll work?'

'I'm a hundred per cent certain. Dead certain. We just need proof.'

My tail stops wagging.

'Damn.'

'What is it?'

'The proof. How can we prove that? We can't just take a picture and show it to Caroline. And Thomas isn't stupid enough to kiss another woman right in front of Caroline's eyes.'

Beck nods. 'That's right – this is still a problem. I have to think that over for a while. But I'm sure to come up with something. Until then, I suggest we step up our surveillance. When the time is ripe, we will enter into evidence procurement.'

Like I said: legal mumbo jumbo.

'But you don't know which apartment Thomas is in with this woman. And even if you did know – how are we going to get in there?'

'You're such a worrier! And you're completely wrong on both counts. First, the apartment is on the ground floor. I saw the woman closing the window. And that makes the second part easier for us too, since even a dog should have no trouble getting into a ground-floor apartment.'

Am I mistaken, or do I detect a mocking undertone? Whatever the case, I decide to ignore it, because no way am I going to be provoked into entering a stranger's house, led by a cat who obviously has a screw loose.

·

'Come on, hurry, I can't carry you any more!'

Beck is groaning and tottering. I'm still hesitating. It's a good few feet to the window ledge, and if I fall down, I will be in for a hard landing. But we've come so far that it would be a shame to give up now and turn around. We've already managed to slip into the house unnoticed with the postman and we got into the garden through the back door. Now 'all' I have to do is get from the stairs at the back door to the window of the apartment in question. So I close my eyes, take a deep breath – and jump.

OK, maybe it was more like a foot and a half. In any case, I land almost effortlessly right in front of the big window. Phew. Two seconds later, Beck lands next to me. Somehow I envy the way cats get around. Even without the collar I wouldn't make it half as far as Beck. We both peer through the window, curious as can be. Sure enough, there's Thomas. And that woman. And they're doing exactly what Thomas recently called 'going strong'. In the dark bedroom, that was kind of hard to see, but here the situation is as clear as day: we are witnessing a mating.

Beck is rejoicing. 'Yup, I knew it! Sex! Call me Supernose! Call me Sherlock Beck! Who says I'm too old? No way! I've got what it takes.'

He's jumping up and down so wildly that I get scared that we could (a) fall down together, or (b) be discovered. Although the latter is pretty unlikely, because Thomas and company are quite preoccupied with themselves.

'So that's what sex is,' I observe drily, once Beck has calmed down again.

'Exactly. And humans make a huge deal out of it. That is, who with whom and when and why. Believe you me.'

Well, dachshund breeders are no different. The mating of

females is always a really big deal. The right male has to be found, Kennel Club authorization may be required, then there is the wait for the female to be in heat and the male to be receptive to mating, etc., etc., etc.... so it's a complicated business. And then, of course, the breeder has to make sure at all times that no other male mates with the female – think of my mother! – or else all the trouble was for nothing and the dream of premium offspring comes to an end. But I digress...

The fact of the matter is that all the hoops dachshund breeders have to jump through are for a concrete reason – to satisfy the breeding and pedigree requirements of the Kennel Club. But humans seem to have something altogether different in mind, something more momentous than bureaucratic hassles in registering their breeding. If they didn't, this issue would not be something that would split up couples, in this case Caroline and Thomas.

'Are you daydreaming?' Beck asks me.

'No, I'm just wondering why this is so important to humans. Why they care about who does it with whom, or why they do it at all.'

'Because of love, of course!'

'Because of love? What's love got to do with it?'

'Man, Hercules, do I have to spell out every little thing for you? OK, here goes: for human couples, sex and love belong together on a really basic level. But it would take a lot of time for me to explain how that works, and we don't exactly have time on our hands at the moment. Right now the important thing is to figure out how we're going to prove to Caroline that Thomas is cheating on her. Everything else will have to wait.'

Well, I've got to admit that when the cat is right, he's right. Then I get a brilliant idea. 'OK, if we don't have a photo, we'll just have to take something else with us.'

Beck looks at me in amazement. 'Take something with us? What?'

'Anything that's such clear evidence that it'll make Caroline realize instantly what happened. Something like …' I scour the scene one more time: '… of course – I've got it!'

•

'You miserable, miserable bastard!'

Caroline is beside herself. I'm delighted. Our plan is actually working!

'But darling, let me just explain …' Thomas stammers. 'This is a really silly coincidence, that's all!'

'I find black lace knickers in the pocket of your jacket, and that's a silly coincidence? How stupid do you think I am?'

She'd be better off wondering how stupid Thomas is. It didn't even strike him as odd that I just dragged his jacket through the hall. That's what comes of not paying attention to pets. It really comes back to haunt you. Caroline, on the other hand, picked up on it right away and looked over at me, which is when she discovered the tip of the knickers peeking out.

'Believe me, Caroline, I haven't the slightest idea how they wound up there. Not the slightest!'

Thomas sounds desperate, but Caroline isn't buying his story.

'I've had enough of your lies, Thomas. I've had a feeling for a long time that something wasn't right. The strange phone calls, all your supposed business trips.'

Caroline's feeling was spot-on. The very moment Mr Beck slipped through the half-open patio door with the knickers in his mouth, I knew that Thomas's relationship with this other woman had not just started up. One quick sniff and I knew where I'd smelled that scent before: in Thomas and Caroline's bed. That was the very thing I couldn't place back then: the scent of this woman. It's perfectly clear that she's been in their bed as well! Can you believe that? Not that I'm an expert on this subject, but I'm pretty sure that that is a huge bump up in the 'cheating' category. I really hope that Caroline doesn't let Thomas sweet-talk his way out of this. He simply deserves to be kicked out on his ear, and the chances are excellent that that's exactly what's going to happen. Caroline's voice doesn't sound the least bit conciliatory.

'The hotel reservation emails in the names of Mr *and Mrs* Brodkamp – supposedly a slip-up by your secretary. The scent of someone else's perfume, which I'm supposedly imagining. Forget it; now it's over for good! I want you to go. Right away! I'm going to Nina's now, and when I come back, you'd better be gone.'

She turns and walks to the door.

'But, but – Caroline!' Thomas is clutching at her arm. 'You

can't do that. You can't just throw me out of here. I thought we're in love!'

Caroline looks right into his eyes, then says in a very firm voice: 'Yes, I thought so too. But apparently I was wrong. Goodbye, Thomas. Come, Hercules. Nina's waiting for us.'

•

I'm so proud of you, Caroline. She pulled that off superbly, without batting an eyelid. She was downright frosty. From my spot on the floor of her car, I can't see her very well, but she's got to be beaming all over. Finally she's rid of that cheater – what a reason to celebrate!

I am certainly happy. In my mind's eye I picture Caroline and me hanging out on the couch for a cosy evening in front of the TV. Wonder if I'll be allowed to sleep in the bed? It's way too big for one person. A little fellow like me would certainly fit – whoops-a-daisy! The car screeches to a halt, and I'm rammed down deeper onto the floor of the car. Ouch! Did we have an accident? I climb back up, and there it becomes clear to me in a flash why Caroline slammed on the brakes. I see her slumped with her upper body on the steering wheel, her face buried in her arms, and – crying. Actually, she's not just crying; she's quivering from head to toe. Her shoulders are trembling, and her sobbing really scares me. What's wrong? Clearly, Caroline isn't happy. I sit next to her without making a peep and think about what to do. How do you comfort a human?

I slowly push my muzzle under her arms and get to her face.

It's really warm and wet. I begin to lick it, very cautiously at first, then a little more. Hmm, really salty. At first, Caroline doesn't react at all, which is astonishing, because normally every human has a very definite opinion about dogs who slobber all over their faces, and in many cases it's not a positive one.

But eventually, Caroline straightens up again, turns to me, and pets my head. 'You want to make me feel better, don't you? That's sweet. I'm really glad I have you.'

I try to make some sort of affirmative sound, which of course I can't do, so I lick her hands as well. She giggles a little. At least that's something!

'It's all right, sweetie. You're probably wondering what's going on, aren't you? You have no idea what's happened, you poor guy.'

Well, I wouldn't exactly say that, but it may be a good thing that Caroline is not especially well informed about the specifics of this matter. She wipes the tears off her face.

'It's OK, don't worry; everything will be fine.'

Is she talking to me, or to herself? In any case, she's stopped crying, and now she's starting up the car again.

Carl-Leopold von Eschersbach, it had better have been a good idea to meddle in this human stuff.

chapter eight 🐾

'Hercules, old buddy, I wish you could speak.' Daniel lifts me onto his workbench and looks at me. 'I wish I knew what really happened with Thomas and Caroline.' He strokes my neck. 'But she doesn't want to tell me – and you *can't* tell me.'

If truth be told, even if I could talk, I wouldn't tell Daniel what happened. I now wish Beck and I had never had the dumb idea with the knickers. When Caroline and I got back from Nina's, Thomas was already gone, but apart from that, none of what I was hoping for has come to pass. We're not sitting on the couch and snuggling up together all nice and cosy, nor am I sleeping on Thomas's side of the bed. No, since Thomas left, Caroline has not been her old self. She cries a lot. She doesn't talk to me any more. She doesn't really talk to anyone. And she hardly sleeps. She paces back and forth in the apartment and listens to loud music. Sometimes it's so loud that it gets to be too much even for other humans – which is saying quite a lot. But when the neighbours ring the doorbell to complain, Caroline just looks at them without saying a word and closes the door. She does turn down the music a little, but nothing else changes. She continues roaming around the apartment aimlessly.

For the past four days, she hasn't even been going to work in the workshop. She grabbed me in the morning and took me down to Daniel She hardly said a word, other than to ask Daniel whether he could take care of me during the day. So for now I'm spending my days with him, and in the evening he brings me back upstairs. He uses every time he hands me over to strike up a conversation with Caroline, but he never gets anywhere.

'Really, Hercules, I'm worried about her. It's horrible that the thing with Thomas has hit her so hard. I think you'll agree with me that the guy was a complete idiot who isn't worth a single one of her tears. And certainly not if someone's as classy a lady as Caroline.'

Woof, exactly! I growl a little at the mention of Thomas's name, but otherwise I wag my tail in approval of Daniel's analysis.

The only good part of the situation right now is the series of man-to-man conversations between Daniel and me. Well, 'conversation' may be overstating it a bit, but Daniel does talk to me quite a lot. I guess it's no wonder; after all, we're usually alone. But in the process I learn quite a bit about humans in general and Caroline in particular. And of course about Daniel. He knew Caroline even before Thomas appeared on the scene. The two of them learned together how to build these wooden things – violins, cellos and objects of that nature. That was somewhere really far from here, in a place with a wonderful name: *Mittenwald*, which means 'in the middle of the woods'. It must have been a really great town to have a name like that.

The violinmaking course that Daniel and Caroline took had lots of girls on it, but none of them was like Caroline. Daniel realized that straight away, and soon they were best friends. They even lived together. They experienced lots of firsts in life: the first spring cleaning, the first home-cooked Sunday roast, the first Christmas without their parents. The only thing they went through separately was the first great loves of their lives, which was a good thing, because they could lean on each other for support afterwards.

When Daniel tells me these stories, I almost feel as though I'm a human myself. At least I feel that I'm starting to figure out how two-legged creatures tick. Of course Mr Beck has already explained quite a bit to me as well, but straight from the human's mouth it somehow sounds more convincing. When I'm with Beck, I'm never quite sure whether he's dreaming up parts of what he's telling me just to make the story more interesting.

Daniel pets me again, then puts me back down on the floor. 'Well, now I have to buckle down again or sooner or later we'll wind up in a big mess here. A special customer is coming in soon. Since you're a dachshund, you probably won't pick up on this – but as a man I can assure you that she's a feast for the eyes! And an excellent musician as well. And what a livewire – ooh la la! That lady's a real winner. Sometimes you have to rein her in a little, but it's always nice to see her.'

He starts to hum a melody and tidy up his workbench.

Now that is really boring. And maybe this excellent musician will also play the violin, which will truly be too much for me. I head to the porch door. Maybe I'll run into Mr Beck in the garden. A nice talk between us pets would be just the thing now.

Sadly, there's no trace of Beck. He's neither behind the house nor in the front garden, but while I'm in the front, I make another interesting discovery: a young woman has sat down right on the low wall that goes round our front garden, and she's doing something to her face. I move closer so I can get a better look. She doesn't notice me because she's so busy doing … what? From the looks of it I would have to say that she's painting herself. In any case, she's holding a little sponge in her hand covered in a bright colour, and she's smearing this colour on her nose. A moment later she takes a pencil and puts some red paste on her mouth. Hmm, that's odd.

The woman stuffs her painting equipment back into her handbag and stands up, then she bends forward quickly and shakes her hair over her head. Looks pretty much like a dog coming out of the water and shaking himself dry. The idea that humans do that without water is further proof that two-legged creatures act totally irrationally, without rhyme or reason. She's now tossing her hair – which is absolutely dry – back over her shoulders. Her hair is very long, very black, and very curly. Looks a bit like the Hungarian sheepdog who once visited us at Eschersbach Castle. I remember wondering how he could even see the sheep he was supposed to watch over.

Now I see that the woman has a suitcase in addition to her handbag. Definitely a violin case, as I now know. So she's probably the musician Daniel was just talking about. I can't judge whether she's especially pretty for the human eye. It's hard to say; after all, she painted her face so much that its original form can't be made out. Anyway, Caroline is the prettiest woman in the world, and that's all I care about.

As the painted lady goes towards the entrance, I run through the garden back to the porch door so I can be standing next to Daniel when he opens the workshop door.

'Daniel, my dear!'

She flings her arms around his neck and kisses him. I try as hard as I can to work out whether it is with or without her tongue. I've certainly learned a thing or two by now. Unfortunately, I can't see the kiss very well because her puffy curls are hiding both their faces. But for my own sake, I hope that this was a normal greeting, because I can't deal with anything else at the moment, even though I was no innocent bystander during the latest developments. The workshop has always been a good retreat from the human whirlwind of emotions, and that's the way it should stay.

'Wow, Aurora, you look fantastic as always! Come in; I've been waiting for you. I'm afraid Caroline is sick and she's not in the workshop this week.'

'Poor girl! What's wrong with her?'

Am I mistaken, or does this show of interest somehow not

sound genuine? I would bet a piece of pork sausage that this Aurora is glad not to see Caroline.

'Oh, she's got a bad cold. She's really congested, and I told her to take all the time she needs to get well.'

'Yes, good idea.' Aurora raises her hand and makes a threatening gesture with her index finger. 'But she had better not spread it to you, not now, when I need you so desperately, my dear.' Finally, she notices me as well. 'Since when have you had a dog?'

'Caroline got him from the animal shelter last month. Sweet little guy, isn't he? I'm pitching in as a dogsitter while she's ill.'

'Nice of you. I'm not much of a dog person; I like cats better. But he's really quite cute.'

Grrr, she likes cats better? Maybe I should give her a nip in the heels, then she'll at least have a good reason to prefer cats.

'So, let me take a look at this gem; I can't wait to see it.' Daniel helps Aurora out of her coat and brings her into his workshop area.

'You'll be glad you did, Daniel. It really is beautiful.'

She hands him the violin case, which he puts on his workbench. He opens it carefully, takes out the violin, and turns it back and forth. Then he whistles approvingly.

'My compliments! Cremona school, without a doubt!'

'I was so excited when the broker called me up. I've been looking for an instrument like this for ages. Last week the expert assessment was complete, and yesterday it arrived from London by overnight express. Do you think you'll be able to restore it?'

'Well, the soundboard has a crack and there's some warping – but, all in all, it doesn't seem too terrible. I would say that there is every reason for hope.'

Aurora whoops with joy and flings her arms round Daniel's neck again.

'I knew it! You're the best! Thank you, thank you, thank you!'

I notice with a sense of satisfaction that Daniel pushes her away gently.

'Don't mention it; this is my job, after all.'

'When can you get started?'

Daniel looks over at the calendar hanging on the wall across the room.

'Hmm, let me see. Well, this week is out, because I'm here all alone for the moment. But I'd already pencilled you in for next week just to be sure, so I can certainly start then. I can't say exactly how long it will take. It also depends on what I find when I open it up.'

Aurora nods and puts her hand on Daniel's arm. 'Just call me when you have a clearer idea. Will you be coming to my performance at the concert hall next week?'

'I don't know yet whether I'll be able to make it. There's so much going on here …' He raises his hands apologetically.

'Then I'll just hope that poor Caroline is back on her feet soon. You would really be missing something. We could go out to eat afterwards and have a little celebration. We do have to make a toast to the new violin, of course. How does that sound?'

'Gosh, Aurora, that sounds amazing. I'll see what I can do.

But now I have to get back to work.' With a friendly, but un-mistakeable gesture, he brings Aurora to the door and helps her back into her coat.

'So we'll see each other next week, my dear! I'm counting on you. Please give it your best shot!'

Daniel smiles. 'I will. And that's why I have to get down to work again.'

He opens the door for her, and before she goes out, she gives him a little peck on the cheek. Without her tongue.

•

Caroline opens the door for us. She looks sort of weird, and she also smells weird. A smell that I caught a whiff of here and there at von Eschersbach's as well.

'Hi, guys; come on in.'

'Is everything all right with you?' Daniel asks.

'Sure, sure, everything's all right.'

That's hard to believe. Even Caroline's voice sounds weird. So slow and garbled. All of a sudden I'm feeling uneasy.

Daniel follows me into the apartment. I head for my basket, and he sits down on the couch in the living room.

'Aurora Herwig was here today,' he says.

'Ooh – the lovely violinist! How is she?'

'She's doing fabulously. She bought an old Italian master-piece in London for a good price. I think it's a Cremona, though I haven't read the paperwork yet. In any case, Aurora was quite happy.'

Caroline starts to giggle. 'Well, isn't it just great that Aurora is so happy. Then all's well with the world.'

'Listen, Caroline, is everything really OK? You seem sort of groggy. I'm really worried about you, quite apart from the fact that I miss you in the workshop, of course.'

Caroline sits down next to Daniel and puts a hand on his shoulder. 'You don't have to worry – honestly. This will all work itself out. Next week I'm sure to be my old self again; I just have to rest up a little.'

Daniel hesitates, then gets up. 'Well, OK, then I'll go home. But promise to call me if you're not feeling well.'

'Yeah, yeah, will do, will do. Now get going. I'm tired; I'm heading straight to bed.'

'So, good night!'

Daniel tries to bend down to Caroline, but she ducks away from him.

'Yeah, yeah, good night.'

Daniel goes, and I stay behind alone with Caroline. I can't say exactly why, but my uneasy feeling is slowly turning into fear. Something's not right here. I feel like running after Daniel and getting him back, but how would I pull that off? Damn. Something tells me that Caroline should not be alone right now – that is, 'alone' in the sense of 'without other humans'. Not that I'm underestimating the pleasure of my company, but this situation calls for more than a small dog. Without a doubt.

Caroline stays on the couch for a while, then she gets up, goes to the stereo, and turns the music back on. It could drive you crazy: she's been listening to this music for almost a week. I feel like knotting my ears together. I run over to her and tug at her jeans a little. Hey, pay attention to me, I'm here too, you know! But she just gives me a glassy-eyed stare, then goes into the kitchen. I run behind her. Even though Daniel has already fed me, I could certainly do with a tasty piece of sausage so she could make it up to me. It would be nice if Caroline thought of me for a change. I'm starting to get a bit insulted.

Sure enough, she opens the refrigerator – but only to take out a bottle. She gets a glass and pours something in. Oh, so that's where the smell is coming from! She's obviously drunk some of that stuff already. When she heads back to the living room, she almost steps on my paws. Ouch! I bark loudly. That is not acceptable! I decide to retreat to my basket.

Quite a while later, I hear a clattering sound. I jump up and run towards the racket to find out what's going on. Once I get to the living room, I see Caroline struggling to her feet. Oh no! Did she fall? I trot over to her and lick her hands. I'm not *that* angry with her.

'Ooh, thanks for checking up on me, Hercules. *Everything's-fineeverything'sfine.* Just wanted to grab something from the shelf up there, but the chair was so wobbly.'

I look up. There are several bottles on the shelf in question. Caroline gets up, puts the chair back in place, and climbs up on it again. This time it works, and she takes down one of the bottles. The liquid is a pretty gold-brown colour, but when Caroline opens the bottle, a strong smell wafts over to me. Ugh

– that's surely the kind of thing that's for external use only. Don't tell me Caroline plans to drink it!

She does. She pours the liquid into her glass and resolutely takes a very big gulp.

'What do you think, Hercules – want to try some too?'

She holds the glass in my direction. I put my tail between my legs and howl. Yuck!

'OK then, don't. Cheers!' She lifts the glass in my direction once again, and some of it sloshes onto the carpet. Caroline giggles.

'Finally that revolting shag rug is getting an interesting pattern. Cognac on crème – there you have it. I never liked it, but Thomas was into this *Better Homes and Gardens* crap. What do you think, Hercules? Should I cut it into the right size to put into your basket? It's nice and cuddly.' She grins and pours herself another glass.

She can't be serious; this has got to be another example of human irony. Even though there is now a bright brown spot on the carpet, that doesn't mean it has to be turned into a pad for my basket. Not that I'd have anything against that, but I can't imagine her really doing it. And yet, sure enough, she's going to the cabinet, getting out a pair of scissors, and kneeling down on the carpet.

'So, let's see if anything sensible can be made out of this piece.' She lifts up one edge, takes the scissors, and cuts into it. 'Ooh, this is really tough. But I'm not giving up so easily – not me!'

She gets down to work, moaning and groaning all the while.

I'm flabbergasted. The carpet was round, but now it looks as though a very large, very fierce animal has nabbed a few bites. Caroline has taken a little break and poured herself another glass. The bottle, which was almost full just moments before, is now almost empty. Caroline looks at me.

'You sweetie, you'll stay with me, won't you?' she whispers.

Or at least that's what I imagine she's saying, because now Caroline's speech is so slurred that I can hardly understand her. I lay my head on her lap. Of course I'll stay with you, Caroline! Even though right now my sensitive dachshund nose is suffering quite a bit from your pungent smell. I hope it goes away.

Caroline strokes my neck almost mechanically. Then she murmurs, 'Have to get a refill,' and tries to get up – and she falls right over. Heavens, what's going on with her now? She struggles to get back on her feet, but she can't.

'I'm not feeling so great,' she murmurs, then she starts to retch. Her whole body doubles over, and it looks as though she's in pain.

Suddenly I'm really scared. What should I do? What's going on here?

Caroline is still retching, and I see that she's throwing up on the light-coloured carpet – or what's left of it. Now I get the picture: Caroline has poisoned herself! Probably with the stuff from that bottle! The last time I saw someone throwing up, it was Mummy's sister Luise, when a mean neighbour put something into her food. We need a doctor pronto, otherwise we'll need to fear the worst!

I run back and forth in a fluster and end up back at Caroline's head. She is now lying motionless next to her vomit. I bark loudly to wake her up, but she doesn't move. What should I do? Caroline needs help right away.

Maybe a neighbour will come if I just make more noise? After all, the neighbours did complain about the music. I bark and growl, and jump up and down. Three minutes, five minutes – surely it's been ten minutes by now. But nothing happens. Exhausted, I take a break. Damn, is this the one time no one's home except us? Not even Beck?

Caroline is still unconscious and her face now looks as white as a sheet. I crawl up to her and listen intently. Turns out she's still breathing, thank God. I lie down at her head, my muzzle on my front paws, and listen to her breathe. Sometimes her breathing stops for a moment, and she lets out a moan. What a dreadful situation. And I got us into this mess. This is all my fault. If I hadn't set a trap for Thomas, he would still be here, and Caroline wouldn't have poisoned herself.

I have another go at raising a racket. This time, I jump up and down right in front of the balcony door while barking. It's tilted open; maybe someone will hear me outside. After a while I'm so busy jumping and barking that I almost don't realize that the telephone is ringing. Is one of the neighbours calling? Oh no! I still don't know how people do that thing with the telephone! But maybe this is my only chance to alert someone. So I have to try to get it – and fast, before it stops ringing. I have figured out that much about using the telephone.

The telephone is on a little table in the living room. Caroline always holds it in her hand when she's making a call, so I run over to it and try to lift it with my nose. But that's not at all easy; the telephone thingy is pretty big. I can't really get hold of it on the first try; on the second go, it falls down. Grrr, nothing's working out right today. I hope I haven't broken it. I cautiously sniff the black thing that's now lying on the floor in front of me. I wonder whether you can still use it to make a call, and if you can, how? When I eye it more carefully, I hear a voice coming out of it that sounds really far away. I bark excitedly! If I can hear that voice, maybe the voice can hear me too. Of course I'm not exactly sure whether the voice knows where I am, but never mind; I'll give it my best shot. I bark, growl, whimper, howl and pant – always straight at the phone. Every now and then I listen again for the voice, which still seems to be there. Unfortunately, I don't understand what it's saying, but I get the feeling that it said my name at some point. Could the telephone actually know my name?

Then suddenly the voice is gone, and all that's left is a beeping sound. I growl at the thing in frustration. I guess all that barking was for nothing. I head back to Caroline and lie down next to her. If she's in such bad shape, at least she shouldn't have to lie there alone.

It's really quiet in the apartment. For the first time in ages I would like to be back at Eschersbach Castle.

chapter nine 🐾

Did I fall asleep? I'm not really sure. In any case, I'm wide awake now, because finally – finally! – something is happening. First the doorbell rings, and a little bit later a key turns in the lock, and the door opens.

'Caroline, are you here?'

Holy pork sausage – it's Daniel! I run right over to him, jump up, and try to lick him.

'Whoa, Hercules! That's a nice greeting. Where's your mistress? We're a little worried about her.'

We? Now I notice that Nina's also standing in the hall.

'Daniel, I have a really bad feeling about this. I mean, it's not normal for Hercules to answer the phone and for me not to get through to Caroline. And the way it smells in there – really disgusting!'

'OK, let's go and have a look.'

He comes into the apartment, and I run ahead into the living room. Come on, follow me! I stop next to Caroline and bark loudly.

95

'Oh God, Caroline!'

Daniel is already behind me, and he kneels next to Caroline. Nina comes into the living room. When she sees Caroline lying there, she covers her face with her hands. 'Oh no! What's happened?'

Daniel takes Caroline's hand. 'Well, at least she has a pulse. Caroline!' He shakes her shoulders. 'Caroline! Wake up!'

She doesn't move. He turns her on her side, away from the vomit, and wipes her face clean with a handkerchief he pulls out of his trouser pocket.

'I don't like this; I'm going to call an ambulance.'

He gets up and goes over to the telephone, which is still lying where I dropped it. He talks to someone for a short time, then he comes back to us. Nina sits down next to us on the floor.

'What's going on? Caroline is unconscious, and the carpet is cut into bits over there. How long has she been lying here?'

'Well, I went home two hours ago. Before that I left Hercules with her. Quite frankly, she already seemed pretty tipsy – but I thought, well, that happens every now and then, especially when you're having boyfriend troubles. Of course, she'd already spent four days out of the workshop because she was feeling so down. But she'd promised me she'd come back next week. Damn, I should have checked in on her more often.'

'You can imagine how I'm kicking myself. I knew she wasn't doing well because of Thomas. But she didn't want to talk about it, so I reckoned she needed her peace and quiet for a while. But when I just called her on the phone and got only Hercules barking…' She falls silent and reaches for Caroline's hand.

'Yes, it was a good thing you called me right away.'

'And it's a good thing you have a key! Hercules couldn't have opened the door for us. Speaking of which,' she says while reaching over to me and pulling me onto her lap, 'you are a very clever dachshund. You noticed that Caroline needed help, didn't you?'

'That's right, Hercules,' Daniel agrees, 'if you hadn't gone to the phone and carried on like that, we certainly wouldn't have come round.'

'How did you manage to get the phone off the hook? It can't be too easy for a little guy with such short legs. Too bad you can't speak.'

How right she is. If I could, I'd waste no time in pointing out to her that my legs are not the least bit short for a dachshund. They are the ideal length.

The doorbell rings again, and Daniel lets three men into the apartment. They look as though they're in costume: they're wearing jackets that look a lot like the ones I've seen on bin men – only I'm pretty sure these aren't bin men. One of them goes straight to Caroline. Before he kneels down beside her, he turns to Daniel.

'What's her name?'

'Caroline Neumann.'

'Your wife?'

'No, a good friend.'

The man now does the same as Daniel did – he shakes her.

'Ms Neumann, can you hear me?'

Of course not! We got that far on our own. He takes her hand and feels her wrist, exactly the way Daniel did. Jeez, why did we call *him*? He's not coming up with anything new. I try to get as close to him as I can so he knows he's being watched. But now he's doing something that we didn't think of: he's opening her eyes with his fingers and looking into them, then he takes something that looks like a pen out of his jacket pocket.

'Hmm, there's a pulse, but it's weak. Pretty wide pupils.'

He opens one of her eyes again and aims the pen at it. Oh, it's a torch! Strange – what's he doing there?

'Hmm, very slow reaction. And she vomited. Do you know what your friend had to drink?'

Daniel shakes his head. But *I* know! I race off and find the empty bottle under the pieces of the carpet that were hacked away. I grab it and bring it back like a true professional. The man with the torch whistles approvingly.

'Well, if that isn't a dog who thinks things through! Very good! Now let's see: Hennessy V.S.O.P. – at least the lady has good taste. But you do have to wonder whether it's really necessary to drink a whole bottle of it. Let's be perfectly frank here: does she have a drinking problem?'

Now Nina chimes in.

'Of course not! What are you thinking? Ms Neumann normally drinks no more than a glass of wine in the evening. But she's not feeling well at the moment; she just broke up with her boyfriend, the miserable bastard!'

'Nina, please,' Daniel interjects, 'that's not the point here.'

Mr Bin-Man-Jacket smiles and shakes his head. 'No, it's quite all right. And actually, that's very much the point. Do you think it's possible that your friend had something besides alcohol? Pills, maybe?'

Daniel and Nina shrug their shoulders.

'I don't think so,' Daniel finally says, 'but I'll take a quick run through the apartment and see if I can find anything.'

The man nods. 'OK. My colleagues and I will take Ms Neumann with us. She definitely has a pretty severe case of alcohol poisoning.'

Alcohol poisoning? I wonder if that's really dangerous.

'I'll hook her up to an IV once we're in the ambulance to bring down the concentration of alcohol, and once we get to the hospital we'll take it from there. She'll probably have to stay in hospital for the next three days. So, fellows,' he says to the two other men, 'let's get this show on the road.'

The two men get a stretcher from the hall, put it down next to Caroline, and lift her onto it. Then they go off with her. The third Bin-Man-Jacket says a quick goodbye to us, then disappears as well. Now I notice that after all the excitement another feeling is creeping in: sadness. And loneliness. A little guy like me needs his mistress! Am I going to have to go back to the animal shelter?

'What do we do now?' Nina looks at Daniel quizzically.

'I think one of us should go to the hospital, so someone's there when Caroline wakes up.'

Nina nods. 'Good idea. She really shouldn't be alone in a

situation like this. How about you go first? I'll clean up a bit around here, then I'll come later.'

'OK. What are we going to do with Hercules?'

The two of them look at me. *Not to the animal shelter!* is what I wish I could shout out loud, but all that comes out is a pitiful howl.

'Look at how miserable he seems to be! He must have been so scared. We can't just leave him alone here. Anyway, he saved Caroline's life; he's certainly earned a reward.'

Finally, a sensible idea from Nina.

'How about I take him with me afterwards? As far as I'm concerned, he can stay at my place tonight, and I can bring him to the workshop tomorrow.'

'Good. Then I'll take the night shift with Caroline, if necessary. And tomorrow I'll take Hercules. See you later!'

Once he's gone, Nina sets about getting rid of the mess in the living room with a bucket and scrubbing brush. When she's done that, she stares helplessly at what's left of the carpet.

'Maybe you can tell me what's happened here?' she asks me, and picks up a piece of the carpet. She turns it back and forth, then a grin comes over her face. 'I know this carpet – Thomas insisted on getting it, and Caroline thought it was hideous. And it was crazily expensive. It almost looks as though some*one* was being cut into tiny pieces in its place.' She puts the piece back down. 'That's fine; it just goes to show that our patient will have a speedy recovery.'

What that has to do with poor sick Caroline is beyond me.

But it is comforting to hear that Nina considers it a good sign.

Before we leave, Nina takes one last look through the apartment to see if everything else is as it should be, and while doing so, she discovers something that I've long since suppressed the memory of. She comes back from the bedroom with the plastic surgical collar. Caroline had put it on the window sill.

'Look what I have here, Hercules!'

Yeah, I see it. Great. What are you planning to do with that? You don't even have a dog, and that thing surely doesn't fit around a human neck.

'We have to take it back to Dr Wagner right away; he must be wondering where it is.'

I don't actually believe that, but if Nina is such an orderly, conscientious person, then by all means. As long as I don't have to go with her and be tortured again.

•

We don't get to the hospital after all. Daniel phones and says that everything is going well there so far and that he can stay longer. This takes a big load off my mind. The very idea that Caroline could be really sick is horrible. What was that stuff she drank? I decide I'll pay closer attention to her from now on so that doesn't happen again.

Nina's apartment is much smaller than Caroline's, and it smells completely different. A bit dusty, if you ask me, but still quite nice. Must be from all those books that are absolutely everywhere. There's a bookshelf on almost every wall, and each is filled with books up to the top. Big ones, little ones, thick ones, thin ones. It's hard to believe that she's read all of them. It's hard to imagine especially for someone like me, since I myself can't read. I'm still in the dark about how reading actually works. What I do know is that you have to stare at a piece of paper with a strange pattern on it for an unbelievably long time, and while people do that, something or other happens to them. Inside their heads, I mean. Every now and then they start to laugh when they look at a piece of paper like that – even though no one said anything and nothing else happened either. Or they even cry. I saw Emilia do that a couple of times. What does the paper do to the human head? Does it give rise to some kind of hallucination? Or dream? If I ever get a chance to see Beck again, I'll certainly have to ask him.

The next important question is of course where I'll be sleeping. I've just realized that I'm incredibly tired. Nina is clearly not going to let me sleep in her bed. The way I size up this woman, even my cutest puppy dog eyes won't melt her heart. Or should I try it just to see what happens? Let's not forget that she herself said that I deserve a reward.

So I do what I can, and tug at Nina's leg a little.

'Well, cutie, you're tired too, aren't you? I'm just trying to work out where you could sleep. I don't have a basket for you.'

Now is exactly the right moment for me to cock my head and look seriously sweet. I try it. Nina looks at me in amazement.

'Are you trying to tell me something? You look so … so odd.'

Odd? The nerve of her! I look totally adorable, good enough to eat, delectable! Come on – take a closer look! I cock my head even more and whimper a little.

'Hmm, are you coming down with something? Or do you want anything in particular?'

I give a short bark and run off. There's got to be a bedroom around here somewhere; this place is not exactly gigantic. I find it behind the next door. I trot inside and plop down. Nina follows behind.

'Well, this sounds a little gaga – sort of like *Prince Charles talks to plants* – but are you trying to tell me that you'd like to sleep in my bed?'

I give her another trusting gaze and now perform a stunt that I haven't done much in my life: I sit up and beg. And it works! I stand for at least a minute, as though I'm carved in stone. Well, if that doesn't do the trick, I don't know what will.

Nina looks – and breaks out in peals of laughter. 'That is hilarious! Hercules, where'd you learn that?'

Insulted, I sit back down. This woman obviously has no idea about art. And she clearly doesn't know how hard it is for a dog to get vertical. For a human, of course, it's nothing at all; they can all do that. But for me that was pretty good. Stupid woman! I don't even want to be in her bed any more. I'd rather sleep on the doormat, and anyway…

'Oh, come on, you little rascal! Hop in!' With a quick movement of her hand, Nina flips back the blanket at the foot of the bed and pats the duvet invitingly.

Did I say stupid woman? Utter nonsense. She's quite a nice lady, is Nina

•

'Good morning, you two. Well, I don't know who looks worse – you or Daniel.'

Nina and I don't go to the workshop the next day, but head straight to the hospital. Daniel has kept vigil at Caroline's bedside the whole night, and he really does look bleary-eyed. That's the disadvantage of not having fur on your face: unhealthy living is much harder to hide.

Caroline looks very, very pale around the nose, but at least she's not unconscious any more. She's sitting up in bed, and she even manages a smile.

'Hi, Nina – nice to have you here. And thanks for bringing Hercules along.'

'Well, dogs are actually not allowed in the hospital, but when I explained to the head nurse that Hercules is the one who saved your life, she went along with it.'

Caroline nods. 'Daniel has already filled me in on that. Come here, Hercules; let me stroke you.'

Only too happy to oblige! Nina puts me on the chair next to Caroline's bed, and then we cuddle a little.

'Oh, guys, all this is so mortifying! How could it have happened? Unfortunately, I can't remember a thing – of course, it's probably better that way.'

Daniel takes Caroline's hand. 'Come on, you don't need to

be mortified in front of us. We're your friends. Besides, we expect you to stand by us if we should ever down a bottle of cognac and cut strange holes in carpets.'

A hint of a blush peeks out from behind her pallor. 'Stop it; I can't even listen to that. It is mortifying!'

Daniel laughs. 'Well, my dears, I'm going home. Work is piling up on my workbench. Just yesterday, Aurora brought in an important restoration project, and I really don't know whether I'm coming or going at the moment. But before that I have to hit the hay for a bit so I don't accidentally drill holes in Aurora's new acquisition where they don't belong.'

After Daniel goes, Nina and Caroline sit in silence for a while. I've put my head in Caroline's lap and am enjoying her scratching me behind my ears.

'Caroline, I'm really worried about you,' Nina finally says.

'Well, what can I say? I'm not used to drinking. I didn't do it on purpose, but I wasn't in great shape, so I drank a bit too much.'

'What? You did not drink a *bit too much*. I mean, 3.2 blood alcohol – just one more cognac and you might have fallen into a coma. That didn't just happen to you.'

Caroline stops scratching me. 'What do you mean by that?'

'You know exactly what I mean. Daniel told me that you didn't come down to the workshop for the entire week. And that he was taking care of Hercules during the day because you were feeling so bad.'

Caroline doesn't say a word.

'Obviously I'm going to be worried. Jeez, Caroline, I know you don't want to hear this, but Thomas isn't worth a single tear. That guy treated you badly for years, and I was really glad that you finally threw him out. Of course you don't feel great, but that's normal, and you'll get over it. Do not start believing that your life is going to be sad forever. That simply isn't true.'

Caroline begins to sob, and Nina gives her a tissue.

'Since Thomas has been gone, I've been so lonely. I'm afraid I'll never be happy again. I always wanted a family and children. But I'm further away from that than I'd ever imagined. When it comes down to it, I only have Hercules.'

What does she mean by *only*? Better a loyal dog than a deceitful scoundrel! I can guarantee that I'll never let Caroline down like that. I quickly slobber over her hands. Nina nods at me.

'You understood that, Hercules, didn't you? But as cute as you are, I can understand Caroline. A dog is simply not a person.'

Luckily! I'd like to shout. At least I can be relied on.

'You know, Thomas wasn't perfect, of course, but who is? I'm not either. I now think that maybe I should have forgiven him. Maybe I was too hard on him.'

Nina sniffs disdainfully. 'Oh, please! That sounds as though you're saying an idiot is better than no man at all. I don't understand how you can sell yourself so short. You'll meet the right man; I'm quite sure of that. And when you do, you will realize that today was your lucky day, the day that things started looking up for you again!'

Caroline looks doubtful. 'Well, if you think so. But where I'm supposed to meet this terrific guy is a complete mystery to me.'

Nina laughs. 'If fate decrees that you'll meet your prince, it could even be in the park behind your building. You don't have to look for long.'

Of course – that's it! I get a brilliant idea. A prince is what's needed! And who here is the expert on nobility? Right you are! Caroline rescued me in my time of need, and now I will rescue her. Even if I have to dig up the entire park to do so.

chapter ten 🐾

I hope we're going straight home. I simply must tell Beck about my sensational plan. I've got the rough outline already, but I need someone with great insight into human nature to fill in the crucial details – someone like Mr Beck.

Finally, Nina stops the car, and walks around it to open the door for me. The moment I hop out, I see that we're not at home. To make matters worse, Nina gets my plastic collar from the back seat. Oh no – I have a bad feeling about this. We're back at the vet's!

The car door is still open, so I quickly hop back onto the passenger seat. Nina can drop off that stupid plastic thing by herself; she doesn't need me for that.

'Hercules, what's wrong with you? Come on out; we want to go to Dr Wagner.'

I growl and bare my teeth. What do you mean *we*? Anyway, I'm in the pink of health. The pain in my ear has been gone for quite a while, and I'm not having any other problems. So why do this?

'Come on, sweetie, jump out!' Nina calls to me.

I shake my head stubbornly. Nina sighs, then rummages around in her handbag and pulls out my lead. Is she planning to drag me in? She is. Nina attaches the lead to my collar with a 'click' and pulls me gently, but determinedly, towards the pavement. Evidently, she means business. I briefly consider whether I ought to put up a real fight with her, and who would lose out if I did. Given the huge difference in our sizes, it'd be me. It's pathetic!

Once we're inside the surgery, Nina goes up to the reception desk with me and hands the receptionist the collar.

'I would also like to talk to the vet and have him take another look at Hercules.'

'But that's really not necessary,' the receptionist replies with a smile.

That's right. Well said!

'Even so. I want Dr Wagner to examine Hercules again. He's such a sensitive, delicate little fellow, and I'm always so worried about him. I just want to make absolutely certain.'

Did I hear that right? Nina is worried about me? *You* can believe that if you like. *I* don't. There must be something else going on here. The receptionist shrugs her shoulders.

'OK, if you insist, but you'll have to wait a minute. There are other patients ahead of you.'

At that moment, Dr Wagner sticks his head through the door of the consulting room.

'Oh, hello, Ms Bogner!' he says to Nina. 'Having more problems with ... uh ...'

'Hercules,' Nina helps him along.

Isn't that great? He still remembers her name, but he's already forgotten mine. Maybe he should switch from veterinary medicine to gynaecology.

'Right, Hercules. The dachshund mix.'

Grrr!

'Well, I wouldn't exactly say problems. But I'm taking care of the little fellow right now, because Ms Neumann has been taken ill. And of course I don't want to make any mistakes, so it would mean a lot to me if you would have another look at Hercules to make sure he's all right now.'

Dr Wagner grins. Yeah, that's very funny – ha-ha!

'Well, then, come right in.'

The next thing I know, I'm back on the examination table, and Dr Wagner has my ear in his hand. He runs his hands expertly over my coat and goes over the spot where the tick had burrowed in.

'I can assure you that everything looks good. Hercules is as fit as a fiddle.'

'Hmm, are you sure? What about Lyme disease? I was just reading that dogs can get it too.'

Lyme disease? I prick up my ears.

'Then close monitoring would make sense, wouldn't it? I mean, I don't want anything to happen to Hercules! I could never forgive myself if it did. I'd better come again next week to have you check up on his progress. Maybe you ought to take some blood from him?'

What?! I dart off the table, shoot the two of them an angry look, and give a short but loud bark.

Wagner laughs. 'There you have it, Ms Bogner. Hercules doesn't think much of your suggestion. And to be quite honest, I don't either. Lyme disease is very rare here in Hamburg, and Hercules seems quite healthy. We shouldn't torment him unnecessarily.'

'Oh, I see.'

Nina looks really disappointed. She is quite clearly a sadist.

'But let me make a different suggestion: before you keep dragging this poor dachshund to me, just go ahead and ask me if I'd like to have a drink with you if you'd like to see me again.'

Nina gasps and looks horrified. Why? I think the suggestion is great.

'Uh, I ... I ...' then Nina bursts out laughing and can hardly settle down. 'OK, you've got me there. So let's get down to brass tacks: tonight? Eight o'clock? At Cavallo's?'

Wagner nods. 'I'd be delighted, Ms Bogner. I'd be delighted.'

•

Nina is in high spirits, and whistling loudly during the drive home. She keeps laughing to herself – then she turns to me.

'My goodness, it's unbelievable. I actually asked him to go to Cavallo's with me tonight. Hercules, you bring me good luck. No question about it.'

That's nice to hear, but somehow it's not entirely clear to me what's so sensational about the whole thing. Wagner did say that she should tell him if she wants to see him. And why did Nina act so horrified about that? It appears that communication between men and women is more complicated than a dog would assume at first glance. So it's not just that he says something and she says something. There must be some sort of secret set of rules that has yet to be revealed to me.

We stop next to our house. I'm finally home again! OK, so I wasn't away for long, but I'm dying to confer with Mr Beck about how to set my great plan in motion. Nina and I walk through the garden to the back door of the workshop. She knocks on the glass, and a couple of seconds later, Daniel opens the door.

'So, did you get a good rest?' Nina asks him.

'Well, so-so. I'll just go to bed a little earlier tonight, then it'll be fine.'

'Listen, can you take Hercules tonight? I'm meeting someone this evening, and it is definitely a not-for-pets occasion.'

'Oh, a date?'

'Sort of.'

'Fill me in on the details!'

'Maybe later.'

'Then I'll just say "tally ho" and "happy hunting"!'

'A-hunting I will go!'

I snap to attention. *Tally ho!* How often I heard this saying at Eschersbach Castle, and it was always the lead-up to a great adventure, even though I was still too little to join in. Only Mummy and her sister were allowed to go along. Grandpa was already too old, but he stayed at home with us and told tales about the great event that is the pinnacle of a dachshund's experience in the world: the hunt. He embellished the descriptions of the hunt in a way that always gave me the feeling of having been there myself. The scent of the rabbits, the trail of the red deer, the whiff of excitement and joy – marvellous! I was so looking forward to my first hunt back then. I could just feel that my true calling in life was to roam through the forests side by side with my hunter!

My nose starts tingling ever so slightly – Nina and Dr Wagner are going on a hunt! I'm so excited that I suddenly don't care in the slightest about my talk with Mr Beck. Dr Wagner now appears to me in a whole different light. A hunter! No wonder Nina wanted to see him again! But why aren't they taking me along? I lie down right in front of Nina's feet and howl. I want to go too! Absolutely!

'One thing's for sure: Hercules's former owner was a hunter. Look how he's reacting to the "tally ho" – the little fellow's all excited!' Daniel bends down to me and rubs my belly. 'But unfortunately, you misunderstood us. The kind of ambush that Nina's going on tonight would be totally boring for little dachshunds. You're not missing out on anything by staying with me.'

There it is again – my communication problem. And it's quite clearly not only between men and women, but also between women and dachshunds. Feeling annoyed, I decide to look for the other four-legged creature here. At least there's one guy who understands me. And even more importantly, I understand him.

•

'Come on, don't be down in the dumps! I don't think Nina's really going on a hunt. Anyway, I can guarantee you that she's not hunting rabbits – it's more like the vet that she's hunting.' Beck grins.

I groan deep down inside. Now he's also starting to speak in riddles! Humans are just not good for us animals.

'When men or women talk about the hunt in regard to the opposite sex,' Beck is now explaining, 'it's not about going into the woods and shooting down the first wild boar they find; it's usually about the art of finding the right partner. Do you get what I'm saying? Men are on the hunt for women, and women are on the hunt for men. But it's not meant literally. Humans just say it that way.'

I shake my head in disbelief. 'But why? Why don't they just say what they mean?'

Beck shrugs his shoulders. 'No idea. For some reason, the person that the other one wants to have as a partner cannot find out about these intentions. Quite the opposite – you have to act as though you don't want anything to do with that person.'

'I see. Then it really is like hunting. Slow, silent stalking. Lull the prey into a false sense of security right to the end. That's how you finish off even the cleverest ones.'

'Well, when you put it that way, you've got a point.'

'So, this whole process of finding a mate is more about stalking than about shooting,' I muse. 'And that's why Nina found it unpleasant for the vet to figure out that she wanted to zero in on him – to stick with the image.'

'Right. Apparently, the man isn't supposed to notice that the woman is out to get him. If he does, the plan falls apart.'

When Beck says that, I realize what I actually wanted to tell him about. 'Have you noticed how bad Caroline is feeling?' I ask him.

'Yeah; relationship problems. She'll get over it.'

'Yes, but she's in hospital!'

'Oh, I didn't know that something like that can put people in hospital. Of course I'm sorry.'

'You should be – it was your idea!'

'Now wait a second. What do you mean it was my idea?'

'If you hadn't set up the thing with Thomas, he would still be there, and Caroline wouldn't be so unhappy.'

Beck snorts furiously. 'Now listen to me – we did all that just for you! You were afraid that Thomas would throw you out; have you forgotten? And Caroline was already unhappy before that; she just didn't realize it.'

I have to admit that the cat is not that far wrong, and I don't want to pick a fight with him, so I strike a conciliatory tone.

'Calm down – I'm not telling you that in order to argue with you, but because I have a sensational idea.'

Beck peers suspiciously at me. Although he doesn't say anything, I notice the tip of his tail whisking back and forth frantically. To lend more weight to my words, I stretch to my full height, then I draw a deep breath.

'So here's the plan: we find a new man for Caroline – a prince. At least a really great one.'

Ta-da! I'm eager to hear Beck's reaction. Unfortunately, he doesn't have one.

'Hey, are you still annoyed with me?'

'No. But the idea is nuts.'

'Why? I think it's spectacular.'

'Yeah, because you know nothing about people, especially women.'

Now I'm the one looking insulted.

'Hercules, how do you imagine you'll find a man for Caroline? I'm pretty sure that young women and little dogs have pretty incompatible tastes in men.'

'But that's exactly the point! Caroline's taste in men! It's not only bad; it's catastrophic! If we wait until she finds one on her own, we may soon have the next Thomas in the house. She simply doesn't know what would be good for her.'

'Oh, and you do?'

'Exactly. I do know. We'll simply find a man I'd be happy to go hunting with. A man who befits her high standards, of course; Caroline is not just any woman. But also someone who would be a loyal master to his dog, who would treat him well, feed him daily and take him for lots of walks, because anyone who would treat his dog like that would surely treat his wife well. But Caroline simply doesn't pay attention to these basic things.'

Mr Beck sighs. 'Of course she doesn't pay attention to things like that. She's a human, not a dachshund. Have you forgotten? Besides, women don't like nice men.'

'Huh?'

Poor Beck; he certainly is a doddering old fool.

'That's right: They don't like nice men. If they did, Caroline would have got together with Daniel a long time ago. I'll bet you he is head over heels in love with Caroline, and she likes him too. But he's simply too nice to her – much too nice – so nothing's going to come of it. Thomas, on the other hand, basically did everything right. Well, almost everything. Mark my words: if you are too nice, other people – especially women – don't take you seriously. My decades of studies tell me that women don't really go for nice guys.'

'You mean women go out of their way to pick nasty guys like Thomas?'

'Exactly.'

'But that's terrible.'

'The fact is that if Daniel or any other guy wants to wind up with Caroline, he has to treat her worse.'

I'm speechless – and bewildered. That can't be true! It would ultimately mean that women like to be treated badly. Mr Beck simply has to be wrong, or else my prognosis for Caroline's future love life is quite grim. On the other hand, Beck is onto something in one respect: Daniel is quite nice, and I also get the feeling that he really likes Caroline, so everything ought to be fine and dandy. There's got to be a reason why Caroline fell in love with Thomas instead of Daniel.

Beck and I sit next to each other in silence for a while. I need some time to take in what I've just heard. My lovely plan … I lay my head sadly on my front paws.

'Now that I really think about it,' Beck eventually says, 'your idea may not be so dumb after all. It's an established fact that we animals have a far better understanding of humans than they have of themselves. Maybe we really *could* spare Caroline from the next disaster. We just have to protect her from her own taste in men.'

'And how are we going to pull that off? You just said yourself that that probably won't work.'

'Yeah,' Beck says, and cocks his head, 'that'll be the interesting part of our new assignment.'

chapter eleven 🐾

'Let's go! This is the ideal hunting ground!'

Beck looks at me doubtfully. 'How did you get that idea?'

'Nina said that this place is swarming with princes.'

'She did?'

'Well, not in so many words. But something to that effect.
OK, maybe she didn't say "swarming", but in any case there are
some of them running around here.'

We're standing in the park looking for men. We're not quite
sure what we're going to do once we've found one, but we've
decided to let the situation be our guide, and we'll improvise
from there. Beck's pessimistic attitude is really bugging me
today. He thinks a rainy day is not a good time to find a man in
the park. But we do have to get down to business, because
Caroline has been home for three days now. She still doesn't
exactly look happy, but at least she's back to work. I take that as
a sign that she's on the mend.

'There! I see one! Back there!'

I run excitedly in the direction in which I just saw a pair of human legs under an umbrella. After going a short way, I notice that Beck obviously has no intention of following me. I stand still and turn round to face him.

'Hey, what's going on? What are you doing back there?'

'Hercules, you crazy dachshund! That is clearly a woman!'

'How can you tell? Only the legs are showing. And in the rain I can't smell whether it's a man or a woman, so we have to go and have a look. Come on, at least make some effort!'

That cat is really awful today. He doesn't act the least bit guilty; all he does is grin from ear to ear.

'You have a lot to learn, my dear. There is a woman under that umbrella – guaranteed. I don't have to sprint halfway across the park to find that out.'

'Oh, and how did you come to know that? For someone who can't tell a plastic toy from a real bird, you're certainly showing off!'

Beck completely ignores my potshot, and instead motions with his paw in the direction of the person in question.

'Take a good look. The umbrella has a really eye-catching flower pattern.'

Well, that's true; there are big and little flowers forming stylish circles all over it.

'So, here's another page out of the *Understanding Humans* textbook: flowers are a woman's pattern. No need to follow that one. I have yet to meet a man who would be willing to be seen with a flowery umbrella. So let's save our energy for when we need it.'

Interesting concept, patterns for women and patterns for men. I wonder what that's good for. Can't women and men recognize each other on the spot? I guess that since their noses are pretty worthless, they have to resort to other means of identifying themselves.

We spend another uneventful ten minutes hanging around the park. It's quite big, but fairly round, so you can get a very good overview from the middle. We see nothing at all. Not a single person is out and about. I'm starting to get soaked despite my thick coat. Maybe Mr Beck is right and we should head home. Just as I'm about to admit defeat to Beck, an intrepid two-legged creature comes into view. And this time it is definitely a man. He doesn't have an umbrella in his hand, and he's going along at a pretty relaxed jog from the far end of the park right in our direction.

'Hey, is he heading straight for us?' I ask in surprise.

'Seems so. He probably wants to take a short cut. It's no fun running around in this weather,' Beck points out. 'Well, he'll be here any second. You said you want to improvise. Now's your big chance. I have no plan whatsoever for how we're going to get a closer look at that guy. We don't want to pick up just any old bloke for Caroline, do we?'

Beck is really getting on my nerves. Why did he even come along if he's going to think everything is silly? If Beck were a hunting dog, his owner would have shot him for defeatism. On the other hand, the jogger really is going to be here any second. And no, I have no great plan. I feverishly ponder my options.

When the jogger is about to pass us by altogether, I decide on the spur of the moment to throw myself right in front of his feet with a heartrending howl. It surely looks as though I'm in terrible pain and in urgent need of help. Let's see if the gentleman is an animal lover and takes care of me. We can find out about the prince stuff later.

Two seconds later, I'm no longer so sure that my idea was such a good one. The man tries to get round me, and he stumbles and falls on his face right in front of Mr Beck. He stays on the ground briefly, then he struggles to his feet, shakes himself off, and rubs his right arm. Once he's up and running again, he comes towards me, looks me over – and yells, 'Why don't you watch where you jump, you stupid fucking mutt?!'

OK, so he's quite clearly not a gentleman in the strict sense of the term. He lifts his right leg to give me a kick, but Beck and I run away and hide behind the nearest bush. Oh no! What a disaster! Beck doesn't say anything at first. Once we've caught our breath, he shakes his head slowly.

'What kind of a manoeuvre was that? That had zero chance of success.'

'At least I *did* something. You just stand around here moaning the whole time!' I reply to defend my unconventional approach in my quest for a master.

'Ha! That was nothing but chasing your tail! I wonder what you would have done if the guy had nabbed you, or if he had landed on top of you. Then you'd be as flat as a pancake now. This is getting ridiculous; I'm going.'

I hang my head. There is some truth in what Beck is saying. I hadn't thought this whole thing would be so hard. When Nina talked about looking for a prince in the park, it sounded so simple. Damn.

I suppose I look very down in the dumps, because Beck nudges me in the side and tries to sound comforting.

'Come on, now – it's not the end of the world just because it didn't work on the first day. You're underestimating the effect of rain on humans. Most of them don't like it much and prefer to stay at home. Take a look at them – not a trace of desire to be active. Apart from the occasional jogger, humans do just fine lying around on a couch for days. That would be too boring even for a cat like me! But you'll see: as soon as the sun comes out again, this park will be jam-packed. Then we'll casually stroll from bench to bench and pick out the best candidates, and you can try out your "I'm a poor sick dachshund" number again. That wasn't half bad.'

I look at Mr Beck in amazement. 'Honestly? You didn't think the plan was so awful?'

'No. It was acceptable – considering that it was cooked up by a dog.'

The coast seems to be clear again, so we leave our hiding place and head home. It's now stopped raining, and sure enough, a few more people have come out. OK, not a staggering number yet, but that doesn't matter, because at the moment I don't feel like establishing new contacts anyway. With my head hanging low, I make my way along the gravel path – and almost fall over Mr Beck, who has positioned himself smack in front of me.

'Hey, little guy, stop! Over there I see exactly the scenario we've been waiting for all along.'

I look up in astonishment. Sure enough, there's a man sitting on the nearest park bench. Although the bench is surely still pretty wet, he's settled down and is apparently preparing to enjoy a little picnic. In any case, he's already put a bottle on the bench and is now rummaging through a bag he brought along. I come up closer to have a better lookout point. He doesn't exactly seem like a prince. He's somewhat rumpled, with long-ish messy grey hair that keeps falling onto his face. He also has a beard that almost reminds me of a wirehaired dachshund's coat.

'Hmm, do you think he's the right one? I have serious doubts about this guy.'

But Beck doesn't accept that argument. 'So what? It's an opportunity – why not take advantage of it? If it doesn't work, at least we'll get some experience. Then we'll be well prepared for the real top candidates.'

That didn't even occur to me. Cats are true strategists. And Beck has come up with even more ideas.

'So, we sneak over to the guy, then you'll do your sick dog act. Step it up a bit, with lots of thrashing about, howling, the whole shebang. If he pays attention to you, I'll try to make him understand that he should go back to our house with you.'

'And how are you going to do that?'

'Just like you, I'll improvise!'

When we get to the bench, I look for a strategic little spot to stage my show. The man is so busy with his plastic bag that he has yet to notice me. Every once in a while he pulls his longish grey hair back out of his face and tucks it behind his ears. I lie down to the left of his feet and roll onto my back. Then I start to whine loudly, thrash my legs about, and writhe from side to side. I'm the very picture of suffering and misery – anyone who wouldn't react to that has a heart of stone and doesn't deserve our Caroline!

Sure enough, the man stops fiddling with his plastic bag and leans over to me.

'Say, what kind of guy are you? And what are you up to, anyway?'

A strong odour wafts over to me – it's a mixture of sweat and … and … yes, that's what it is: the stuff that Caroline drank on that horrible night. Awful memories well up in me, and I would like nothing better than to call off the whole business. But out of the corner of my eye I see that Mr Beck is sitting only a couple of feet from us, off to the right, and watching me like a hawk. He seems to be tickled pink. If he thinks I'm giving up now, he's sadly mistaken. I'm seeing this through to the end – woof!

I thrash back and forth a little more, and try to bring even more drama into my act by rolling my eyes and twitching my nose.

'Man, you poor thing, you're in really bad shape! Come on, Willi will pick you up.'

As he says this, the man, Willi, gently grasps me under the chin and stomach with his big hands and carefully lifts me onto his lap. I stop thrashing; I don't want to fall down and really hurt myself. The man rubs my belly, which is actually quite pleasant, except for the fact that he smells even more strongly like that stuff Caroline had to drink. Yuck – that must be something awfully bad. I hope the man doesn't start to vomit; if he does, I'm certainly in a very vulnerable position.

'Well, little chap, you're not trembling any more. So you're all better, aren't you? But what is Willi going to do with you now?'

That's a very good question – and it's exactly the right point for Beck to jump in. I hope he's not asleep at the wheel, and has come up with some way of luring the man to Caroline, even though I'm now utterly convinced that he is neither a prince nor any other kind of acceptable candidate. Come on, Beck, where are you?

'Well, what do you know, there's another little friend! Where are you all coming from at once?'

So telepathy among us four-legged creatures really does work. I quickly roll over onto my belly and watch Beck sweep around Willi's legs. Now he jumps onto the bench and plops down right next to us.

'Meow, meowwwww, meowwwwww!'

OK; cats can't howl to save their lives, or I guess I should say that they can't howl at all. Beck sounds like one of the violins that Caroline works on every day. Or even worse. I wonder what he's trying to accomplish.

'Oh dear, I guess you're not doing so well either. What's going on here today? Are you both sick, or did you two get lost?'

Willi pets Beck's head with one hand and looks at him pensively. Even if he's not a prince, he's certainly a nice guy. Maybe that's all we need. Beck puts a paw on Willi's arm and tugs at him a little.

'Ouch!'

I guess he's using his claws; in any case, Willi is startled, and pulls back his arm. Beck hops back down from the bench and now goes for one of Willi's legs. As well as it is possible with a paw, he pulls at his trouser leg and keeps on mewing.

'Now would be a good time to be able to talk to animals. I would really like to know what you want from me. Should I come with you?'

I lick Willi's hands wholeheartedly. The way they taste – well, how should I say this? – takes some getting used to.

He laughs. 'Hey, my little friend, you're getting really excited. Was that the answer to my question? You want me to come with you?'

It's insanely easy to talk to humans. I thought it would be much harder. Or is Willi especially receptive? Well, it amounts to the same thing. I jump from his lap down to Mr Beck, who is looking at Willi expectantly with his tail racing back and forth. Willi stands up and sways from side to side a little as he does so. Once he is steady on his feet, Beck runs around him twice, then he heads towards Caroline's house. Since I don't have any better ideas, I do the same.

'So I guess I'm supposed to follow? A dachshund and a cat want to take a walk with me. If I tell this to the lady from the Salvation Army, she'll just blame it on the brandy. Well, off we go!'

At this command, Mr Beck and I head to the end of the park, which is right in front of our garden. Every now and then I peer over my shoulder, and, sure enough, Willi is still following us. He hesitates for a moment only when we get to the garden gate.

'This is it? That's a nice house. I don't want them to think I'm a burglar.'

That's funny! A watchdog who brings the burglar home himself! I wonder how Willi got that idea. A moment later we're standing in front of the terrace door of the workshop. I scratch at the glass with Willi standing right behind me and peeping through the window. Finally he knocks. Daniel comes and opens the door – but just a crack.

'Yes?'

Willi clears his throat. 'Hmm, yeah, how can I put this – those two down there sort of brought me to you.'

Daniel looks down, and now seems to notice us for the first time.

'Oh, Hercules and Mr Beck – what are you doing there?'

'Well, the little dachshund seems to have had some pretty bad convulsions, and he collapsed in front of the park bench I was sitting on. Then his friend came and wanted me to come along with them.'

Daniel looks through the crack of the door and lifts one eyebrow, which looks rather funny.

'Oh yes. The cat wanted you to come along with them. I get it.'

'Look, I know that sounds strange, especially coming from someone like me, but believe me, that's how it happened. Then the two of them brought me here.'

At this moment, Caroline appears behind Daniel.

'What's going on here?'

'The … uh … gentleman here claims that Hercules and the cat brought him to our place after Hercules had a dizzy spell in the park.'

Caroline comes up next to Daniel and opens the terrace door.

'So, you two? What did you do? Hassle people sitting quietly in the park?'

She smiles encouragingly at Willi. Hmm, maybe she likes him after all. Daniel, on the other hand, rolls his eyes in annoyance. Of course, Caroline can't see that, but Willi can. He runs his hand through his messy hair, looking uncertain.

'So, as I was just telling your husband, the two of them actually brought me here. What I mean is, first they jumped onto my bench, then the cat pulled at my trouser leg, and then …' Willi hesitates; suddenly the whole thing seems to embarrass him. 'I don't want to take up any more of your time. The dog seems to be all right again. I'll be off now.'

Just as he's about to turn round, Caroline takes a step towards him in the direction of the garden.

'Thank you so much for bringing the two of them home.

They must have wanted something from you, but unfortunately they can't speak. Maybe I'll take Hercules to the vet later. Better safe than sorry.'

'Yes, better safe than sorry,' Willi echoes. 'That's certainly a good idea. I wish you a good day.' Then he goes.

Oh no! Well, that certainly backfired! To the vet. I should have known that this whole act would land me back at Dr Wagner's. I hang my head forlornly, with Beck standing there next to me smirking.

'Well, Hercules, come in,' Daniel finally says, and waves me through the door. 'And you go around the outside, Beck. It seems to me that the two of you have done quite enough together for one day.'

Daniel seems to be annoyed. I scurry back to my box.

'Do you believe the story?' Caroline asks Daniel. 'I mean, did the two of them really drag him along, or did he just want to get a closer look at our back entrance so he could break in here?'

'He didn't look as though apartment buildings would interest him. More like someone who would break into an off-licence to get some booze.'

'But then why would he think up a story like that? Or can you seriously think that Hercules and Beck dragged him here? And if they did, why?'

Daniel shrugs his shoulders. 'Quite honestly? I have no idea! But Hercules certainly doesn't look sick to me. Maybe the old man was hallucinating. That's what happens when you've had a bottle of cognac. It's not so good for the health, is it?'

Daniel grins, and Caroline blushes. She turns on her heel and goes back to her room without another word. Daniel hesitates for a moment, then runs after her.

'Hey, I'm sorry; that was silly of me.'

Caroline doesn't reply. She is really angry at him; even a nearsighted four-legged guy like me can see that. I'm not sure why, but Daniel seems to have caught on right away. He's now standing really close to her and I think he's trying to work out what to do. He eventually goes for the option that I, as a dog, would have picked too: physical contact. He puts his arms round Caroline and pulls her very close.

There's suddenly tension in the air. It's as though the old von Eschersbach had turned up the electricity on the paddock fence to the max.

chapter twelve

'He's so sweet! Honestly! I don't think I've met such a great guy in ages!'

Nina's eyes are sparkling, and as she talks, her hands talk right along with her. Even though Operation Caroline's Prince has yet to be crowned with success, at least her best friend seems finally to have hit the jackpot. Nina has been sitting on our couch for a solid hour singing Dr Wagner's praises. Ugh – the very idea of Nina choosing to spend time with that tormenter of dogs is bizarre beyond belief. A man who has blood on his hands! Maybe even my own! On the other hand, what do I care? The only thing that matters to me in the end is Caroline's wellbeing.

While Nina's voice drones on in the background, my thoughts wander. When the weather improves, Mr Beck and I want to get cracking again. Anyway, the thing with Willi wasn't a total flop. Beck was right – it was good practice, and we got pretty far. I'm not sure why Caroline thought that Willi might be a burglar. Could it have been something to do with his peculiar smell? But there's no way that Caroline noticed that; her nose isn't nearly good enough, and Willi was never standing right next to her. Beck and I have to fine tune our approach. I'll go and look for him in the garden, assuming Nina stops talking at some point and I can go back to the workshop with Caroline. But unfortunately, it doesn't look as though that'll happen any time soon; Nina is gushing like a waterfall.

'And his looks – just fantastic! A super physique! And all his lovely brown hair! A little like Hugh Grant, don't you think?'

I prick up my ears. Maybe this conversation isn't so boring after all. So Dr Wagner is good-looking. This brings us to a topic that is pretty puzzling to dogs: what makes a human look good to other humans? Does a person need to have a lot of hair? Or is less hair better? Does being tall make someone look nice – or being short? Are the standards for men different from those for women? Oh dear, when it comes down to it, I've taken on a huge project with this 'matchmaking service'. Which makes what Nina's now saying all the more interesting.

'Didn't you notice right away how unbelievably blue his eyes are?'

Ah. The colour of someone's eyes is apparently an important point.

'No, I didn't catch that.'

Neither did I. Then again, I'm not able to tell colours apart very well.

'You must have seen his eyes; they're so striking. Cornflower blue!'

'Nina, I don't know if you still recall, but when we were at the vet's, I had a very ill-tempered Hercules with me who howled the whole time, and then tried to kill two cute little rabbits, and utter chaos resulted. Excuse me for not having had the chance to catch a glimpse of the deep blue eyes of your Supervet.'

Caroline sounds a little annoyed. I wonder if it's because she's recalling the terrible visit to the vet, and the way I carried on there. So embarrassing!

'Good grief, are you in a bad mood! I thought it would interest you that your best friend had a date.'

'Forgive me; you're right. I'm sorry I'm so grouchy. I solemnly vow to do better! So, besides the cornflower-blue eyes: how does he kiss?'

That seems to be an especially important point, or else Caroline wouldn't ask about that first. But how do you recognize that? How are Beck and I going to find a man who kisses well?

Nina giggles. 'You're not going to believe me when I say this, but I don't know. We haven't kissed yet.'

Now I get it. It's not a feature you can see by looking at people. You have to try it out for yourself.

'You haven't kissed yet? I thought you spent the whole evening together.'

'We did. And we had a great time. Marc was quite charming and witty. But we didn't kiss. It doesn't matter, though. I want to try to take it slow.'

'Hmm,' Caroline says doubtfully. '*Try to take it slow?* You? That's quite a new tactic. Since when have you been doing that?

There was no sign of that at the vet's surgery. That looked more like laying it out as clear as day. I mean, you wound up in his arms.'

Nina snorts angrily. 'Now wait a second – I just tripped over your stupid dog! And what do you mean by a new tactic? That sounds as though I always hunt guys down with a scattergun.'

'Yeah well, you've never exactly been the prim and proper type when you like someone. More scattergun than sharp-shooting.'

'Caroline, it's easy to see that you haven't been on the market for quite some time. I'm young and single, and when I like a guy, I don't wait for him to come riding in like a knight in shining armour on a steed. I take matters into my own hands. Call it the scattergun approach if you like – but what's wrong with that?'

Market? Steed? Scattergun? Nina is talking in riddles – but Caroline seems to get what she's saying.

'OK, OK. You're right that I haven't been out there for a long time. I have to get used to the idea first.'

Nina nods vigorously. 'Yes, and I'm telling you – don't just sit around waiting for the right guy to show up! That only happens in fairy tales.'

How wrong you are, my dear! That also happens when Carl-Leopold von Eschersbach sees to it personally. Then you don't have to spend your evenings with a vet. So, girls, how about we finish up here so I can regale Mr Beck with my latest discoveries?

'Say, do you think Hercules has to go?' Nina looks at me musingly.

'Why?'

'Well, he's suddenly started pacing around, and he seems so fidgety. Let's hope he doesn't leave a little package under your couch.'

'Actually, I took him for a quick walk before you got here. But maybe we're boring him. I can let him run in the garden; I have to go back to the workshop anyway.'

'That's a pity. I thought you might take a little time off and we could grab some coffee together.'

'I'd love to – but I've really left Daniel hanging in the last few weeks. I have such a bad conscience.'

'Oh, come on. You weren't well, and Daniel was surely glad to be of help.' Nina grins at Caroline and gives her a pat on the back.

'You don't have to look at me like that. Of course Daniel was glad to help, but I don't want to put any more strain on him. He has enough on his plate. The reconstruction of Aurora's violin alone will take forever.'

'Well, boo hoo. Frankly, I'd rather see Daniel take care of you than work on that stupid violin belonging to an even stupider violinist.'

'Aurora is an outstanding musician.'

'She's a nincompoop, and as if that weren't bad enough, she keeps hitting on your partner,' Nina insists.

'Daniel is only my business partner. In his spare time, anyone who wants to hit on him can go ahead and do so.'

Nina rolls her eyes and sighs. 'Yeah, yeah, likely story.'

'Nina, don't start that again. Daniel and I are friends, that's all. Hercules, let's go!'

•

'Our ideal candidate has blue eyes and is good at kissing.' I'm sitting in the sun next to Mr Beck and reporting my latest findings on the matters of humans and choosing a partner.

'Then the issue is as good as settled. This'll be child's play. I'll take a careful look at their eyes, and you kiss the guys. I just hope you have some way of judging what passes for good kissing.'

I give Beck a dirty look. 'Why do I get the feeling you're not taking me seriously?'

'Because I'm not. Your ranting is not getting us anywhere, especially because we don't even know whether Caroline is also into blue eyes. What if she likes brown eyes better? Or green ones? And besides, a human eye isn't exactly huge. From our perspective we can hardly tell from a few feet away what colour a man's eyes are. And then the thing with the kissing – we're not even close to that. If we can get a guy near enough to Caroline for them to shake hands, that'll be pretty good.'

'All right, then, if I'm such a dumb little dog, I suggest that you take over here and I'll just tag along behind you.' Yeah, that stupid cat can kiss my ass.

'Don't get all offended again! Our plan is good. We'll go back to the park and stage the same routine we did with Willi. Eventually, the right guy will show up. The scattergun approach at work.'

'That's funny – Nina was just talking about that too.'

'You see? And she knows quite a bit about this subject. Since I've been living in this house, I've seen Nina show up here with at least five or six different men. We'll do it exactly the same way – have as many men as possible in tow. Like Nina. Believe me, she's an expert.'

I look at him doubtfully. 'Is that so? Then why doesn't she have a man yet? Her selection process doesn't seem to be working so well. Now she's even winding up with that horrible vet.'

'Who knows? Maybe she doesn't even want to hold onto these men for the long haul. Maybe they're just sort of… used up after a certain amount of time. Then a new one has to take the place of the one before.'

'That'd be the first time I've heard anything like that about human couples. I thought the idea was to swear undying love. You said it yourself. Otherwise, Caroline wouldn't have got so upset about that thing with the knickers, right?'

Mr Beck cocks his head. 'Hmm, you're right on that score too. Yeah, what do I know? I'm just an old cat trying my best to understand humans. It's not always going to work. So, what do we do now? Shall we go to the park?'

'All right.'

Operation Scattergun can now begin.

•

The weather is nice today, so more people than we can comfortably check out are enjoying a day in the park. We decide to focus our efforts on the park benches near our house, which will spare us the effort of having to lure the men over half the grass if they wind up following us. Unfortunately, there are only women on the first two benches – and Willi, with his plastic bags, who gives us a friendly wave. So those benches won't get us anywhere.

At the third bench, we finally strike it lucky: a young man has sat down there to tie his shoelaces. I can't tell what colour his eyes are, but we didn't want to take them into account on our first go anyway. Mr Beck and I creep closer, then we get the show on the road.

Or should I say, we *would like* to get the show on the road. Before I can even really get going, a young woman suddenly makes a beeline for the bench and bends down to the man and kisses him. I struggle back to my feet, give myself a little shake, and sit down next to Beck.

'Damn, he already has a woman.'

Beck giggles. 'But we could ask her whether the guy is a good kisser. That was one of your newly discovered criteria.'

'Ha-ha! Very funny.'

I'm a bit disappointed because I found the man very appealing for my dachshund taste. The last thing I need is snide remarks from an overweight cat.

'How about you pick out the next man?' I suggest, and I sound more miffed than I wanted to let on.

'I'd love to, my dear, I'd love to. I've already sighted one – take a look over there!'

He heads along the grass for a bit, then stops in front of a bench next to a flowerbed. OK, I have to admit that the guy doesn't look too shabby. He's reading the newspaper, which would seem to be a sign that he's reasonably well educated, and also makes it possible for us to lie down right in front of his feet without being noticed. So once again I roll onto my back and begin to yelp my heart out.

After a while, the man looks up from his newspaper and watches me carefully. Or at least I think so, because of course I can't see him very well from my vantage point. It seems to me, though, that the man is not showing the least bit of sympathy towards my impersonation of a deathly ill dog. Damn! It worked straight away with Willi. I'm now writhing right in front of his feet and howling as pitifully as I can. All the howling and panting has even made some foam form around my fangs. Despite this, the man just gives me a bored look and moves his feet slightly to the side, then stands up, turns round and walks away. I'm speechless. This can't be happening! Beck comes trotting up to me.

'Hey, what was that? Did he just take off? And left you to your sad fate? Unbelievable how heartless these humans can be!'

We gaze after the man, who is now standing still and looking back at us. Is he feeling bad about walking away? He's rummaging around in his pocket. Maybe some pork sausage? No – he's taking out his mobile phone and starting to make a call. I sneak up a bit closer to him, because something tells me that it's going to be about me.

'Hello, police? Yes, my name is Diekamp. Well, you may be surprised, but I would like to report a suspected case of acute rabies.' He stops talking for a moment. 'Yes, yes. Right, here in Hamburg. OK, connect me.'

Another moment of silence, while the man stands and listens intently to what is being said on his telephone. 'Hello, my name is Diekamp. As I was just telling the other officer, I would like to report a suspected case of rabies. In a dachshund. In Hamburg. Exactly. Uh-huh, uh-huh...'

The man is walking back and forth and staring in our direction. When he sees that I've come closer, he backs away a little.

'You want to know what signs of rabies I'm seeing? I would say... sudden excessive clinginess, convulsions and a hint of foam at the mouth. Ah, Hamburg is not a rabies area? All of Germany is not a rabies area for pets? I understand – but maybe you can send someone over just to make sure?'

Now Mr Beck is also standing next to me. 'Say, that man's awfully worked up! Who's he talking to?' he asks.

'I think it's the police. He told them I have rabies. I must be a damned good actor if people think I'm rabid! You know, usually only foxes get that. Grandpa told me that. It's very dangerous, and a good hunter always has to be careful not to get bitten. A good hunting dog is careful too, of course.'

My voice has taken on a slightly boastful tone, but that's all right; after all, I really do know a lot about hunting. Theoretically, at least.

'What?' Mr Beck shakes his head and laughs.

'Yeah, it's funny, isn't it? And now he wants them to make a special trip out here.'

Beck's laughter dies down. 'Really? Uh, oh. In that case, we'd better get out of here, and fast.'

'Why? Now things are finally getting interesting. Obviously, I'm not a matter of indifference to that guy after all, and maybe he wants the police to find out where I live.'

I think that Mr Beck is simply jealous of my acting talent and the magnificent impression I make with it.

'That's such nonsense, you stupid dog. What do you think the cops do with an animal that they think suffers from a very dangerous disease like rabies? They don't take him home – they haul him in! Maybe even put him to sleep on the spot!'

'They put him to sleep?' I echo a bit uncertainly.

'Exactly. They kill him. Just like that. Nothing will stop them!'

I hear a terrified squeal, and just when I start to wonder at the strange sounds that Beck can make, I realize that *I'm* the one squealing. The look on Mr Beck's face shows me that the situation is urgent.

'Precisely, my friend. You heard me right. And if you ask me, there is only one option left to us at this point.'

We shout in chorus: 'Beat it!' and we run off without another glance at the man. As fast as we can, we scoot out of the park, past Willi, who's sitting on his usual park bench and watching us in amazement.

When we get to our house, I'm drenched in sweat. Not from all the running, but from fear. *Put to sleep*. What a horrible,

horrible thing to say! We slip through the garden gate and lie down in the shade of the big tree. We're too exhausted to talk at first, but then I get up again.

'I don't know, Mr Beck. I guess my plan wasn't so great after all. Or at least not suitable for hunting for a man the way I was doing it.'

Beck's head sways back and forth. 'Don't give up so fast. The basic idea is certainly right. Maybe we just have to narrow down our selection a little more. Not every man who sits in the park when the weather is nice is automatically a good candidate.'

'But that was our exact approach – and by the way, it was *your* idea. I just say scattergun.'

'So what? What do I care about the junk I said yesterday? What's wrong with me learning as I go? I think the secret of our success will lie in a selective preliminary screening. And then we strike!'

'I don't know,' I grumble, 'how would that preliminary screening work?'

Beck thinks it over for a second.'We have to see the men through Caroline's eyes.'

'That's great; how would we accomplish that?'

Instead of answering, Beck jumps up. 'Come on!' he shouts to me over his shoulder. 'I've just had a brainwave.'

chapter thirteen 🐾

I feel a bit silly jumping up and down in front of Caroline with my lead in my mouth, because I actually hate walking attached to a lead. But if Beck's theory is correct, the suitable men in the park are easier to identify if we have Caroline with us. So the plan is to take a walk with her and see who captures her attention. And then … well, what happens then is still a bit unclear. I can hardly pull off the previous act with Caroline standing right next to me. But I'll come up with something, and besides, we'll be tailed by Mr Beck, who claims he'll size up the situation. It would be nice, of course, if Caroline finally got it through her head that I want to take a walk with her.

I jump up again as high as I can, and scratch her jeans with my front paws. She looks down and laughs.

'Hercules, don't get so wild! I know what you want, but let me just finish what I'm doing here. Then we'll go out, I promise!'

She takes one of those small wooden plates from her table and wedges it between the base and the strings of a violin.

Sheesh! Work always comes first around here, even though my issue is far more important. I growl a little.

'So, does Hercules want to go out?' All of a sudden, there's Daniel standing next to Caroline.

'Yeah, he's making it as plain as day. Not that I blame him. The weather is really great outside; it's much too nice to spend the whole day hanging around in the workshop. I'll go out to the park with him in a couple of minutes. It'll do me good as well.'

Daniel nods. 'You're right. Would it be all right if I tagged along for a while?'

Oh no! That's not what I had in mind at all. After all, I'm doing all this in order to find a new man – with an emphasis on new. Bringing another man along is sure to get in the way.

But no one's asking me what I think anyway, so when Caroline finally clips my lead to my collar, Daniel also reaches for his jacket, and the three of us head out of the workshop together. Once we're in the garden, we walk past Beck, who has positioned himself to tail me.

'Hey, what's going on here? He's coming along? You don't take beer to a bar!' he whispers to me.

'You think this was my idea?' I whisper back. 'Tell me what I could have done to prevent this from happening!'

Beck shrugs his shoulders and seems to be about to say something, but by then we're already past him.

While we head to the park, I think about whether my plan has any chance of success under these circumstances. Will Caroline even notice other people if she's talking to Daniel the whole time? It's enough to make you want to tear your hair out – I can't mimic a sick dog because Caroline is here, and watching Caroline's reactions to the men isn't going to accomplish anything, because Daniel is here. Grrr!

'It's kind of odd – here I work right next to such a beautiful park, yet I almost never come to it.'

Exactly, Daniel, I'd like to say, so why did you have to pick today?

'Yes, we don't come nearly as often as we should, although I must say that since I've had Hercules I spend much more time outside than I used to. I have to admit, though, that recently I've been criminally negligent to him, and I feel so bad about that. Just now he even came up to me with his lead to remind me of my duties as his owner.' She leans over to me without breaking her stride, and strokes my head. 'Isn't that true, Hercules? You haven't had an easy time of it with your mistress lately, have you? But wait and see – everything's going to get better now. I hope you're not wishing you were back at the animal shelter.'

Me? Wishing I were back at the animal shelter? Perish the thought! Even if the quest for a master is not exactly running smoothly, Caroline doesn't seem to understand how uncomfortable it can get in a ten by ten cage with guys like Bozo and Boxer.

Since the weather really is nice, and we're not going to get rid of Daniel anyway, I decide just to enjoy the walk for what it is. It's certainly true that Caroline has not been out with me very often in recent days. Actually, she hasn't been out with me at all. We trot along one of the meandering gravel paths, and I have a great

time sniffing at every tree on both sides of the path. Fabulous!
My nose tells me that important dogs have come by here, and
thanks to all my practice in the garden, I can now add my own
scent mark like an expert. Which I go ahead and do – in ample
quantities. Caroline and Daniel are walking along at more of a
stroll than trying to get somewhere in particular, so I have plenty
of time for the things that matter in a dachshund's life.

Now, however, they've slowed down too much even for my
taste; I guess it's because they're so absorbed in their conversation. Humans never stop talking. I pull at the lead a bit. Hey,
let's get moving! I've already peed at every bush!

But Caroline and Daniel pay no attention to me. Instead, they
head for the nearest park bench and sit down. What happened
to her idea that she's been neglecting me and absolutely has to
do something about that? Well, this is certainly not the way! But
the very least Caroline could do is to take off my lead and let me
go on sniffing for a while. So I jump up onto the bench and lay
my head on her lap.

Hey, am I just imagining things, or is there that strange
tension in the air again? Daniel seems to be nervous, and
Caroline smells upset as well. That would come as no surprise.
If I hadn't been outdoors in as long a time as those two, I would
be jumping out of my skin. Somehow humans are just big
animals; they simply don't want to admit it. I try to find Caroline's
hands so I can lick them. Maybe that'll calm her down.

But to my great surprise, before I can slobber over the back
of Caroline's hand, Daniel's hand lands on my nose. Hey, what

do you think you're doing? There's no joking around when it comes to my nose; I'm really sensitive there. I let out a quick growl, and Daniel pulls his hand back as fast as he can. I've obviously frightened him – but he's frightened me as well! What does he want with my nose? I look up at him, but he acts as though nothing's happened. Strange. For a couple of minutes it's really quiet; neither Caroline nor Daniel says a word. It's actually quite nice. Then Daniel clears his throat.

'Say, how about we do something together this week?'

What kind of nonsense is that? They already do something together every day. Caroline apparently sees the situation the same way as I do. She giggles.

'What did you have in mind? Does it involve a cello or a violin?'

'Ha-ha, very funny.'

'Just my way of getting back at you for what you said about the cognac the other day.'

'All right, so now we're even-stevens.'

Now there's silence again.

'Cook,' Caroline says after a while, 'we could cook something together, the way we used to when we shared an apartment in Mittenwald. We haven't done that in ages, and it was always so much fun.'

She smiles at Daniel, with the exact same smile that caught my eye back in the animal shelter. Distinctive, and so beautiful. In an instant, it's much warmer on our bench. Fabulous! I cuddle up to Caroline and savour the moment.

This time I see Daniel's hand in the nick of time, before it can land on my nose, and I duck away. Has he gone crazy? Though I have to say it's obvious that I'm not on his radar at all – only Caroline is; in fact, he's now reaching across my back for her hand and pulling her towards him. Caroline looks astonished, but she's not pulling her hand back. What does *that* mean? When does a man hold a woman's hand? Too bad Beck isn't here; I'll bet he knows the answer. I decide that this can only be a good sign, since humans are usually so sparing with physical contact. I wonder what'll happen next.

'Hey, you!' a loud, surly voice booms out just then.

Caroline and Daniel flinch, and he lets go of her hand.

'Yeah, you!' the voice roars.

Now the man with the unfriendly voice comes into view, and he stands right in front of our bench. I give a quick bark – doesn't this guy notice that he is very much in the way? But he stays rooted to the spot and stares at Caroline and Daniel. Or is he staring at me? I sense that this can't be good.

'Excuse me for coming up to you like this. My name is Holger Diekamp. But the dog you have on your lap behaved quite strangely here yesterday, and I'm afraid he has some kind of dread disease. Frankly, I think it may even be rabies, although the police didn't think so yesterday.'

'The police?' Caroline and Daniel echo in chorus.

'Yes, of course I alerted the police right away. But before they could get here, the dog had disappeared, along with the fat cat that was there the whole time. But I was alarmed, and I took it upon myself to be on the lookout for the dog. After all, rabies is a deadly disease. I know that might sound somewhat excessive on my part, but the dog went into convulsions and was foaming at the mouth. He also struck me as clingy in the extreme – all the classic signs. Any chance that you took him to North Africa recently?'

I feel myself going rigid with fear. What happens if I have to go to the police, and they really want to put me to sleep? Oh no – all this is happening just because I came up with an idiotic plan! I try to make myself as small as possible and squeeze myself really tight between Daniel and Caroline. Clinging to Daniel's trouser leg, I notice he's starting to tremble. How awful! He's obviously really scared of me. My fate is sealed; the two of them are sure to hand me over to the police. I lower my muzzle and start to howl.

'Rabies!' Daniel exclaims in a choked voice, and trembles even more. 'That's the silliest thing I've ever heard!'

Well, what do you know! Daniel isn't trembling with fear – he's shaking with laughter! I jump spontaneously onto his lap in relief and lick his face.

'Whoops, Hercules! As you can see, Mr Diekamp, this little fellow is quite chipper. Whatever was going on with him yesterday was certainly not rabies. Maybe you've mixed him up with another dog.'

Diekamp glares at me.

'No, this was no mix-up. But if you want to put your own health in jeopardy by not following this up, be my guest!'

Diekamp snorts indignantly one more time, then turns on his heel and heads out of the park.

Daniel shakes his head. 'There are certainly some real wackos out there. Rabies – what nonsense.'

'Hmm, I'm starting to get a little worried now.'

'Worried? Why? Hercules is as fit as a fiddle. Just take a look at him. There's nothing wrong with him.'

'Yes, but do you remember last week? The hobo? He also said that Hercules was acting strangely. Maybe he *is* sick.'

Caroline's voice sounds quite upset. Damn – what have I done!

'I mean, convulsions, foaming at the mouth – I once read somewhere that dogs can have epileptic fits. And once you know what they have, you can treat it, the same way you can with humans.'

Daniel sighs. 'Well, OK then, let's stop by your vet if that'll make you feel better. It's also a nice walk from here in this lovely weather, so it's a good idea anyway.'

Caroline nods. 'Yes, I'll call Dr Wagner right away.'

•

'I can already tell you something reassuring at the outset, Ms Neumann. So far, Hercules appears to be in the best of health. Clear eyes, a cold nose, good body tension – so I would rule out an infection.'

Once again, I'm on the cold metal table in Dr Wagner's consulting room, letting him fiddle around with me, resigned to my fate. I feel so miserable that I don't even take advantage of the opportunity to check out Dr Wagner's blue eyes. But what can I say? It's my own fault. It would of course be only fair for Mr Beck to share some of this retribution, but that's not the way the world works. Wagner pats my head, then he turns back to Caroline and Daniel, who are standing next to the table and watching the whole procedure attentively.

'As far as epilepsy goes, it does exist in dogs, but unfortunately it's pretty hard to diagnose. However, it often runs in families. Do you know whether there's any history of epilepsy in Hercules's family?'

Caroline shrugs her shoulders. 'No, sorry. I got Hercules at the animal shelter. I don't know anything at all about his family, but he supposedly comes from a very reputable breeder. The only thing is that he's not pedigreed, so they gave him up.'

Dr Wagner looks at me thoughtfully. 'Hmm, reputable breeder … I have to say I had the feeling right from the start that I'd seen Hercules somewhere before. Must have been a dachshund breeder, and I know nearly all of them. Maybe it was at the old von Eschersbach's place?'

VON ESCHERSBACH! The very mention of his name almost knocks me off the table. I jump up and start barking loudly. Exactly! It's me! A true von Eschersbach! A real good one!

'Easy there!' Wagner says, while gently placing me back in the middle of the table. 'You clearly know this name very well, little chap. I would say: Bingo!'

What Bingo has to do with any of this is a mystery to me,

but for the first time since we met, I almost like Dr Wagner. Finally, a person who recognizes my true origins.

'My father looked after the von Eschersbach breeders. I was there just a few times myself, and the dogs are quite healthy, thank God. But I can ask von Eschersbach whether he's had any problems with epilepsy in his dogs. Diagnosing it can be very time-consuming and expensive, so we ought to have a more concrete suspicion first. Maybe the seizures are caused by something altogether different. Give me a very specific description of what the attacks are like.'

'Well, I can't give you any specifics, because I was never there when they came on.'

'Hmm.' Dr Wagner looks over questioningly at Daniel.

He shakes his head. 'Neither was I, I'm afraid.'

'Then how do you know that Hercules had seizures?'

'This will sound a little strange, but in the past five days two people have told us about these attacks. The first time, someone brought Hercules home from the park to us and filled us in on what he'd seen, then it happened again: a man approached us in the park and claimed that Hercules had gone into convulsions and howled in front of him, and that he was foaming at the mouth. The man was even afraid it could be rabies, because Hercules was suddenly so clingy around him.'

Dr Wagner laughs. 'Well, it's certainly not rabies. Once it reaches the convulsion stage, the animal is already close to death. Also, I can't recall a single case of rabies in dogs in Germany in my career as a vet. But you're right that it's odd.'

He turns back to me and strokes me under my chin. 'Hmm, so you're clingy and strange? Did Hercules have anything traumatic happen to him lately that might have really rattled him? I'm not an animal psychologist, but something like that can have a negative effect on an animal's behaviour. You told me he came from the animal shelter. Separation anxiety, perhaps? Have you ever accidentally locked him out or something of that sort?'

Caroline studies the floor, looking shamefaced. 'I was a bit ill recently,' she whispers more than states.

'Right, I remember. Ms Bogner mentioned it when she brought Hercules for a follow-up examination.'

'Oh, did she?' Caroline blushes.

'So do you think Hercules may be reacting to that?' Daniel asks. 'That's really interesting. Maybe he's worried about you and wants to find someone to look out for you – let's face it, so far he's pulled this act only in front of men.'

I've been found out! I draw in my tail guiltily.

Caroline looks daggers at Daniel. 'I hardly think there's a connection there.'

'Come on, Caroline, I was only kidding.'

Phew, that's a relief! It would have been so unpleasant to have my plan come out into the open. Caroline would certainly not approve.

'Well,' Dr Wagner interjects, 'I don't think the idea I brought up is that outlandish. Dogs do develop a rather protective instinct for their social pack. So if there's reason to suspect that,

I would certainly pursue the idea. Exactly what happened to you?'

'I don't think this is getting us anywhere,' Caroline lashes out at him. 'I'm just fine. But do ask this breeder; that strikes me as a more promising way to get to the bottom of this.'

•

'I mean really, the nerve of him to interrogate me like that! This Wagner is just impossible. I'd like to know what Nina thinks is so great about him.' Once we're on our way home, Caroline gives vent to her irritation. I trot next to her and Daniel, and hang on to every word. After all, this is partly about me.

'Relax; he wasn't trying to be mean. He just wanted to make as sound a diagnosis as he could. He has no way of knowing that you're so sensitive about this.'

'I'm not sensitive!' Caroline shouts.

'Well, maybe just a little,' Daniel replies.

'So what if I am – is it any wonder? Picture this: my vet thinks that Hercules is acting like a psychopath because I'm such a basket case.'

'Come on – no one said anything of the sort. And besides, the idea is totally outlandish.'

'Is that so?' Caroline turns her head to Daniel, who's grinning.

'I really hope that Hercules looks to me to rescue you before dragging in some complete strangers.'

Now Caroline has to laugh as well. 'That's true. I hope so too!'

Oh, so now I get it. Maybe Daniel isn't too nice for Caroline after all. I desperately need to talk to Beck. Maybe our plan is in need of a fundamental revision. Oh, what am I saying – I'm hoping our plan will soon be unnecessary altogether.

chapter fourteen 🐾

'I don't think we need to keep looking; we have our man!'
Assuming an air of importance, I announce to Mr Beck the
next day my new discovery in the matter of choosing a partner
for Caroline. We're sitting under our tree in the garden and
enjoying the warm afternoon sun.

'How do you work that out? First you went to the park with
Daniel, then to the vet, and today Caroline has been out and
about without you the whole day – how can you have found a
prince for her?'

'Quite simply: we've had the prince close by all along.'

'Huh? I don't get it.'

'Daniel. I think Daniel is the right man.'

'Oh, come on. I've already explained to you that his case
looks dire because he's too nice. And there is an extenuating
circumstance that will render his verdict even more severe,
namely his good nature.'

Mr Beck, Esq. I don't appreciate his lawyer talk at all.

'Have you ever considered the idea that your theory might be wrong? I've watched the two of them carefully. First of all, there's a tension in the air when they're together. It's hard for me to describe, but it's clearly there, even if it can't be seen. Like the electricity on a pasture fence.'

Mr Beck looks unimpressed, and enjoys a good long stretch. 'Electricity on a pasture fence? You're a real country bumpkin, my dear. I have no idea what you mean.'

Ignoring his argument, I list more of my evidence: 'And second, Daniel held Caroline's hand. On the park bench – right across my back.'

'So what? They've known each other forever. What does that really mean?'

'And third, Caroline said herself that she would like to have Daniel as her rescuer.'

So, cat, what do you think about that?

'You have quite a lot to learn, my canine friend. What people say and what they actually think and do are two completely different things. Completely different. Sometimes I even think that the faculty of speech is totally wasted on humans, because they almost never use it for sensible things. Honestly, if people could not talk to each other, basically nothing would change. They never tell each other the truth.'

'That's ridiculous. I think you just want to be proved correct.'

'I don't want to be proved correct – I *am* correct.'

My goodness, he certainly is stubborn today. I sigh and stop talking. After all, it doesn't matter what that cat thinks. The important thing is for everything to get sorted out for Caroline once more, and then we'll be a happy family again, with a master, a mistress and a dog. Beck and I continue to sit in silence for a little while, and I decide to head back to the workshop. Caroline is out at some appointment, but maybe I can get in a little love and affection from Daniel.

I arrive just in time to witness a grand performance by Aurora. She's going on about her latest concert and embellishing her description with sweeping gestures. It was apparently a huge success; she makes that perfectly clear. My knowledge of good breeding in humans tells me that this much self-praise is considered bad form. The old von Eschersbach, at any rate, would have given Aurora a very stern look. 'You don't show off. It isn't proper,' was his favourite piece of advice to all castle visitors. Of course von Eschersbach is much older than Aurora, so it's possible that his views are somewhat old-fashioned. Or that thing with self-praise doesn't really apply to artists.

'Thrilled – the people were just thrilled, Daniel. But I really outdid myself that night. It's too bad you weren't there, by the way.'

'Yes, too bad. I'll come for the next one – certainly by the time I'm finished with your new violin. I promise.'

Aurora wrinkles her nose, which looks very interesting. 'Hmm, I get the feeling that you'll come on account of the violin, and not because of me.'

'Come on, that's silly, Aurora. You know very well how much I enjoy hearing you play. I've just been too busy lately.'

'You mean you're too busy taking care of your partner, right?'

'With all due respect, that is none of your business.'

Daniel now sounds a little angry. That's good!

'But I am right! Since Caroline got rid of that Thomas, everything's been going haywire over here. I can hardly get you on the phone, it's virtually impossible to make appointments with you ... not that I'm knocking romantic stuff, but you have a workshop to run, not a rehab centre for broken hearts.'

'Aurora, we've known each other for five years now. Have I ever done bad work for you?'

'No, that's not what I—'

'Well, there you have it. And has Caroline ever done bad work for you?'

'You just don't want to understand me – what I wanted to say is only—'

'That you feel neglected. Yes, I get that.'

'Daniel!' Aurora's voice takes on a weepy undertone. 'Don't be angry with me. I'm just a little disappointed that we see so little of each other these days, that's all. I thought you were interested in my art.'

Oh, how I wish I could roll my eyes! Even without Mr Beck's professional judgement, I realize that Aurora is not really talking about Daniel's interest in her art. But Daniel is apparently choosing to ignore this remark; in any case, he suddenly switches gear and tries to smooth things over.

'Let's not fight. I solemnly swear that I'll come to your next concert, with or without the new violin.'

Instantly, Aurora begins to beam at him like a kid. Hmm, I

wonder if that goes down well with human men. As a dachshund, I find it extremely silly.

'Oh, thank you, Daniel! That means so much to me! And in case that doesn't work out again, in the autumn I'll be looking for someone to accompany me on my next concert tour. It'll be in Italy, and while I'm there, I want to look at a couple of violins that I've been offered. What do you think?'

'Well, you did just buy a masterpiece. Besides, I can't leave the workshop alone for such a long time.'

'I can see that you don't want to say yes right away. But I won't accept a no now either. I'd rather wait a while.' She pats his arm. 'So, off I go. I have quite a lot on my plate.'

She turns round – and steps on the tip of my tail. OK, she probably didn't mean anything by it, and it didn't hurt all that much, since she didn't really get too much of my tail. But I probably won't get this opportunity again any time soon, so I howl pitifully and take a swift but firm nip at her. Quick as a flash. Grrr. Fabulous!

Aurora lets out a sharp cry and jumps up. 'Ouch! Damn it – are you crazy?'

She stares at me, and I try to look as innocent as I can, and howl a little more just to drive the point home. Aurora is rubbing her calf – you can see my tooth marks pretty clearly.

Daniel looks unmoved. 'Well, I guess you must have come down hard on poor Hercules's tail. He's usually so sweet.'

Aurora gasps. She seems to want to say something mean, but decides against it.

'Really sweet, for sure. Say hi to Caroline for me – see you soon.'

She sweeps out of the room. Daniel looks at me, then he bends down and pats my head.

'Well done, fatso.'

•

'How do I look, Hercules?' Caroline has a knee-length flowery dress on, and she's turning back and forth in front of me. Very pretty, I have to say. Besides, I'm happy that she's choosing a flower pattern for her evening of cooking with Daniel. If I understood Mr Beck correctly, that's definitely a woman's pattern. I deduce that Caroline absolutely wants to look like a woman. That's a good sign! I sit down in front of her and wag my tail.

'Oh, so you like it? That's nice – then I'll keep it on. And should I wear my hair down or put it up?'

With a skilful sweep of her hand, she gathers up her long hair and holds it on her head in a bun. I give a short growl. Down is much prettier – you see the hair much better, and no dog would ever get the idea of hiding his beautiful fur, most certainly not if it has a silky shine like Caroline's. A member of the wirehaired dachshund family like me can only envy her. In this regard, Caroline is a real Irish setter, or more like a golden retriever. She lets her hair fall back down.

'I get it, down. Well, that may look better, but it's a little impractical for cooking.'

I cock my head. No – down is much prettier!

'OK, how about a compromise? While I cook, I'll put my hair up, then I'll let it loose again. Exactly. Good idea. Thanks, Hercules!'

You're welcome – glad to oblige. I'm happy when I can help out.

Caroline zooms through the apartment in good spirits, and tidies up a bit. She sets the table, opens one of those horrible bottles, and with one quick motion of her hand pours the contents into another bottle that is bigger and rounder. A big splash of red liquid lands in the container. Looks really pretty, but what purpose that serves is a mystery to me, though I saw this at the old von Eschersbach's place from time to time as well. Maybe it's a ritual? A magic spell? For a successful evening? Being a dachshund, I'm not especially superstitious, but if it helps today, I'm all for it. It would be so great to see the dazed expression on Beck's face if I could tell him that Caroline and Daniel have become a couple after all.

The doorbell rings. That is certainly Daniel. Man, am I keyed up! Caroline is too, apparently, because she's dashing to the door, but then she slams on the brakes in front of the mirror to the right of the door and gives herself a critical once-over before opening the door. I'm eagerly glued to her heels and ready to act as the supportive reception committee. Caroline flings open the door, I stand on my hind legs – it's Nina. Oh no! What's she doing here?

'What are you doing here?'

'That's a warm welcome! I'm fine, thanks, and I'd love to come in.'

'Listen, this isn't a good time.'

'Hmm, I can see that. You're all dolled up compared to the way you usually dress. Who's coming?'

'Daniel. We're going to do some cooking.'

'Oh, Daniel. Then I can surely stay for a minute. I thought you had a date.'

Caroline sighs, then takes a step to the side. 'What's so urgent?'

'I think Marc Wagner is not my type after all.'

'I see. How did this sudden change of heart come about?'

'Hmm, I'll explain it to you in a second. Can I have a glass?' She points to the bulbous glass bottle into which Caroline just poured the contents of the other bottle. 'I have to have a drink first. Today was a complete disaster.'

'Yes, well, I actually wanted to …'

'Thanks, I could really use this now.' Nina takes a glass from the cabinet, pours herself a drink, and takes a quick sniff of the red stuff. 'Hmm, delicious; this is a fabulous wine. Are you celebrating something special? Picked up another hundred-thousand-dollar violin for Aurora at an auction?'

'No, I just wanted to spend a relaxing evening cooking with Daniel and drinking a glass of wine.' Caroline gives Nina a dirty look, which she can't see, because she's too busy with her glass.

'Well, then you're lucky that I've dropped in on you, otherwise you'd just talk about nothing but business the way you always do.'

I notice that Caroline is about to say something about that, but at this very moment the doorbell rings again. It's Daniel.

'Wow, Caroline, you look terrific!' He greets her with a little kiss on her left and right cheek. I've never seen the two of them do that before – I knew my theory was right. Then he sees Nina. 'Oh, hello, I didn't know you were here too.' He sounds disappointed, and I know humans well enough by now to realize that he really is. Only Nina seems to be oblivious to this fact. She waves at him merrily.

'Yes, I joined in on the spur of the moment. I'd rather have a girls' night, but you can certainly stay.' She laughs.

Daniel manages a smile. 'In view of the fact that I, unlike you, have an invitation, that is a very generous offer.'

'My pleasure.'

Nina beams at Daniel. Apparently, she has no intention of clearing out.

'So what are we cooking?'

She heads to the kitchen. Caroline looks at Daniel and shrugs her shoulders. Then the two of them follow Nina. When they get to the refrigerator, they all stand still.

'I have all the makings of a coq au vin. We just need to slice up the potatoes while the chicken is in the oven. So sit down and I'll give you both paring knives.'

Caroline, you really are too good for this world. We'll never get rid of Nina this way. And Daniel and you will never be a couple. And I will never be the super I-always-knew-it dachshund.

It turns out just as I fear: after half an hour Nina is still here. It's no wonder: the chicken is now giving off quite a tempting smell. Of course she wants to have a taste of it, and I can't even blame her. I'm also speculating on a little taste of my own. To improve my starting position, I slip next to Caroline, who is now sitting on the kitchen bench, lay my head on her lap, and look at her as heartrendingly as I can, unfortunately with limited success, because Caroline, Nina and Daniel are so engrossed in their conversation that they don't even notice me.

'So Dr Wagner is not your dream guy after all?'

How can you keep talking about someone who's just a vet? And that's the verdict you came up with? With all due respect, that was a foregone conclusion. If you'd asked me, Nina, I could have told you that right away. Nina pours herself another glass of wine.

'We've gone out three times now. It's enjoyable every time, but it doesn't lead anywhere. And today wasn't even particularly nice, because several large families brought their bratty kids along and managed to spoil our trip to the beach. It was so annoying.'

'What a surprise – and here you are such a fan of children. It must have been really bad.'

Am I mistaken, or is Daniel making fun of Nina? I guess he is, because Nina really tenses up.

'So what? Not everyone dreams of having loads of children. I don't have to want to be a mother just because I'm a woman.'

Daniel backs off. 'Fine. Then no children. It's not a must.'

'Well, in any case, absolutely nothing is happening with Marc and me, so it makes no sense. I'm not looking for a buddy; I want a lover. Maybe he's gay.'

Gay? What might that be? Another word for shy?

Daniel grins. 'Not every man who doesn't want to get involved with you automatically has to be gay. Look at me: I'm living proof.'

Nina glares at him. Hmm – it must mean something other than shy.

'Thanks a lot. And don't worry, I won't make untoward advances to you.'

'Good, I'm glad we've got that out of the way,' Caroline declares with forced cheer. 'I suggest we go ahead and eat.'

An excellent idea. I quickly put on my most innocent look, and this time I get a reaction from Caroline.

'Listen, guys, Hercules would like a little appetizer as well. If I'd known that there would be four of us, I would have bought more.'

'Now listen, you're not trying to equate me with a dog, are you? Besides, no one told me that a cooking event was taking place tonight, otherwise I would have signed on in the proper way. Or...' – Nina hesitates for a second – 'did you two want to be alone?'

You guessed it! I feel like shouting, but neither Caroline nor Daniel replies. Instead, Caroline takes the roasting pan out of the oven. A warm breeze of chicken aroma wafts over to me. Hmm, tasty! I lick my lips. Nina sees that and looks at me pensively.

'Say, is coq au vin the right thing for a dog? I mean, there's alcohol in it.'

Well, that really takes the biscuit! First she invites herself over, then she tries to deny me my rightful portion. Of all the nerve! I growl at her.

'All right, all right! I just don't want you to be caterwauling tomorrow.'

Cat – what? What does Mr Beck have to do with the chicken? Here's where things stand: there's far too much talking going on tonight for my liking, and it's all Nina's fault. Everything looked just right – without that stupid Nina, Daniel would certainly have held Caroline's hand again, and maybe the two of them would even have kissed. I decide that it's time to step in and change the way the evening is going – once I've finally got something to eat, that is.

Daniel, being the dog lover that he's always been, prepares a little plate for me. The finest chicken meat, without bones or tendons. It smells heavenly, but also a bit out of the ordinary. That's surely because of the red liquid that Caroline poured into the other bottle, and also into the roasting pan, in large quantities. I wonder if that's the alcohol. And why would it be harmful? Or is that the very same stuff that sent Caroline to the hospital? Oh, so what – my appetite is winning over my doubts, and after the first taste I'm enchanted by the fabulous flavour. I have to hold myself back from just gobbling up everything. But after five mouthfuls, the dream comes to an end, and I lick every last speck off my plate so as not to waste a single drop of the exquisite sauce.

Unfortunately, the others like it just as much as I do, so I'd just be fooling myself if I hoped for a second helping. But that's all right, because now it's time for Operation Freedom for Caroline and Daniel. I scoot out of the kitchen to the closet and grab my lead, and run back with it in my mouth and sit up and beg right in front of Nina. She looks at me in amazement.

'Do you want to go for a walk with *me*?'

Of course I do! I hop up and down to confirm this.

'Oh no, I'm settled in so nicely here. Better ask your mistress – or even better, ask Uncle Daniel.' She grins at Daniel.

'I get it; you two want a little hardcore girl talk. Come on, Hercules, let's take a spin around the block.'

No! No way! That is the exact opposite of what I want! I quickly drop the lead and run out of the kitchen. Annoyingly, Daniel interprets this all wrong, and comes behind me with the lead, heading for the apartment door. I growl a little, but it doesn't accomplish anything. Daniel puts on his jacket, then he attaches my lead, and two minutes later we're on the pavement in front of the house. We march off without a word. When we get to the park, Daniel clears his throat.

'It's probably weird to talk to a dog about this – but for the time being, you're the only man around, and I just have to vent my frustration. If I'm being honest here, I pictured this evening somewhat differently. More romantic, more intimate, and above all, more just-the-two-of-us. What in the world was Nina doing at our evening together? Can you tell me that, Hercules?'

I shake my head and hope that Daniel appreciates this superb feat of communication between dog and man.

'Oh, I don't know either – I thought there was something more between Caroline and me. But obviously she was quite happy tonight when Nina just dropped by.'

I give a short bark.

'Or was she? But why didn't she say anything?'

I hang my ears sadly. That, my dear Daniel, is something I frankly don't know either. I agree with you that she should have shown Nina the door. We walk a bit further in silence.

'But it's probably my own fault. I have to make it clearer that Caroline means more to me than a colleague and friend, otherwise she'll always consider me her good buddy Daniel. It's high time I did something about that.'

Good idea! I, for one, would be strongly in favour of that, and to show how I feel, I jump up on Daniel's leg for a second.

'You think so too, huh?' He looks around, then laughs. 'I wonder if anyone's watching me having a man-to-man talk with a dachshund... and whether you can be put away for that. I bet it looks really weird. So what? We'll take another spin around the block, then I'll act on my decision.'

Now you're talking! I step up the pace, so we can get home pronto!

●

Once we're back in the apartment, we find that Nina's finally gone home. Caroline is clearing up in the kitchen and she gives us a cheery greeting.

'There you are! Did you have a good walk, Hercules? This must have been a boring evening for you – too much chit-chat, wasn't there? But I'm certainly glad you liked my chicken.'

'I liked it a lot too, by the way. Thanks again very much for the invitation. Shall we have another glass of wine?'

'Sure, why not? Though I am a bit tired. I can't stay up late tonight.'

She gets two clean glasses from the kitchen cabinet and puts them next to the bottle that is still on the kitchen table. Daniel pours, and gives Caroline a glass.

'So, here you are. To our cooking evening for two!'

They both laugh.

'Hmm, I guess Nina was absolutely determined to ignore all our hints. But she got so bogged down in that vet story that she was in urgent need of emotional support today. I'm sorry. This was not how I was expecting our evening to turn out.'

'That's all right. I can live with women's solidarity. I was just afraid you were OK with Nina's visit.'

Caroline shakes her head and yawns. 'Not at all. But now I really have to get to bed. I have to meet a client tomorrow – at 8 a.m., sad to say. Let's make a new date for our cooking – and this time it'll take place at a secret spot.'

She stands up, and Daniel does too. That's just great – so much for 'It's high time I did something'. Now Daniel goes home and nothing gets done. What a disaster. I won't be able to show my face to Mr Beck. He was right after all. Daniel really is too nice. And not assertive enough.

The two of them are standing in the hall, and Caroline opens the door for Daniel. For a moment it seems as though he'll go past her, but then he hesitates – and shuts the door again.

'Listen, Caroline, I have to tell you something. I, uh, no, I have to do something.'

Then he puts his hands on her shoulders, pulls her close, and kisses her – on the mouth. Just as quickly as that happened, he lets go of her, mumbles 'Bye', and disappears.

chapter fifteen 🐾

D amn! I really wanted to tell Mr Beck about last night as soon as I could. I was already picturing the look on his face when he realized that I was right all along. But unfortunately nothing comes of it, because instead of strolling into the workshop in the morning and then slipping out into the garden, I'm running behind Caroline, who's lugging a huge suitcase and is clearly in a big hurry. Now she's throwing me a glance over her shoulder.

'Come on, Hercules, pick up the pace! This is not the time to make friends with every single tree!'

She tugs hard at my lead, and I don't like that one bit. I'm not going to let her get away with this kind of behaviour. I plop down in protest.

'Hercules, what's that supposed to mean? Come on; we're late. I have to deliver this thing on time.'

The tugging starts again. I go into reverse. Caroline snorts in annoyance and puts down the big case.

'You're a naughty dachshund! Your mistress has to work so she can buy pork sausage for you. We have an appointment, and the people are waiting for us.'

Huh! What do I care? You could have parked me with Daniel if I'm in the way. Caroline thinks for a minute, then she bends down to me.

'Hercules, darling, be a good dog and come along now. I promise you that I'll make it quick. I just have to drop something off, then we'll go back home to Daniel. Please!'

Am I mistaken, or does her voice take on a really warm tone when she says the name 'Daniel'? It may be wishful thinking on my part, but in any case, the thought of getting home quickly calms me down. I give up my resistance and take a step towards Caroline, who gives my neck a swift rub.

'Thanks, sweetie. I'll make it quick.'

Shortly afterwards, we're standing in front of the revolving door of a big building.

'Do you want to wait outside?'

No, I don't. I cling tightly to Caroline's leg.

'Well, then, come in with me. But let me take off the lead for a second, so you don't get caught in the door.'

She bends down and unhooks the lead from my collar, then we squeeze ourselves and the case through the door, which is no easy matter. Although I'm small, I'm also long, and getting through a revolving door without jamming my tail in it is rather a challenge. Humans don't have that problem, or else they wouldn't have come up with such a stupid construction. The glass brushes the tip of my tail, but then we're inside. In front of us, there's an enormous hall with lots of people walking back and forth. To the left and right there is a colonnade, which lends the hall a certain similarity to the ballroom in Eschersbach Castle.

I'm sure I've never been here before, and yet this place seems familiar. Not only because of Eschersbach Castle – I was in a room like this with Caroline before. On the side walls there are large contraptions that look like a combination between a cabinet and the kind of television set Caroline has in the living room. When people stand in front of these cabinets and type something under the television set, the cabinets start to rattle and spit out printed paper – the kind that Caroline always carries around with her, and uses to buy tripe at the butcher's and coffee in the restaurant, as I've seen her do on numerous occasions.

Further up in the hall there are people milling around and chatting in front of and behind high tables. This seems to be some sort of meeting place. But I have yet to sniff anything to eat, which is strange, because normally there's always food when people make plans to get together. Well, maybe this is a place to play instead of eat. In any event, if Caroline keeps to her promise, we'll be back outside soon, so it's not worth working out the exact purpose of this hall.

While Caroline talks to a man somewhere up front, I roam around a little, look at the people, and eventually sit down at the side. I'm bored. When humans chat, they obviously lose all sense of time. Maybe I ought to mosey over to Caroline and pull at her trouser leg a little. Speaking of Caroline – I don't see her right now. Where did she go? Maybe I ought to look for her, otherwise this is going to take forever.

Just then, there's an unbelievably loud bang. I squeal in terror and press myself against the wall behind me. What was that? Up front at the high tables, there's a racket, with people running all over the place. Then there's another bang, and someone shouts, 'Everyone down on the floor, now!'

And sure enough, people instantly start dropping to the floor. It's as though they've been given the 'Sit!' command. The dog training area Mummy told me about a few times must have been like this. Great event! The only question is why any of this is happening. And where's Caroline? Is she also lying around here somewhere? I slowly make my way to the front, trying my best not to disturb all these goings-on. The man who shouted seems to be at the front of the hall. In any case, he's the only one still standing. Not only that, but he also has something in his hand that he's waving around, and he seems to be giving more commands. What's going on? I try to sidle up closer as unobtrusively as I can. I have to get a better look.

Once I've crept up until I'm just a few feet away, the man suddenly turns in my direction, and now I can see what he's holding in his hand: it's a gun. How embarrassing – I should have been able to tell that from the sound of the bang! Now really – seeing as I'm a descendant of famous hunting dogs, I should be able to pick up on these kinds of things. The sense and purpose of everything going on here still escapes me, though, because the man does not look like a hunter. He's dressed all in black, and his face can't be made out because he's wearing a black cap that goes from the top of his head down to his neck, with just a slit for his eyes. Very strange.

I'm so distracted by this interesting scenario that I don't notice a man next to me also crawling to the front until he jumps up and pounces on the man with the black cap. The two of them wrestle and eventually wind up on the floor, where they continue to battle it out. Unbelievable! More happens here in five minutes than in Caroline's workshop in two weeks. The man without the cap is clearly trying to get to the gun, and the guy holding it tries to fight him off with all his might. The two of them roll back and forth, so entangled that you can hardly tell who the various arms and legs belong to. Then there's suddenly another loud bang – a shot has gone off. The man without the cap rolls to his side, moaning loudly, while the other man stands up and brushes himself down. Then he takes the gun, which is now lying on the floor, goes up to his assailant, and takes aim!

I know what that means: a coup de grâce! The cap guy wants to kill the other man. No! I want to scream out loud. That's a human, not a rabbit! I feel hot and cold all at the same time. And then, without further ado, I come out from under cover and lunge at the man with the cap. It's all so unreal that it's almost as though I'm watching myself do this. I leap up and sink my teeth into the man's trouser leg before he can fire again. The black fabric is not especially sturdy, and right away I realize it's starting to tear. Next thing I know, my teeth are on his leg. The man jerks back, bellows in pain, and yanks his leg up. I let go and fall down in front of him. He pulls his cap off his head and stares at me angrily.

'What the hell is that? Can someone tell me where this dog came from?'

Suddenly, people are running towards us from all directions. The command to lie on the ground seems to be called off. But the biggest surprise is that the man who was shot and was writhing in agony on the floor suddenly sits up and looks sympathetically at his tormentor.

'Shit, Jens, does it hurt?'

'Sure does!' The guy I bit pushes up his trouser leg, and his calf displays a perfect outline of my teeth. 'Helen! I think I need an ice pack or something.'

A young blonde woman comes out from behind one of the columns and an older grey-haired man who looks sort of like the old von Eschersbach emerges from a group of people. The young woman kneels in front of the man named Jens and looks at the bite, and the older man turns round to the other people.

'So, out with it – who brought that dog onto the set?'

Silence.

'Who?' the grey-haired guy demands again.

I'd love to clear out of there, because I have a feeling that the grey-haired guy is really angry, and Caroline will be in hot water. I still don't know why; after all, I stopped a crime in progress. But no one seems to care about that. Everyone is acting as though it were the most normal thing in the world to aim a gun at someone. But before I can even work out whether there's some clever way to wriggle out of this, I hear Caroline's voice: 'It was me. I brought the dog here.'

Now I finally see her: she's standing next to one of the columns on the left side.

'I'm sorry,' she continues, 'I didn't notice that Hercules ran away. I thought he was still standing next to me and—'

She's just about to explain something else when the man starts to shout, 'Are you crazy? Do you know how expensive this whole shoot is? Every hour that we hang around costs big bucks! And then you bring your ill-behaved dachshund here with you. I hope he didn't really hurt Jens – without him, we can kiss this production goodbye. He's our lead actor!' He snorts again, then takes a deep breath and continues in a somewhat calmer voice. 'By the way, who are you?'

Caroline, who is now looking green around the gills, answers in a near-whisper, 'My name is Caroline Neumann. I brought the cello case for the gun. I'm really sorry about what happened with Hercules. He probably thought it was a real bank robbery and wanted to protect the man over there.'

Exactly! I'm not ill-behaved. I'm just helpful – and quite brave!

In the meantime, this Jens has moved over to us and is giving Caroline the once-over. He looks much better without that cap. He has the blue eyes that seem so important for relationships with men. His hair is very dark and really messy. That last part may be because of the cap, of course.

'Let it go, Roland. I'm OK. The little guy did give me a good hard nip, but I think I'll survive.' As he says this, he winks at Caroline, who actually smiles back. Then he bends over to me. 'So you thought I was really robbing a bank? And you wanted to help Uwe? Good dog.'

Rob a bank? What on earth does that mean? And why do Jens and Uwe seem to be friends? They were just trying to do each other in! A really major confusion is shaping up in my head. How is a dog supposed to understand that? The grey-haired guy, in any case, seems to have had enough of all this idle chatter. He claps his hands quickly and authoritatively.

'OK, kids, let's take a half-hour break to let things settle down around here. Jens, keep your leg elevated for a moment or two. Extras, please be back in position in twenty minutes. And I'm going to calm down with some herbal tea.' Then he looks at me again. 'And get that dog out of here this instant.'

Caroline nods and bends down to put me back on my lead. 'Well, we'd better go right away before you create even more havoc.'

I'm insulted. After all, I still don't know what I supposedly did wrong. But I'm not happy about having caused all this trouble for Caroline either, so I trot along nicely beside her.

She turns back to Jens again. 'I'm terribly sorry, and I hope you're not in too much pain. If there's anything I can do for you, do let me know. I'm so embarrassed by this whole thing.'

'It's not all that bad, Ms Neumann. But there is one thing you could do to make me very happy and ease my pain quite a bit.'

Oh no! I bet he's going to say something along the lines of 'Take that wretched beast to the animal shelter'.

Jens rummages around in his trouser pocket, then puts a slip of paper into Caroline's hand. 'Would you please have dinner with me? You'll find my phone number there. I'll be waiting for your call.'

•

'That's crazy! Jens Uhland! JENS UHLAND! Germany's hottest young actor wants to have dinner with you! I can't believe it! Crazy, crazy, crazy!'

Nina is out of her mind with excitement. The guy with the cap seems to be important in some way. Since Caroline told her over lunch what happened this morning, Nina has not stopped for a single minute to catch her breath. She's been chattering away non-stop. According to Mr Beck, that's a sure sign of great excitement in humans. But I don't understand why Nina's so excited. Nothing all that major really happened. Jens didn't end up with any lasting damage, the grey-haired guy eventually stopped cursing, and in the end, we got back home safe and sound – minus our cello case. I still don't get all that stuff with the gun and the shot. Jens very clearly shot at that other man – so why was the guy jumping around in the pink of health afterwards? I didn't understand Caroline's explanation: film, set, shooting? What does that mean? Nina, on the other hand, seems interested in only one thing, namely the aforementioned Jens. That woman is awful.

'And have you called him yet?'

'Of course not – when could I have? This happened just three hours ago.'

'Oh, right – but you *will* call him, won't you?'

'Well, I don't really know.'

'You don't really know? I don't get it – you're young, you're single; what's there to think about?'

'Come on; just because he's a celeb, it doesn't automatically mean he's my type. Of course I thought he was very sweet, but that's about it.'

'You never know what'll come of it. And "very sweet" is the understatement of the century. Jens Uhland is a real hunk. He's stunning and witty. And he seems to be charming as well.'

Caroline rolls her eyes. 'Has it ever occurred to you that I might not be looking for a new boyfriend right now?'

'Nope! I find that idea utterly absurd. But even if it's true, and you're not actually looking, you can still snap at the chance if the right man comes along.'

All this is extremely interesting. Nina thinks that this Jens falls under the category of 'right'. I don't understand why. Quite the opposite – I'd put him in the category of 'armed and violent criminal'. Besides me, no one seems to have picked up on that. Instead, *I'm* now labelled a violent dachshund. And another thing that's really upsetting me is the idea of Caroline looking for a boyfriend. We've already found the ideal candidate for her, namely Daniel. That Nina is really starting to annoy me. First she interrupts the cosy tête-à-tête with Daniel, and now she's trying to talk Caroline into going after that silly Jens. She's impossible! She ought to take care of her own love life, and she'll have her hands full.

I decide to throw a monkey wrench into the 'Jens' project. I've already bitten him, so we're not about to become close friends anyway. If he turns up again, I'll just piss on him – literally.

chapter sixteen 🐾

For a dachshund like me, there is something hilarious about women standing in front of their closets for an endless amount of time, and taking out one piece of clothing after another, holding it up to their bodies, then going in front of the mirror to look at themselves. OK, I now know that people put on what amounts to a different coat for every occasion – but I'm still puzzled about the criteria for the choice of coat. Why put on a flowery dress one day and black trousers the next? And while we're on the subject of dresses, the length of the dress seems to be a critical factor too. Right now, Caroline is putting three black dresses next to one another on her bed, and they seem to be absolutely identical, except for their different lengths. She looks at the dresses in silence, then she turns to me.

'Hmm, what do you think, Hercules? Mini, midi or maxi?'

I'm stumped. Of course I'd love to give Caroline advice, because if she's getting together with Daniel again this evening, it should finally work out for the two of them. And I'm sure that a crucial step towards success has been made if Caroline feels good in her own skin, or should I say her own clothing? But the length of a skirt is something I've never given a moment's thought to, and in view of the length of my own legs, it would also be pretty absurd; even if there were such a thing as skirts for dachshunds, they would have to be very short. But what would a woman be trying to express with the length of her skirt? I run back and forth uncertainly in front of the bed. What's better: showing a lot of leg, or not much? What do human men pay attention to?

It's obviously much easier for dogs, and for dachshunds in particular. The World Canine Organization defines the general appearance of a dachshund in its Breed Standard N° 148/13.07.2001/GB as follows: *Low, short legged, elongated but compact build, very muscular with cheeky, challenging head carriage and alert facial expression. His general appearance is typical of his sex. In spite of his legs being short in relation to the long body, he is very mobile and lithe. With the distance above ground level of about one third of the height at withers, the body length should be in harmonious relation to height at withers, about 1 to 1.7 – 1.8.*

And the German Dachshund Club of 1888 lists very clear guidelines for the coat of a wirehaired dachshund: *The wirehaired dachshund has a short, thick, tight, wiry outer coat with an adequate undercoat. The muzzle has a distinct beard, and the eyebrows are bushy. On the ears, the hair is shorter than on the body, almost smooth. The hair on the tail corresponds to the hair on the body; it is tight and tapers to a point.*

That's how easy it is with dachshunds. How do I know all that?

Well, as a mixed breed, I had to listen to plenty of commentary about what was wrong with me. My legs are clearly too long, and my coat is too soft and too fuzzy for a genuine wirehaired dachshund. And although Grandpa loved me dearly, he never forgave his daughter for her affair. All his other grandchildren had always been champions.

But to get back to the real question: what is the standard for humans? I'm quite sure there is one. That would be the only way to explain why, for example, Caroline makes such a fuss about dressing up every time she's planning to get together with other people. Otherwise it wouldn't matter in the slightest, and she could simply go looking the way she looks. But annoyingly, I don't know what this standard is. If I did, I could figure out, for instance, whether Caroline's long legs are better off hidden or highlighted. I plop down on my behind and take a good hard look at her. In my opinion, she is an extremely pretty human. But is she pretty to other humans?

'Hey, Hercules, you're looking so thoughtful! Are you trying to give me good advice? Well, here's the thing: I can't decide between this short black dress and the long charcoal-grey one I just had on. I don't like the black trousers so much after all. This is a tough one, isn't it? My grandma always says that beauty is in the eye of the beholder – which means that each of us finds different things beautiful.'

Come on, give me a break! What kind of a saying is that? Once again, my grandpa knew better, and Caroline's grandma obviously doesn't have a clue, or else she wouldn't say such nonsense. Maybe there really is no clearly defined standard for humans, but there must be something of the kind. I can't imagine that every person decides for themselves what they consider beautiful. By the way, the other day I was watching TV with Caroline and we saw a programme that was structured sort of like a dog show, but with women instead of dogs. Just as in a dog show, the women came up one by one and walked in a circle in front of the judges, then the judges told them whether they were beautiful or not. I realize that the grading scale didn't run from 'excellent' to 'unsatisfactory', but apart from that, it was exactly the same thing. The women who got high scores seem to have won something – the head judge said something along the lines of 'You can go to casting', and the woman in question was thrilled. And when the judge told the worse women that their scores were not high enough, they cried. What weren't they high enough for? I have no idea. Maybe for breeding? So I have seen for myself that beauty does *not* lie in the eye of the beholder, for humans any more than it does for dogs. It can be measured.

So – jeans or a skirt? What's better? I cock my head and try to visualize Caroline in both next to each other. Caroline nods at me encouragingly and holds the short dress up to herself again.

'What do you think? Which one will Jens think I'm prettier in?'

JENS?! Caroline isn't going out with Daniel? This bad news literally knocks me off my paws, and I roll onto my side with a plaintive howl.

'Hercules!' Caroline shouts. 'Are you having another one of those attacks?'

She drops the dress, kneels down beside me, and pets my head. Then I get an idea: if I'm sick, she's sure to cancel her date with this Jens. So I launch into another one of my famous park performances, with every bell and whistle I can come up with. I howl, tremble and writhe around, throwing in spasms for good measure. Caroline looks at me in horror, then she jumps up and runs out of the bedroom. Phew! I get a little breather. Acting is quite an exhausting profession. I hear Caroline talking on the phone, obviously to Nina.

'Nina? Do you have Marc Wagner's home phone number? Hercules is having another one of those attacks, and it's far too late for his surgery hours ...' A brief pause. 'Thanks, I'll tell him.'

She comes back into the bedroom with the telephone in her hand. Now I'm lying on my back and just twitching a bit here and there. I think I'm doing a very impressive job.

'Dr Wagner? This is Caroline Neumann, you know, Nina's friend with the dachshund. I'm sorry to disturb you at this hour, but Hercules just had one of those attacks, and now he's lying there looking really listless. I'm so worried ...' She kneels back down next to me. 'Oh, yes, would you do that? That's very, very kind. 12 Helvetia Street, a big art nouveau-style building. Right; see you soon.'

No sooner does she finish that conversation than she dials another number. 'Jens? It's me, Caroline. Listen, I'm really sorry, and I know this sounds ridiculous, but my dachshund has just had another epileptic attack, and the vet is coming here for a house call. Could we move it to another evening? I wouldn't feel right leaving Hercules alone today. OK with you? Thanks – I'll be in touch tomorrow. Bye!'

If I weren't in the middle of playing a sick dog, I would let out a howl of triumph. But if I did, my cover would be blown, so I keep it to myself. Instead, I just lie draped over the bedside rug and yowl every now and then. Caroline pets me and hums away to herself. I guess she's trying to calm me down. Then the doorbell rings. It's Dr Wagner. Not that he's the man I want to see here either, but I'd rather have a couple of check-ups from this vet than see Jens mess up my plans for Caroline and Daniel. After all, it's in a good cause.

Caroline lets him in and brings him right into the bedroom. 'Thank you for coming so quickly. Look at how badly he's still suffering!'

Wagner has a bag with him, which he puts down next to me. 'Hmm, let's have a look and see what we can do about this.'

He sits down on the floor beside me and grabs a kind of thick pen from his bag. He aims it directly at my eyes, and a bright beam of light blinds me.

'Pupil reflexes are normal.' He gets up again. 'It doesn't look as though Hercules has just had an epileptic seizure. If that were the case, his pupils would be dilated and would not contract when the light hits them. We could make sure with an EEG, but I don't think that's necessary. Whatever Hercules had, it seems to have been something else. But I have an idea.'

He rummages around in his bag again, then takes out a metal thing with two cords and a kind of pliers, and sits back down next to me. He sticks the pliers into his ears, and puts the metal thing on my chest. He seems to be listening for something.

'Nope, his heart also sounds perfectly normal. His heart rhythm seems to be completely unaffected.' He pulls the thing back out of his ears. 'Irregular heartbeats can also bring on seizures. You see, an irregular heartbeat can lead to a drop in blood pressure in the brain and a loss of consciousness with convulsions can result.' He strokes me. 'I realize the seizure is already over, of course, but generally it takes a while until the rhythm is completely back to normal. Hercules, just what are you up to?'

Caroline studies me with a worried look on her face. 'Maybe he has some other kind of bad disease?'

Caroline's voice sounds so nervous that I decide to be totally healthy again. I don't want to overdo this whole thing, so I stand up and shake myself off.

'Ms Neumann, the way Hercules looks now, he seems completely healthy to me. Of course we can examine him from head to toe next week at my surgery, but something tells me that there is no health problem here. Call it my veterinarian instinct if you like, but I think Hercules is not doing as badly as we think. You're probably worrying over nothing at all.'

Grrr, you traitor – stop talking like that! Caroline would certainly be angry if she realized that all this was only for show. I decide to put the seizure act on ice. I think Wagner is already too hot on my trail.

FRAUKE SCHEUNEMANN

'But didn't you say you know the breeder Hercules came from? It would certainly ease my mind if you were to look into that.'

'Glad you reminded me. I'll be there next week anyway, and I'll ask about it. But still, you should assume for the time being that there's nothing seriously wrong with Hercules.' He gets up from the floor again and grabs his bag. 'So, I'll be off now. You clearly have plans for tonight. You look as though you've just been having a little dress rehearsal here.'

Caroline laughs and stands up too. 'You're right. But if you like, you can stay for a glass of wine. After all, you gave up your evening for us, and I'd like to thank you for that.'

Wagner hesitates. Get going, Mister, take off – Caroline is just trying to be polite. The fact is that no one here wants you around!

'But you surely have plans, and I don't want to be in the way.'

Good thinking, Wagner. Bye!

'Quite the contrary! I'd love you to stay. I've changed my plans for tonight anyway because of Hercules.'

'Then I'll be happy to fill in.'

Oh no! No sooner are we rid of one of them than we're stuck with the next one! Well, all right, at least Wagner is not a danger for Daniel, but that is his only advantage. Caroline smiles at him. 'My name is Caroline, by the way.'

'Oh yes, thank you! I'm Marc.'

Caroline nods. 'I know.'

They both laugh – somewhat shyly, it seems to me.

'How about you go into the living room first? It's right across from the front door. I'll just change.'

'Not on my account – I think you look enchanting.'

Caroline laughs in embarrassment. 'Well, OK, if you can stand me in jeans and a baggy sweater, I'll stay like this.'

'I certainly can; no problem.'

And instead of Wagner taking his stupid medical bag and making himself scarce, there he is, not even two minutes later, sitting on our living room couch. Feeling out of sorts, I lie down right in front of it and watch Caroline get two glasses out of the cabinet. She's just too nice. Why didn't she let Wagner go? Instead, this 'wine-drinking business' is starting up again. I really hate to say this, but humans are sometimes just endlessly boring, for example when they drink wine. Here's how it'll go: Caroline will soon pour one bottle into another, then the two of them will pour the stuff from the second bottle into two glasses. With any luck, they'll simply drink it up, and we'll be rid of Dr Wagner in no time. Unfortunately, this outcome is extremely unlikely. What *will* happen, in all likelihood, is that they'll spend an inordinate amount of time sitting on the couch and going on and on about things that are supposedly important in life. Bottom line, there'll be talk instead of action. If Dr Wagner were Nina, most of this talk would be about men, which would at least be of some interest to me because I might find out more about how Daniel's chances with Caroline stand. But with Wagner she'll probably talk more about the other topic that's always on humans' minds: work. Another favourite subject is the old days. Yawn. Or they like to combine both topics and chat about work *and* the old days. They can easily fill an hour just exploring the question of when they were young, what they wanted to be when they grew up and why that choice didn't work out. I don't understand how people can be so deeply concerned about things that can no longer be changed anyway. But humans are true masters in the art of contemplating the what-ifs. No self-respecting dog would ever bother with issues like that. In other words: *drinking wine* is apparently a synonym for a highly inefficient method of killing an evening for people who can't be bothered to go for a good run in the park – and most people are like this.

I sigh deep down inside and lay my head on my front paws. While the voices of Caroline and Wagner merge into a vague background noise, I think about how I can nail this thing with Daniel. Maybe I could somehow lure the two of them into some kind of trap so that they're finally alone. Then the rest would fall into place. But how?

I desperately need to talk things over with Mr Beck again. Cats are famous for being master strategists, and he is sure to have an idea about how to do this. It's truly tragic – just recently, the two of them had become so close! If Nina hadn't shown up, they could be an established couple by now. But since that evening, Daniel and Caroline have barely seen each other, apart from brief encounters in the workshop, and there were almost always customers around. Obviously, nothing is going to come of that. If there's one thing I've learned by now, even without any instruction from Mr Beck, it's that when it comes to finding mates, people seem to be a really shy species. In any case, this tingle of excitement between Daniel and Caroline vanishes the second other people come along. I've seen the same thing happen in the park: the couples who are kissing usually stand off to the side or sit on a bench where no one else is sitting. People like to kiss in cars, but almost never in the supermarket. In the breakfast café where Caroline and Nina often get together and where every last seat is always taken, there's nothing happening in the way of smooching couples. Maybe a little kiss here or there, but definitely nothing on the scale of the real mating Beck and I observed back then with Thomas and the other woman. We dogs are markedly more assertive in that arena. A male dachshund who discovers his sweetheart on the other side of the street would certainly not be put off by a few pedestrians going by. It's sort of strange. After all, humans don't exactly tend to be shy in general.

Meanwhile, sure enough, Caroline and Wagner have arrived at the topic of work. I'm telling you: little by little, I'm getting a feel for these two-legged creatures. Wagner, in any case, is now wearing out Caroline with an extremely detailed description of his career.

'And then I knew that I'd rather become a vet, so I switched over from human medicine to veterinary medicine, although I had actually sworn to myself never to do the same thing as my father. And now I've even taken over his practice and live in the same house, just as he once did. At the beginning, it was definitely a strange feeling, but now I can say that it was the best decision of my life. My profession makes me happy.'

So, who cares about that? I certainly don't. I certainly hope that Caroline gets rid of this conceited bore soon. OK, I admit that I'm not exactly an innocent bystander in his being here, but the essential purpose of Wagner's visit has now been fulfilled: Jens is out of the picture for this evening, so Wagner is just in the way. He should drink up his glass and head back to his basket – figuratively speaking, of course. Caroline is bound to be trying to work out how she can get him out of the apartment as pleasantly as possible.

'I think it's great that you followed your inner voice. People should do that more often. Speaking of more – would you like another glass of wine?'

I must have heard wrong – more wine? But apparently, Wagner is not getting on Caroline's nerves as much as he is on mine. It can't be explained away as pure politeness any more. Does she actually find his stories exciting?

Caroline fills both glasses again, then sits down next to Wagner. 'I live over my workshop too. Nina always claims it would get on her nerves if she lived and worked under one roof, but I find it ideal.'

Wagner nods. 'Yes, that's how I feel too. How did you come up with the idea of a workshop? It's not exactly a run-of-the-mill job. Or is that a family business as well?'

Caroline shakes her head. 'No, not in the slightest. My father is a lawyer, and my mother a housewife. But even when I was still at school, I knew I wanted to become a violin maker. You know, I love music, I've played a lot of violin myself, and I wanted to do something with my hands. Then I did an internship in a violinmaking workshop and realized: this is it!'

Caroline is positively beaming, and Wagner is studying her. What am I saying – he's looking at her the way a fox might eye a goose! Surely he's not thinking of making a pass at my – or Daniel's – Caroline!

He clears his throat. 'That gives me an idea. Would you like to go to a concert with me next week? I have two tickets for the concert hall and no one to go with.'

Caroline hesitates. Of course it's not easy to give the brush-off to the guy who rescues your dog.

'Well, I, uh …'

Come on, spit it out, Caroline! It's time for us to get rid of this guy.

'I'd love to!'

chapter seventeen 🐾

'**K**iddo, you can't rush something like this. Forget it.'
 I admit that doesn't sound as though he agrees with me,
but I'm not going to lose heart that fast. After all, I would not be
Carl-Leopold von Eschersbach if some insipid remark by an old
cat were to throw me off my game. We're sitting back at our
favourite spot under the tree and I've just given Beck a quick
update on the twists and turns of the past three days on the
subject of Caroline and men.

'Believe me, Mr Beck, there's something going on there! You
didn't see the two of them – Daniel actually did kiss her. That has
to mean something.'

'Yes, that means that Daniel is in love with Caroline, which
doesn't necessarily mean that she's also in love with him,
otherwise she would have kissed him, not the other way
around.'

I'm starting to get really annoyed with Beck. 'That's just
splitting hairs – what difference does it make whether he kisses

her or she kisses him? It all comes down to the same thing – they kissed each other.'

'I can see you haven't got a clue. There is a HUGE difference. Let me tell you: Daniel is rather pathetic. He's been drooling over Caroline from a distance for absolutely ages, but when push comes to shove, even Nina gets in his way.'

'That was really bad luck. He couldn't do anything about that. And that's why we have to help him – he just needs another chance, an opportunity to be alone with Caroline.'

'Oh man, Hercules, get it through your thick skull. A guy who has to rely on a fat cat and a short-legged mongrel to get the point across to a woman is a hopeless case. A loser. A big zero. I told you that right at the start.'

I feel rage rising up within me. My voice sounds really hoarse when I snap at Beck, 'You take that back right now! Right now! Or else our friendship is over.'

'Jeez, all right, sorry. Excuse me for calling you a mongrel.'

'That's not what I mean.'

'All right, excuse me for saying short-legged. Happy?'

'I mean the loser part. Daniel is not a hopeless case. He is a very nice man, and he happens to mean something to me. He's my friend.'

Mr Beck rolls his eyes. 'You dogs and all your "my friend the human" nonsense! Let me put it to you straight: a dog is not man's best friend, and the same goes the other way round. Daniel is a man, and man's best friend is man. And just because some humans don't find other humans to be friends with doesn't mean that they can be friends with an animal. Whenever a human talks to you and tells you all kinds of personal stuff, he doesn't mean you, but himself. He's talking to himself, get it? But in order not to feel too nutty and lonely, he talks to you. When this happens, you're basically something like that little plastic friend belonging to that dumb parakeet. A substitute. So stop whining that I shouldn't talk that way about your friend Daniel – that's completely ridiculous.'

If I were able to cry, now would be a good time to do so. And if I were into violent confrontations, ditto. I wouldn't have thought that Mr Beck could be so mean. But I know one thing for definite now: even though Beck may have pulled together some knowledge about humans, it doesn't mean that he really knows them. Of course a human can be a friend. The way Daniel talks to me has nothing whatsoever to do with the plastic bird that pathetic parakeet on the third floor works away at every day. Daniel means me, not himself. I know it – I feel it. I admit that humans can be quite nasty – Thomas is a case in point. But at the same time they have something that makes them unique in my eyes – and precious. They have feelings – compassion. They can be happy for others, and sad for others – and furious, when their friends are angry. And they can love – including a little dog like me. I will never forget Emilia's tears when von Eschersbach put me in that carton and she knew she would never see me again. Caroline is my friend, and Daniel is my friend. I know it for a fact. Now the two of them just have to become a couple. And I will see to that, with or without Beck. In this case probably without. So I turn round and just walk out on Beck.

'Hey, little guy, don't just clear out of here! That wasn't meant to be mean!' Beck calls after me, but I act as though I don't hear him, and keep on going. Beck comes up behind me. 'I like Daniel too, but you have to be a realist. Hey, stand still, Hercules!' I'm almost at the terrace door. 'OK, fine: Carl-Leopold! I'm sorry!'

Hmm, he does seem to mean business. I stand still. No one can claim that I'm pigheaded and unforgiving. Mr Beck runs around me and sits down in front of me.

'I didn't want to hurt your feelings. If you've become so attached to all these humans, it's your business, of course. They certainly really care for you. Maybe I'm just a little envious.'

I cock my head. All right; that sounds better already.

'But there's one point I'm not budging on: if Caroline is not in love with Daniel, the two of us can't do anything about it. The human heart can't be swayed much, and it's only a teensy bit receptive to rational considerations. What I'm trying to say is that even though we both know that Daniel would be a super guy for Caroline, there's not a whole lot we can accomplish in a case like this, no matter how many opportunities we create to give the two of them time alone.'

Hmm, that does sound pretty convincing. Even so, I don't want to give up quite yet.

'Yes, but we don't even know whether Caroline isn't in love after all, so I think that we have to try it just one more time, and if it doesn't work then, I promise I'll give up!'

Mr Beck sighs. 'Man, are you stubborn. I think all these

near-dates with actors and vets mean the odds are totally against it, but – suit yourself. What's the plan?'

'I don't have one yet,' I admit somewhat sheepishly. 'That's why I asked you – because you're such a strategist.'

Mr Beck grins and stretches out in front of me. 'Yes, that I am. I will give it some thought.'

•

There's not much going on in the workshop today. Daniel and Caroline are at their separate tables, quietly tightening and planing some pieces of wood. Boring. And besides, I get the feeling that the atmosphere between the two of them is no longer crackling with tension, but just plain tense. Caroline has not looked Daniel in the eye once today – while he, on the other hand, keeps stealing glances at her when he thinks she's not watching. Very odd. Maybe Beck is right, and we should abandon our plan before we've really seen it through.

Daniel clears his throat. 'Say, Caroline,' he says, as he comes out from behind his table and walks over to her. Ah! Finally things are getting going here!

'Yes?'

'Uh, do you have any rosin handy? I can't find any here.'

Argh! What kind of talk is that? Rosin? Not that I have any idea what that is, but I'm pretty sure that it's not a code word for 'I love you; may I please kiss you?'

'Yes, I have some; here you go.'

Clunk! A small translucent brown block falls out of the little box that Caroline has just handed to Daniel without really looking his way. Now both the box and the block are on the floor. Caroline kneels down to pick them up. Daniel leans over too. For a brief moment, the two of them are really close, almost face to face. *Come on, Daniel! Do something!* is what I would love to shout. Unfortunately, I have no choice but to think it out loud to the best of my ability. And sure enough, the telepathy between dachshund and man works. Daniel reaches for Caroline's hand and holds it.

'Caroline, is something wrong?'

Caroline gives him a quick glance, then looks back down at the floor.

'No, why?' she mutters.

'You're avoiding me.'

'No I'm not; you're just imagining it.'

'Is it because of what happened the other day?'

'I don't know what you mean.'

'Come on, let's at least talk about it. Is it because I kissed you?'

'No, well, I …'

Daniel sighs. 'I knew it. I knew that it was a mistake.'

Daniel lets go of Caroline's hand and sits down on the floor next to her. The two of them don't say anything at first, then Daniel pokes her in the side.

'Hey, Caroline. Come on, don't take it so seriously. You don't have to explain anything to me. It's absolutely all right. It was just one of those moments: you looked great, and I was a little tipsy. I couldn't help myself.'

Caroline nods. 'Yes, it was a lovely moment. But now…'

'Now, in the light of day, the whole thing somehow seems different, I know,' Daniel finishes her sentence. 'And you're wondering whether it was such a good idea, with me, your buddy and partner.'

Caroline nods.

'No, it probably isn't,' Daniel goes on to say. 'Although it was a very nice idea, you and me as a couple. For a moment, at least.'

'And you're not angry with me?'

'Nah; I've been thinking the same thing. So now stop walking around looking so down in the mouth. That's an order!'

Daniel laughs, and eventually Caroline joins in, though a bit hesitantly.

I, on the other hand, feel more like sobbing. My beautiful plan! Well, all right, my half-baked scheme! It would have been so great to have Daniel and Caroline as my master and mistress. A real little family. And the worst part is that all that looking around has to start again from scratch, and there's still the danger that we reel in another idiot like Thomas. And I was so sure that Daniel is the perfect man for Caroline. Oh, what am I saying: not 'was' – I'm *still* sure that he is. But Mr Beck is right in saying that if Caroline's heart doesn't see that for itself at some point, it makes no sense to pursue it. With my head hung low, I creep back to the terrace door to let Beck know about my defeat. If he's truly my friend, and he meant that apology, maybe he'll cheer me up.

But before I get outside, the workshop doorbell rings. Normally, I love running up to greet visitors, but I'm so down in the dumps that I can't bring myself to do so. It's probably that stupid Aurora again, wanting to flirt with Daniel. It rings again, and needless to say, I'm now pretty curious after all. On the other hand, the sun is shining so brightly outside and the idea of lying under my tree and pouring my heart out to Mr Beck with the grass tickling my belly is also tempting. But in the end, curiosity prevails, and I run to the door.

Caroline's already opened it. There's a man in a brown uniform standing in our hallway, and handing her a small package.

'Are you Ms Neumann? If so, I'll need your signature here.'

Caroline puts the package on the floor so she can sign. My curiosity piqued, I sniff at it. Hmm, it smells kind of yummy. I wonder what's in it. When Caroline takes the package to her table in the workroom, I run behind her.

'Was it for you?' Daniel asks.

'Yes.'

'What is it?'

'No idea. I didn't order anything.'

'Who sent it?'

'Let me take a look. It's from …' She pauses. 'It's from Jens Uhland.'

Daniel shrugs his shoulders. 'Don't know him. A client?'

'In a way. He works with the film crew that recently borrowed that cello case.'

'I see. Well, maybe you left something there?'

'Yes, perhaps.'

Personally, I don't think that's it. After all, I was there, and

I'm sure that we left with everything we arrived with, that is, other than the case, of course, but there's no way that's in this package. It's much too big, and the cello case smells completely different. Not nearly as tasty. What's in it? I sit up and beg, which brings me up to the height of Caroline's knees. She's wondering what's going on.

'Hey, sweetie, what's up with you? You're getting rather excited.'

'Well, maybe this Jens is sending you a kilo of coke, and Hercules has what it takes to be a top drug sniffing dog.' Daniel grins. 'You know how those film people are. They're all into that scene.'

Caroline shakes her head. 'A kilo of coke? That's a bit pricey to send to someone you barely know. But what could it be?' She uses a knife to get the tape off the top of the box. 'There's a card. Let's see.'

She reads it and a grin spreads over her face. Daniel comes to her table and tries to read it over her shoulder. Just as she is about to move away from him, he reaches over as quick as a flash and pulls the card away from her.

'Hey, what are you doing? Didn't anyone ever tell you that mail is private? This isn't addressed to you.' Caroline sounds annoyed, but Daniel just laughs.

'Well, my dear, it's not for you either. It clearly says *"Dear Hercules".*'

What? The card is for me? I run right over to Daniel. Never in my life have I received a card. How exciting! But also a bit odd.

Who writes to someone who can't read? I sit down in front of Daniel and look at him expectantly. He gets the hint and starts reading it out loud.

Dear Hercules,

I really hope you're feeling better today. To help you get back on your feet nice and quickly, I'm sending along a top-quality gourmet sausage for you, which is sure to be yummy. Let me know when you're back to your old self.

Best regards,
Jens

Wow, he must be an insanely nice guy, despite the gun. I'm delighted! No wonder the box smelled so good. I have to try that sausage right away.

'How did this Jens get the idea that Hercules might be sick?'

'Um, he had another one of those attacks.' Caroline's voice sounds funny.

'While you were in the bank?'

'Yes, that's right. It even made them interrupt their filming.'

Hey, that's not true at all! What is Caroline saying?

Daniel looks worried. 'Hmm, that doesn't sound good. Have you spoken to Wagner again? He wanted to have a talk with the breeder.'

'That's true; it slipped my mind. I'll call the surgery later.'

She doesn't seem to want to tell Daniel about Wagner's

rescue operation. This whole thing is getting more and more mysterious. There were two whopping lies in only a handful of sentences. That's not the Caroline I know. And to say things like that to Daniel! Even if she doesn't want to have him as the man in her life, he's still her friend! Why is she doing this?

I can't help thinking of all those times von Eschersbach held forth on the subject of dishonesty. To him, dishonesty was one of the worst character flaws a human being could have – maybe even the very worst. Lying came well before greed and lack of discipline. *Deceit and lies are signs of weakness!* he often preached. *The brave are honest, and dishonesty is the sister of cowardice.* In a nutshell and in simple terms that any dachshund can grasp: bad people lie, good people tell the truth.

Still, we have to give bad people credit for coming up with the idea of telling lies on purpose. That is pretty clever, and I'm not sure whether something like that would occur to me on my own. But in the end, no matter how clever dishonest people may be, they are always bad. At the same time, that tells me that Caroline did not really lie, because there is no question that she is a great person. But if she didn't lie, what was that? Maybe she's suffering from a disease and has no clear recollection of what really happened with Jens and Dr Wagner?

Before I can continue to ponder this difficult topic, however, Caroline puts down a bowl for me with a heap of gourmet sausage cut into small pieces. I wolf most of it down in an instant – divine! We should take a closer look at this Jens after all. Maybe it was a mistake to sabotage his date with Caroline. After all, he seems to be a great lover of dogs, or at least someone who likes dogs. I put two more pieces in my mouth. Yummy! On the other hand, if the two of them had got together last night, I wouldn't have had this delicious sausage. So it wasn't a mistake. No more than a little detour.

•

'Am I getting this right? The thing with Daniel is over and done with, and the new, hopeful candidate is named Jens, and he knows everything about dogs?'

'Right.'

'That tells me only one thing.'

'What?'

'That you can be bought. You were just moaning about how Daniel is your friend and we absolutely have to help him and so on and so forth. And now? No sooner does some actor come along and send you a piece of sausage than Daniel is old news. Who ever started the rumour that dogs are as loyal as gold?' Mr Beck shakes his head in disgust. 'I thought you wanted to tell me about a great plan; instead, I'm stuck listening to this gourmet sausage garbage. My time is too precious to waste on that.'

'But, but,' I stammer sheepishly, 'you said yourself that you don't think anything is going to come of Daniel and Caroline, and I was just going to tell you that you're absolutely right. Why are you so annoyed with me now?'

'Maybe I'm disappointed that I'm right. Maybe I had kept hoping that you would turn out to be right and that a cat and a dachshund could achieve more than I would ever have thought possible after all. Somehow you carried me away with your optimism. I would have been glad to see it work out between the two of them. And now this!'

I hang my head. 'Sorry,' I whisper.

'Don't misunderstand me – you can't help it that nothing is coming of Daniel and Caroline. But the idea of you running straight to this Jens!'

'OK, fine! I was just glad that he was worried about me. And it's the first time in my life that a human has written me a letter!'

'Good grief, are you naïve! He wasn't worried about you! He wanted to impress Caroline! That's it. And then he'd get a chance at another date.'

'You think so?'

'It's quite obvious. What did Daniel say about it? It can't be all that great when you yourself have just been given the brush-off and the next guy is already standing on the doorstep. It must have hurt him to find out that Caroline actually planned to go out with Jens last night.'

'Yeah, that really was odd: Caroline didn't tell him that she actually had a date with Jens and that it fell apart because I was sick. She claimed that I had keeled over back in the bank, and that Jens noticed it.'

'Ah, a little white lie.'

'White lie?'

'Think about it. Caroline didn't want to hurt Daniel's feelings with the story of how Jens came to send a gourmet sausage for dogs. After all, he's her best friend.'

'And then you're allowed to lie? Even though dishonesty is such a bad thing? At least that's what my old master kept saying.'

'He's right about that as a rule. A white lie is still a lie. But sometimes people lie so as not to hurt someone, and that's not quite as bad. It falls more into the category of putting a good spin on things.'

My head is ready to burst. Lies, white lies, putting a good spin on things – how am I supposed to understand that?

'But why would Daniel be hurt? He said himself that his kiss was probably not a good idea. He even said that everything was perfectly fine.'

Mr Beck shakes his head. 'Hercules, I thought that by now you would have got to know people better. This is a matter of the heart. No human likes to admit to falling hard for someone. They prefer to act as though it's not an issue. I explained that to you already – the person you're interested in is never supposed to know how much you love them. That's a cast-iron rule. Otherwise you've had it.'

I fear that Mr Beck is right on this point as well. It doesn't surprise me in the least that when it comes to love, there is so much chaos among humans. Their rules are just utterly absurd. A dog would never come up with nonsense like that.

chapter eighteen 🐾

Today is a totally boring, unremarkable day. Marvellous! I'm lying around in my workshop box, taking a peek into the garden here and there, then heading back to the aforementioned box for a snooze. The only thing I could imagine to make my happiness complete is a nice bowl brimming with tripe or offal. I mull over whether I ought to ignore my growing hunger pangs – I'm just too lazy to run over to Caroline and demand my next meal. But eventually, my stomach starts growling so loudly that I can't manage a proper nap, so I get back on my feet, head to Caroline, who's sitting at her desk, and nudge her with my nose.

'Time to eat?' Caroline looks at her watch. 'You'll just have to wait a little longer. We have something else to do first.'

Oh no! I'm hungry now! I nudge Caroline again. She laughs, and strokes my neck.

'Hang in there, Hercules. We're about to do something you'll like too, and then there'll be something to eat as well.'

Hey! I don't want to do anything! I want my tripe now, then I plan to continue lying around. Yesterday would have been a fine time to do something. The whole day I had such a need for fresh air, sniffing around for rabbits and catching flies. But instead, she was so busy that I couldn't even pry her away for a little walk in the park. *Tomorrow is Saturday, then I'll have more time, I promise.* As though that could console a dog. You've got to seize the moment as it comes. But people just don't seem to get that.

I head back to my box. I was in such a good mood, but that vanished in an instant. With my head on my cosy pillow, I mutter to myself about how offended I feel. We always do what Caroline wants. That is so unfair. Meanwhile, the feeling in my belly has gone from a healthy appetite to full-blown ravenous hunger. I begin to whimper a little. Caroline might as well know that she's teetering on the verge of cruelty to animals.

'Don't make such a fuss!' she says pitilessly from her room. 'We're getting out any minute now. We just have to get something from the apartment, then we'll go. Our chauffeur ought to be at our front door in about thirty seconds.'

Our chauffeur? Now *that* sounds exciting. I haven't heard that word for months, and it brings back fond memories of the good old days. Naturally, there was a chauffeur at Eschersbach Castle. The old von Eschersbach was extremely reluctant to get behind the wheel himself. 'My eyes have just got too bad, and I'd pose a danger to the public at large,' he'd tell people while he was waiting for his car to drive up to take him to a hunting party. Most people might wonder whether it was actually a good idea to go hunting with von Eschersbach in light of this limitation. But as far as I know, nothing bad ever happened; probably his claim that he needed a chauffeur was just an aristocratic way of showing off.

The doorbell rings, and Caroline walks past my box to open the door. It's Jens!

He greets us with, 'Good morning, Caroline. Good morning, Hercules!'

I have to admit that without a black ski mask and a gun, Jens actually looks quite nice.

He gives Caroline a kiss on both cheeks. 'So, you two – all ready for our picnic?'

'Sure. I just have to get the basket from upstairs. I put a few of the things in the fridge; I'll go and pack them up.'

She hops upstairs, and I stay with Jens.

'So, are you all right again?' he asks. I look at him eagerly. 'Did you like the sausage?'

I realize that, according to Mr Beck, the bit with the sausage was pure bribery, but since I'm a polite dachshund and the sausage really was delicious, I wag my tail a little. Then I start to think that where there's one sausage, there could be another, so I pick up the pace.

'I knew it, you good dog!' He bends over to me and scratches me behind the ears.

At this moment, Caroline comes downstairs with a gigantic basket. 'It's so nice that the two of you are getting to be friends. The last time you met wasn't exactly harmonious.'

Jens laughs. 'I still have a bruise where Hercules snapped at me. But let's forget it; after all, he was trying to come to the rescue. Besides, now I'm finally up to date with my tetanus injections. It turned out that I was long overdue for one. So something good came of it. And I can see that my little present arrived in good shape.'

Caroline nods. 'Yes, it took Hercules about ten seconds to polish off the sausage. He loved it.'

Oh no! If they keep talking about gourmet sausages, I'm going to collapse. I'm so hungry I could faint. I hope it doesn't take too much longer until I get something to eat. I do have to admit, though, that the basket Caroline brought from the apartment smells as if there's something quite yummy in it. I can't help starting to drool.

'So we can get going, right?'

'Yup, we're ready to go!' Caroline calls out cheerfully and opens the front door. Jens walks past her and heads for the car that is parked right in front of the house.

'Please get in!' He flings open the passenger door.

'Come, Hercules!' Caroline calls to me – but I hesitate. The car looks kind of funny. Sort of dangerous. At first, I can't work out what's bothering me so much, but when Caroline lifts me up to put me in the car, the problem is as plain as day. The car has no roof!

•

Twenty minutes later, my misgivings about getting into something that goes very fast and doesn't keep you from falling out have faded away. I'm sitting on Caroline's lap and pointing my nose out into the glorious summer air, and my ears are blowing in the wind. A dream come true! Jens and Caroline are having a cheerful conversation. I can't really tell what they're saying, because the wind is whooshing in my ears so loudly that I can't hear very well. But it doesn't matter. At this moment, I feel as though I'm flying, and the feeling is fantastic. The trees at the side of the road are rushing past and blurring together to form a bright green hedgerow. The sky above us is blue and wide-open; I could keep going like this for hours – sort of, anyway. The reason I'm saying 'sort of' is that my belly is still hurting from not getting anything to eat, so I hope that the time will soon come for Caroline to take the basket with the tasty titbits out of the boot.

Sure enough, Jens starts slowing down, and the green wall is turning back into individual trees. Eventually, he stops.

'So, here we are. Just a second; I'll help you!'

Jens jumps out of the car, runs around it, and opens Caroline's door. Very attentive, I have to say. I hop off Caroline's lap, then Jens holds out his hand to Caroline and helps her out. Hmm, it smells good here. Like woods and water, and a wee bit wild. Armed with the picnic basket, we head to a little thicket on a hillside. A set of steps leads down to a clearing. We stand still there for a minute.

'Look at that.' Jens points ahead. 'Isn't that a fabulous view?'

'Yes, it looks lovely when the Elbe glistens in the sunlight like that.'

Sounds good, but in case anyone cares, I can't see anything

at all. My short legs bring me right to the level of the nettles that have sprouted up like crazy to the left and right of the steps. Is either one of them planning to pick me up? I want to see too! I sit up and beg.

'I think Hercules is famished.' Caroline completely misinterprets what I'm asking for. 'Normally, he gets something to eat by eleven o'clock.'

'We'll be there in a second. The beach begins just here.'

OK, that's good news too. Finally, I'll get something to eat. But what's a beach? Once we get to the end of the wide landing, there are no woods any more, and we cross over a little path. Now I can also see where the smell of water is coming from: there's a big river in front of us. A really, really big river, to judge by the size of the ship that is passing us right now. Gigantic! I've never seen anything like it! It looks like a huge, travelling house. I yap with excitement, and Caroline laughs.

'You're amazed, Hercules, aren't you? Up to now we've only been to the Alster, and Hercules hasn't seen anything bigger than sailing boats.'

'Then it's high time he sees a real ship. You can't live in Hamburg and not get to know the Elbe!' Jens tells her almost reproachfully. We keep going towards the shore – and wind up in an enormous sandpit. I come to a dead halt, because sand on my paws is a sure sign that any minute now, a human mother will come round the corner to give me a good tongue-lashing. But it's strange that I haven't seen any wooden border to this sandpit. I sit down uncertainly.

'Now you're going to tell me that your dog has never been to the beach. He almost seems a little afraid.'

'No, he never has. I haven't had him very long, and so far I've only taken him to our park or to the Alster. And we haven't been on holiday together yet, so this is his very first time.'

Jens takes a step towards me and lifts me up. 'Take a good look around, little guy. On a day like this, Hamburg is without a doubt the most beautiful city on earth, and this is the most beautiful part of it. You just have to get used to the sand on your paws, and you'll soon realize how great it is here. From here you can run as far as you like in any direction. But when you see the first sheep on the embankment, you'd better turn round or else you'll lose sight of us.'

He puts me down again. Run as far as I like – an excellent idea. But before that I need: right, you guessed it! Something to eat.

Caroline has brought a blanket in addition to the basket, and she spreads it out on the sand. The river is just far enough away that the waves can't reach us, even if another big ship comes past. Now Caroline opens the basket and takes the things out. Hmm, yummy. Then I spy a bowl with offal for me. She puts it a little to the side, and I lunge at it. While I wolf down my meal, I see out of the corner of my eye that Caroline is serving up a storm of sausage and cheese, and she has even brought a cake. Jens takes off his backpack and puts it down.

'So, to celebrate today, I've brought along something nice too.' He pulls a piece of fabric out of the backpack and unwraps it, and two long-stemmed glasses are revealed. Then he grabs his pack again, takes out a green bottle, and gets straight to work on it. The cork jumps out with a loud plop, and Jens pours the liquid into the glasses. It looks bright yellow and spurts out quite nicely.

'Here you go: champagne! A beautiful drink for a beautiful lady!'

Caroline giggles, looking a little embarrassed, then she takes the glass Jens gives her.

'Thank you. And – thanks for this good idea.'

'I'm the one who should be thanking you! I'm so glad that our date worked out after all. And now: here's to a great day!'

They clink their glasses.

'Yes, to a great day.'

●

When we get back home late in the evening, I'm tired, but feeling fabulous. For the first time in my life, I've gone swimming in a river, which is much harder than in a lake. While I was in the water, I almost caught a fish. I ran until I saw the sheep. Jens threw at least a hundred thousand sticks for me. I munched on pork sausage and strawberry tart in addition to dog food. I lounged around and dozed off on the comfy picnic blanket, and just watched Jens and Caroline talk. And at some point, all three of us were lying on the blanket, looking up at the sky, watching the moon rise and later the sun slowly sinking into the big river. It was the perfect day.

Now I'm lolling about on the couch in the apartment, covered with sand, and I'm really happy. Caroline puts the empty picnic basket back into the kitchen and then goes to the little box next to the telephone that tells people who called while they were out. *You have two new messages. First new message.*

'Hi, sweetie, it's Nina! So, how was it? I'm dying of curiosity! Call me right away!'

Second new message.

'Hello, Caroline, it's Marc Wagner. You know, the trusty old vet. Just wanted to find out whether we're still on for Wednesday. Shall we get a bite to eat before the concert? On Wednesdays I always close a little earlier, and I could come and pick you up. Speak to you soon, I hope.'

There are no more messages.

Marc Wagner – I'd already forgotten about him. And if Caroline's being efficient about finding a mate, she might as well cancel the appointment. Jens makes a fine impression; I couldn't find any fault with him today. He smelled good, his hair was combed, and he had on clean clothes, so why waste time on that unappealing Wagner? And Caroline definitely had a good time too. I haven't seen her so happy and relaxed in ages. So go ahead and call Wagner and cancel! But Caroline looks hesitant. She gazes at the black box, lost in thought, then she grabs the telephone.

'Hi, Nina. I know it's late – but would it be OK if I came by? Really? Thanks, that's nice of you. I desperately need someone to chat with.'

That's just great. Of course it doesn't even occur to her that she could tell *me* what's on her mind too. I'm not happy with the idea of getting in the car all over again right now. I'm lying here so comfortably. But when Caroline stands up, I rush to my feet too. After all, I don't want to be a spoilsport.

'Hercules, you can lie back down again. I'm just going to drive over to Nina's, but you stay here.'

What's that all about? Are they keeping secrets from me? I jump off the couch. I'm not *that* tired!

'No, really, Hercules. You can be alone for one little hour every now and then. Look, you're full of sand, and I don't feel like bathing you now. And Nina will not be pleased if I get there with a dirty dog. So lie down in your basket like a good dog. You've had plenty going on today already.'

Harrumph. She really doesn't want to take me with her. I'm not all that dirty. Silly Nina.

Once Caroline has pulled the apartment door closed behind her, I fall back into my basket in a bad mood. It's mean somehow for us to have spent the whole day together, and then I'm not allowed to come along later. I feel so … rejected. Only a minute ago I was part of things, and now I'm just the pet. It's the pits. To make matters worse, I'm not even a bit tired any more.

I stay in my basket for a while, then get up again and head into the kitchen. Maybe there's still some food in my bowl that I could dig into. Von Eschersbach always says that boredom makes for chubby dachshunds. I think he's right. Unfortunately, however, my bowl is so sparkling clean that I can almost see my own reflection in it, so eating is not on the cards for me. I head back, and as I pass the apartment door, I smell a familiar fragrance. Mr Beck! He must be standing right in front of the door; I suppose he's off for a night-time stroll. A little chat with him would be just the thing to distract me. I bark loudly.

'Well, buddy?' I hear his voice through the door. 'How's it going?'

'OK. I'm really bored, and Caroline just left me alone at home.'

'That's bad luck. I'm on my way to the park. I'd take you along, but without Caroline we're not going to be able to get you out of the apartment.'

'Yeah, that's the stupid thing. I'd love to come with you, but it's not as though I can squeeze through the letterbox.'

I hear Mr Beck giggle. 'Nah, don't try that. You'd just get stuck in it, and that'd be pretty uncomfortable.'

'Well, I can't think of any other option. I'll just have to stay here and carry on being bored. Give my regards to the park and the rabbits.'

'Hmm. Will do.'

Now it's quiet again. But just as I'm about to turn round and head back to my basket, I catch another distinct whiff of Mr Beck.

'Hey, Hercules! I've just had an idea – but it's only good for a daring dachshund.'

Well, who else would that be but me?

'What is it?' I ask.

'You remember our trick with the knickers?'

'How could I ever forget that?'

'Do you remember how I got inside? Through the tilted window. Now run over to Caroline's bedroom as fast as you can. Maybe we'll be in luck and the balcony door is tilted open too. That's how you'll get out.'

Only a cat could come up with an idea like that.

'Beck, your faith in my artistic ability is all well and good, but I can't do that. Even if the window is tilted open, never in a million years would I fit through. Even though you're – pardon me for saying this – fat, you can squeeze through tight spaces in a way I'm simply not capable of. I would get caught there, without a doubt.'

'You have no ambition at all. Let's at least take a look. I'll go through the garden to your balcony, and then we'll size up the situation. It would be great to take an evening stroll together without any humans around.'

Mr Beck – or his smell, at any rate – vanishes. That cat. This is never going to work out. And I'm certainly not bored to the point where I'm willing to risk my neck. On the other hand, some nice roaming about alone at night in the park for a change is of course also a tempting idea. I sigh to myself, then head into the bedroom.

Sure enough, the balcony door is tilted open. Then again, the opening doesn't begin to widen out until a spot way over my head. Just then, Mr Beck jumps down onto our balcony from the ivy-covered wall outside the building.

'Well, that does look good!' he calls over to me cheerfully.

'What, pray tell, is good about that?'

'The door is tilted. That's great.'

'Yes, but down here I can't fit through, and I can't get any higher up. No way will this work.'

'Can't you jump up there?'

'No; how could I?'

'How about if you climb up on the curtain one paw at a time?'

'Mr Beck, you clearly have the wrong idea about my claws. I can't use them to hook into anything the way you do. They're much too straight and smooth for that.'

'In that case, it'll be tough.'

'That's what I've been telling you.'

We sit there for a while and look at each other through the balcony door. Eventually, I get a good idea. I take a quick look around the room, and, sure enough, in the corner I see the chair that Caroline puts her clothes on at night when she goes to bed. It is pretty massive and also has a high back, which means that if I use it as a ladder, it might even work. I trot over to the chair and try to push it to the balcony door. Wow, it's heavy!

'Can you manage, or should I come in?'

'You'd better stay where you are. Either I'll get it there on my own, or we'll forget about our little outing.'

I lean all my weight against the chair, and eventually it moves a tiny bit. Then I lean against the left leg and it goes a bit further. Then I try the right one again, then go back to the left one – and bit by bit, I use my chest to push the chair through the room. It's really hard work, but eventually it's done. The chair is now standing right in front of the balcony door opening.

I hop onto the seat. Yup. From up here, things look quite promising. I may almost be able to fit through.

'Come on! What are you waiting for?' Beck eggs me on.

'Keep your cool! I have to concentrate.'

It won't work without a little jump; after all, I don't want to get stuck. But in order to jump, I need a bit of a running start, and that is impossible on the chair. Damn, I really need to be just a fraction higher on the chair. If I were, it would be so much easier.

'Hercules, see whether you can get to the handle with your muzzle. Maybe you can open the door all the way if you can grab the handle with your teeth. Then all you have to do is pull it down.'

What does he mean by *all you have to do*? Are we in the circus? Little dachshunds opening closed doors clearly falls into the category of stunts.

'Just try it! It can't be all that hard!'

That's easy for him to say, sitting over there on his behind. On the other hand, maybe the idea isn't so bad after all. In any case, it's better than getting stuck in the door. So I sit up, get a good grip on the door handle, latch on, then drop back on the seat. With a jerk, the handle moves down – and the door swings open! Sensational! I, Carl-Leopold von Eschersbach, have just opened a balcony door!

However, my euphoria quickly fades. Two seconds later, I'm

standing next to Mr Beck on the balcony, but I now realize that we didn't think through our wonderful plan. God only knows how I'm going to get down from here!

chapter nineteen 🐾

I am a hero, a superman, a superdachshund!

'Did you see that leap? Wasn't that phenomenal? A real sensation?'

'Yes, it was quite nice.'

'Quite nice? It was PERFECT! I've really got what it takes, my dear.' Mr Beck doesn't seem to quite get the fact that this was the achievement of the century. 'I mean, have you ever seen any other dachshund jump from the second floor? I would say I could now pass for a cat.'

Beck shakes his head. 'Well, as I just said, it was OK. But first of all, that was more like a mezzanine, and second, you jumped into ol' lady Meyer's laundry basket. If I hadn't found that, you would still be perched at the balcony railing, crying.'

Can you believe this guy? That fat cat! I don't know of any other dachshund who has ever executed such a daredevil manoeuvre. The superb feat of squeezing through the bars of the balcony railing towards a near-certain death, and then the leap itself: straight into the laundry basket with Mrs Meyer's towels. And I did all this in the dark! I admit that if ol' lady Meyer hadn't left the laundry basket outside, it would have been a bit more complicated. But the operation was certainly a bold one. After all, I could just as easily have made an unfortunate landing next to the laundry basket and broken all my paws.

'So, once you've pulled yourself together in the aftermath of your heroic deed, we can get going, right?'

I glare at Beck, but sadly, he can't see that because it's already dark. On the other hand, it's also boring to keep sitting around behind some towels, and so, in an act of true largesse, I decide to forgive him, although he did not apologize.

I hop out of the basket and trot behind Beck, who is already moving towards the garden gate. A gentle wind is blowing around my nose, and I'm starting to catch a whiff of adventure. Even though Mr Beck is a stupid cat, he is of course absolutely right on one score: a walk like this without Caroline is the best opportunity to finally go on a hunt. I instantly feel that pleasant tingling in my nose, and my tail whisks upward automatically. On guard, you rabbits! Carl-Leopold von Eschersbach is coming after you – and he will get you!

Once we get to the park, there appears not to be a single rabbit in sight or in smelling distance. I wonder if they're all tucked up in bed in their burrows. Even if they are, I'll hunt them down. Mr Beck's speciality lies more in the area of birds, so at least we won't get in each other's way. I walk along the gravel path with my nose close to the ground. After a few feet, I come across a promising scent. A rabbit must have come hopping down this way not too long ago, probably heading to his burrow. I go crazy with excitement! There are bound to be more of his kind in the burrow, so I'll get one or other of them. Sure enough, the scent grows stronger. I leave the path and trot over to the lawn, where there are several big bushes. It must be right here. I use my nose to root through the grass in an ongoing quest for the opening to the burrow. Finally, a tuft of grass right in front of me gives way, and I discover a deep hole under it. The scent is now quite intense, and I can't help but whoop with joy at the top of my lungs. Hurray!

'Hey, are you OK, Hercules?'

Mr Beck is suddenly right beside me.

'Everything's absolutely great! I have just unearthed the first rabbit burrow of my entire career as a hunting dog!'

'You do know that this kind of rabbit burrow is pretty tiny, don't you?'

What an idiotic question.

'Of course I do. And now, if you will excuse me, I have work to do.'

Instead of leaving me to go about my business in the burrow, Mr Beck sits down right in front of me. The nerve of him!

'With all the hunting instinct you're building up here, I hope you'll keep in mind that you're not really a dachshund.'

I take a deep breath. 'So what? That just goes to show how wrong von Eschersbach was: I may not be pedigreed, but I found the burrow in an instant. Any reservations about me are totally unfounded. I'm a hunting dog through and through. Would you please move aside now?'

'Sorry, you've got me wrong. I wasn't trying to get into a discussion about your bloodline. All I wanted to say is that you're a bit bigger than a dachshund. I just don't want you to get stuck in the burrow. If you did, I have no idea how I'd ever get you back out. And at this time of day there aren't exactly a lot of people around here to help us.'

'That's ridiculous. Get stuck – what do you think my claws are for? Maybe I can't use them to make my way through the ivy, but they're outstanding for digging. So don't worry about me. And now I have to get cracking, or else the rabbits will be gone again by the time we finish chatting about this.'

I stick my nose deep into the hole and begin to dig a larger entrance to the burrow. What a great feeling! I've finally found my true calling – though it is a pity that I don't have a passionate hunter with me. All I've got is Mr Beck, who's nothing but an old fusspot.

After a few minutes, I'm almost completely under the earth. The scent of rabbits has now grown so strong that my nose feels really tense and double its usual size. The tingling has spread throughout my body, and I'm so excited that my heart is racing. Just a little bit more and I've got those rabbits! I start imagining that I can already hear them. They're probably sitting in their cave rigid with fear, and are not even thinking about how to escape. The whole thing is almost a bit too easy. I push hard with my paws and nose in the direction I figure the cave is in – then the ground in front of me gives way, and suddenly my whole front half is in a hole. Yippee! I'm in the cave!

Then comes the big letdown. Even though it's pitch black in there, my nose tells me immediately that the rabbits are long since gone. The scent is no longer as distinct as it was only a few minutes ago. What a bummer! I must have just missed them – and it's all Beck's fault! If I'd started digging sooner, I would surely have got those guys down here. But this way, they obviously had enough time to dig a new hole and make their escape. I have no choice but to look for another burrow.

I go into reverse – or should I say, I *try* to go into reverse. It turns out to be no easy matter if your front paws are dangling in the air, the way mine are right now. I try to pull myself back with my back paws so I can steady myself again in the front. But no matter how much I brace myself from behind, nothing comes of it. I'm stuck. It's as though I'm in the neck of a bottle and can't move either forward or back. I try it a few more times, then I take a break because I'm so warm already. And to make matters worse, it's also awfully musty down here. My nose starts to tingle again, but not because any of the rabbits have come back. No, what I'm feeling now is fear. How the devil am I going to get back out of here?

I hope Mr Beck is still up there. I bark as well and as loud as I can under the circumstances. I wonder if he can even hear me. He himself keeps saying that he can't see too well any more. Maybe his hearing isn't so good either. That would be a real catastrophe. I'm getting hotter and hotter, and it's becoming almost unbearable. Stay calm, Carl-Leopold! Don't panic! After all, someone knows where you are. At some point, Mr Beck is sure to wonder why you haven't resurfaced. He's not going to go home without you. And what do I do if I irritated him so much that he *did* go away? I'll bet I really annoyed him with my stupid drivel about being a hunting dog. I keep barking. Dear, dear Mr Beck, I definitely didn't mean any of the stupid stuff I ever said to you. You are a dear friend of mine. Actually, you're my only friend. Help!

'Hercules? Is everything all right down there?'

Hallelujah! He's heard me!

'No! I'm stuck!'

'What was that? I can hardly make out what you're saying.'

'I'M STUCK!'

My throat is tickling, and I'm gagging. Come on, Mr Beck – do something!

'Damn. I was afraid something like this would happen. This whole rabbit thing was a really stupid idea. How do we get you out now?' He doesn't say anything. Then he asks, 'Are you deep down?'

'No, it's not bad. The tunnel is quite high up.'

'I'll see if I can find some help for you.'

'No, please don't leave me alone! I'm scared!'

'I have to find someone who can dig you out. Preferably a human. There's no other way. I can't possibly do it myself. Just stay calm, or else you'll use up too much air. And try to relax.'

Relax? Very funny. I'd like to see how relaxed Mr Beck would be in my place. But of course he's right. We need help.

'OK, but hurry!'

'Of course – I'll be as quick as I can. Hang in there!'

•

Mr Beck has probably been gone no more than a couple of minutes, but it feels like an eternity. It's really quiet down here, as silent as the grave. I'm terribly afraid, but I try to follow Beck's advice and stay calm. How could I be so stupid as to get myself into this mess? Beck is quite right. And I'm an idiot. In any case, I'm totally unsuited for hunting. As Grandpa always said: passion is a very bad guide. And false pride as well. Why can't I stick to being a cute little pet? A bit of pork sausage every now and then. Maybe chase after a pigeon here and there. Nothing dangerous. Dear dachshund God, on the off-chance that you exist, please make Mr Beck find someone to help me. I promise that from now on I'll always stay on my lead, I'll never make a night-time getaway from the apartment again, and in every way possible will be the best dog ever. And never go after a rabbit again.

Right above me I suddenly hear rumbling off in the distance. Human footsteps! That simply has to be my rescue! My prayer to the dachshund God was evidently answered, and Mr Beck has found someone.

'Hey, Hercules! You won't believe who I brought along!'

This is most certainly not the time for guessing games, but I resist the urge to say so – and anyway, I'm too weak to shout out loud by this point.

'Willi. I found Willi. I admit that although he ranted and raved about both of us, he still came along with me. Bark again so he can tell what we want from him.'

I gather all my strength and bark as loud as I can.

'Oh, I get it!' I hear Willi's voice booming from above. 'Your little friend is stuck down there, isn't he?'

Even though I can't see what Mr Beck is doing now, I certainly hope he manages to show Willi that he's on the right track.

'In that case, I'll try to dig him out. I hope he's not in too deep. Getting him out without a shovel – with just my bare hands – won't be easy.'

There's still a lot of thudding on top of me. Willi seems to have knelt down. For quite a long time, I don't hear anything, then the ground on top of me begins to quake again. Willi is digging. Thank dachshund God!

I hear Willi moan and groan. Digging seems to be pretty exhausting for humans. It's no wonder; without claws, it can't be easy to get it all out of the way. But the quaking gets closer and closer, and every now and then some earth from the top of the cave falls onto my nose.

'Man, you really picked out a great underground spot for your little outing! The ground here is so muddy – this is really hard!' Willi curses. Then he stops talking and just keeps on digging in silence.

'Are you still all right, Hercules?' Mr Beck asks.

'Yes!' I gasp. By now, I'm barely getting any air.

'You should be pleased that Willi was sitting at his usual spot and hadn't knocked back too many beers yet. It didn't take me long to make him see what I wanted.'

Just as I'm about to answer that no matter how fast this is going, it's starting to close in on me, I feel a gentle breeze on my tail.

'Finally!' Willi shouts. 'I have the tunnel. So, this will be done in no time!'

I can't see anything yet, but Willi has already got as far as my behind. I hear his panting and snorting almost directly behind my neck. Now he's freed up my back paws altogether and is stroking my back.

'Man, what have you got yourself into? Now I'll carefully dig out your head, and then you'll be free from this.'

Earth keeps falling onto my nose, but since I know that it's because of Willi, who is digging directly next to my muzzle, I stay calm. There! Willi lifts the top off the cave, and I'm finally free. I shake myself and look up. Gee, I'm sitting in a pretty deep hole. Willi lifts me up carefully and sets me down at the edge of the big hole he dug for me. Then he climbs out himself and sits down next to me.

'Wow, Willi could use a breather. I'm a little dizzy from all that hard work. I'm not used to it any more at my age, ha-ha!'

Mr Beck comes running over to us, and the three of us sit under the dim light of the park streetlamp off in the distance.

'You were lucky that your buddy found me, my friend – if he hadn't, you wouldn't have got out. Boy, am I exhausted. I'm not feeling so great. Well, it's no wonder, when you consider how out of shape I am.' Willi runs his hand through his messy hair. 'Er, I'm feeling really bad all of a sudden. I feel so ...' He leaves the last sentence hanging in the air – and topples onto his side on the grass. He's just lying there. Good grief! This can't be happening!

'What's wrong with him?'

'Whatever it is, it doesn't look very good.' Mr Beck goes closer and pokes Willi's face with his paw. He doesn't move. 'Damn, Willi, don't do this!'

I run around for a minute to think over what to do, then I jump onto Willi's chest. If he doesn't react to that, this is serious.

It *is* serious. Even when I run up and lick his face, he doesn't move, yet he's breathing really fast and unevenly. I realize that I'm panicking.

'Beck, I think Willi's in a bad way. What are we going to do?'

'Shit!' Beck bursts out. 'This is all your fault! If you hadn't been in that stupid burrow, and if Willi hadn't had to dig you out, he wouldn't be lying here. That was obviously too much for him. We need help desperately!'

I hang my head. Beck is right. It is all my fault. And there's no one around.

'Was anyone else around earlier?' I ask Mr Beck, but all he does is shake his head.

'Not a soul. Not even couples. No one at all.'

Willi lets out a pitiful groan. *Think, Carl-Leopold, think. Who could help us now?* Then I get a brilliant idea.

'I know!' I bark excitedly. 'I got Willi into this mess – and I will get him out of it. You stay next to him so he won't be alone. See you soon!'

And before Mr Beck can say another word, I race off.

chapter twenty 🐾

O nce I'm out of the park, I take the small street right to the
end. Then I tear across it, heading left, until I get to the big
tree at the corner with the hugely impressive scent of the black
Doberman I've often admired from afar. After crossing over a
bigger street, with no cars at this time of night, I run as fast as I
can without losing my way. At the next corner I'm unsure of
where to go at first, but then I take in a whiff of the bakery I've
walked past with Daniel and Caroline. Yup; I'm still on the right
track here. This street is pretty long, and I have to stay on it until
I hit a sharp curve. By the time it finally comes, I'm panting like
crazy.

At last, I come to the almost familiar stench of a dry cleaning
shop, and I've reached my destination. Diagonally across is Dr
Wagner's surgery. Its windows are dark, of course, but luckily,
the apartment on the floor above it is brightly lit. Dr Wagner
seems to be at home and awake. Without a moment's hesitation,
I plop down on the pavement in front of the house and begin to

bark loudly. Incessantly. At some point, someone is sure to hear me. I can't give up now – I owe it to Willi.

It doesn't take too long for a window to open – unfortunately on the third floor, and a woman peeks out.

'What kind of goddamned noise is that! Get out of here, you stupid dog!'

Undeterred, I keep on barking, though I'm getting kind of hoarse.

'Beat it, or I'll call the police!'

What do I care about that? For a change of pace, I howl a little. The woman closes the window. Nothing happens for a while. Doesn't matter. Don't give up, Carl-Leopold – don't give up. We're talking about Willi here!

Then I hear a clatter, and the front door opens. The woman comes out onto the street – and she has Dr Wagner with her! They talk to each other while they approach me.

'I don't know what makes you think that this could be a patient of mine, but I'll take a look to see what the problem is.'

'Well, why else would a dog make such a scene? Thanks for coming down.'

The two of them stop in front of me. Wagner stares at me. I stare back. I hope he recognizes me, or else they really might call the police.

'Sure enough – I *do* know this dog. He belongs to a girlfriend of mine.'

Hey – that part is not really true. Caroline is not your girlfriend! But in this situation I don't want to stand on ceremony, so I jump up on Wagner and wag my tail to say hello. Wagner strokes me for a minute, then he looks at me thoughtfully.

'What's wrong over at your place this time, Hercules?'

If I could simply tell him what's going on, I wouldn't have to stand here making such a fuss. I jump up at him again and pull at his sleeve. The woman, who was freaking out just moments ago, now has an amused look on her face.

'It looks as though he wants you to go with him.'

'Yes, it does seem that way, doesn't it? Is something wrong with Caroline?'

I jump up and down. I admit that's a bit of a lie, but the important thing is that he'll come along with me, so luring him with Caroline probably makes good sense. He'll soon see for himself that it is not a beautiful young woman who needs his help, but rather an ugly old man.

'Where is Caroline? At home?'

I run three steps ahead of him, then I turn back to Wagner and wag my tail. Wagner shakes his head in amazement and pulls a mobile out of his trouser pocket and calls a number. He holds the phone to his ear and listens, but after a while he puts it back in his pocket. 'Hmm, I can't reach her – all I get is her voice mail. OK, Hercules, I guess I just have to follow you. Wait a minute; I must get my jacket.'

The woman looks at Wagner. She is utterly bewildered. 'Hey, I was just joking! You don't seriously believe that this dog is actually asking you to go with him?'

'Yes, that's exactly what I believe, Mrs Loretti. This dog

doesn't mess about. He's dead serious.'

Then he turns round and goes back into the house. I'm elated. Wagner may be an idiot, but he does know his dogs.

A moment later, he's standing next to me once more.

'Good, Hercules. I am really quite curious to find out the reason for your beautifully staged performance.'

I wag my tail again and set off, and a brief glance over my shoulder assures me that Wagner is following me. On the way back, I don't have to think about where I'm going, which makes things much easier. Soon we go past Caroline's house, and Dr Wagner starts to turn off the street to the entranceway. I give a quick bark – no way!

'Ah, not there. So where are we heading?' Wagner looks at me questioningly, and I continue towards the park. No slowing down – we'll be there any minute now.

At last I head straight for Mr Beck, who is sitting next to Willi as we agreed. Willi is still lying on the grass just the way I left him. Mr Beck stares at me.

'Goodness me, that is a truly brilliant idea – you got the vet.'

Now Wagner comes up. 'What's happened here? You two found this man here? And fetched me to help? That is just incredible.' He kneels down next to Willi. 'Hello? Can you hear me? Hello?'

Willi doesn't react. Wagner pulls up Willi's sweater and puts his ear to Willi's chest, then starts massaging him. No, it's more like beating him up. That looks really brutal. I hope Wagner knows what he's doing! After a long time of massaging and hitting, Wagner puts his ear back to Willi's chest. Apparently, something now seems to be working better, because Wagner is smiling with satisfaction. He sits up and fishes out his mobile phone, then he dials a number.

'Hello, my name is Marc Wagner. I just found an unconscious male lying in Helvetia Park, aged between fifty and sixty. It is difficult to conduct a thorough examination here, but my guess is that it could be a heart attack. In any case, his heartbeat is quite irregular, but after a cardiac massage it seems to be better.'

He listens again. Someone on the other end of the line seems to be asking him something.

'Well, not really. I'm a vet. I've now put him into a stable position on his side, and he doesn't appear to need more cardiac massage. You'll find us to the right of the children's playground. See you soon!'

Wagner hangs up, then he gives Mr Beck and me a sombre look. 'I think this man had a heart attack. In any case, it seems to be something serious. It is good that you went for help.' First he pats my head, then Mr Beck's. 'Well done!' He falls silent for a moment, then he adds, 'Even though no one will believe this wacky story, your mistress least of all, I'll bet, Hercules. Where is she, anyway? And why are you running around at night alone in the park?' He studies me curiously. 'It's too bad you can't talk.'

He picks up his phone again and dials a number. 'Hi, Nina, this is Marc. Listen, can you give me your friend Caroline's mobile number? Hmm. Yes.'

How clever of Wagner – he seems to have called up Nina.

'No, I just wanted to tell her something that might interest her. So if you could do me this favour…' Silence again. 'Oh, hello, Caroline! Such a coincidence that you're at Nina's. Well, this is going to sound strange, but I'm in Helvetia Park with Hercules. Do you think you can come here?'

•

The paramedics lift Willi onto a stretcher. Wagner has a brief conversation with the human doctor who just examined Willi.

'I think it was a heart attack too. He was really lucky that you came along.'

'Well, normally my patients are much smaller or much larger, and usually much hairier, but if need be I can also take care of someone without fur.' The two of them laugh.

'We're going to take the gentleman to the university hospital. Goodbye, then!'

Marc Wagner nods briefly, before turning to Caroline and Nina, who are now standing next to us. 'Have a nice evening, ladies!'

Caroline doesn't say anything at first, but just takes me in her arms. 'Hercules! What are you doing here? What in God's name happened?'

Wagner says with a wry smile, 'Well, here's what I've been able to piece together: Hercules was with the cat in the park, and while they were there, they found this homeless man. Being the clever beasts they are, they understood that this was an emergency, and so Hercules went to get the only doctor he knows, namely me.'

Nina laughs out loud. 'Excuse me, Marc, but do you realize how crazy what you just said sounds? The dachshund and the cat want to save a bum, so they go and get you? Have you been drinking?'

What a nerve! Why does that sound crazy? That is pretty much exactly what happened. It's strange – Nina seems to be really anry with Wagner; in any case, she sounds quite annoyed. I wonder why.

Wagner defends himself. 'Why are you so upset? What do you imagine really happened? You think I kidnapped Hercules from Caroline's apartment, brought along the cat, and then I attacked this poor old man? Or that our two friends here assaulted the man? I can only tell you what I saw with my own eyes. And what I saw for myself was that Hercules showed up in front of my surgery and barked until I came outside. Then he guided me here, and this man was lying on the ground, apparently being watched over by the cat. I admit that I have no idea how the two of them got outside Caroline's building and into the park, or what happened to the man. I suspect he had a heart attack. In any case, he doesn't appear to be drunk – I didn't pick up any smell of alcohol. Oh, and I'm not drunk either.'

Nina gasps, and Caroline hugs me tight.

'I can't imagine how Hercules got out of the apartment, but luckily he made his way to you. I know that man; one day he came to our front door and seemed to be a bit confused. Thanks for helping him. Who knows what would have happened if you hadn't.'

Nina looks at the two of them and giggles – a little unkindly, it seems to me. 'Why? What do you picture having happened? Anyone else could have called the paramedics just as easily. I doubt that Marc's veterinary training was of much help.'

Wagner's smile grows even wider. 'Dear Nina, if you're lying unconscious in the park some day, you'll be glad if someone who is at least a vet finds you.'

Precisely! Better than a psychologist, I would think, even though I'm not exactly sure what that is.

'So, ladies, we've said everything that needs to be said, and I'll be on my way. Have a nice evening.'

He gives Nina and Caroline a friendly nod and heads out of the park. When he has gone five steps, he turns round again.

'Oh, before I forget, Caroline – Wednesday night, six thirty? I'll pick you up, OK? See you then!'

Caroline nods and quickly waves goodbye. Nina doesn't say anything, at least as long as we're still in the park. But on the way home, she makes up for lost time.

'You have a date with Marc? Why didn't you tell me?'

'I wanted to, but …'

'I mean, you go out of your way to stop by and go on and on to me about your great day at the Elbe with Jens and how romantic it was and how well you two got along – and you don't say a word about your date with Marc?'

'Yes, but—' Caroline starts to say, but Nina doesn't let her finish.

'And I really thought your stupid dog was sick, when all you actually wanted was Marc's number! Did you even ask yourself how I would feel once I found out? Really crappy, I can tell you – really crappy!'

'I wanted to tell you, which is why I made a point of coming to your apartment tonight. But then Marc called, and I didn't get around to it.'

'A likely story. We talked for a good hour first. I suppose that's far too short a time for you to get round to something that unimportant.'

'What do you mean? You asked about Jens the second I walked through the door. Nothing else interested you in the slightest.'

'Of course not. How was I supposed to know that there was something else to report?'

'He invited me to a concert – that's all.'

'Oh, that's so nice. And how artistic of him.'

'Besides, you told me he's not really the guy for you. I had no way of suspecting that that's not the case.'

'Right. You couldn't suspect it, but you could have known it if you'd bothered to ask me recently how I'm doing. Instead, all we talk about is you and your relationship problems. And when I came to your place not too long ago and really needed a friend, your stupid cooking with your buddy Daniel was suddenly incredibly important, and I even felt as though I was in the way. Great friend you turned out to be – thanks a lot. I will remind you of that next time you need a friend to talk to.' She turns on her heel and strides off.

Caroline remains behind with me. 'Oh, damn. I suspected there'd be trouble. I guess her thing with Marc isn't over and done with after all.' She sighs. 'Well, let's go home, sweetie, and then you can tell me all about how you got here in the first place.'

I'll be happy to oblige. But could someone do me a favour and tell me what just happened between Nina and Caroline? Nina had decided that the vet was just as silly as I'd originally thought. So why is she so angry? And leaving that aside for the moment: what is going on with Jens now? It was a great day with him. Does Caroline really know what she wants? I think the answer is no.

•

When we get home, I run into the bedroom, riddled with guilt, and plop down in front of the chair and the open balcony door. Caroline's eyes go back and forth between Exhibit A and Exhibit B.

'You're not going to tell me that you got the door open by yourself, are you? That is unbelievable. You can perform in the circus with that one. But how in the world did you get down from the balcony? Did you jump?' I give her my best innocent look and sit up and beg. 'Hercules! Are you crazy? You're not a cat! There is no way you have nine lives!'

Huh? Nine lives? Does a cat have nine lives? That would, of course, go a long way to explaining Mr Beck's behaviour. Or is that just one of those human proverbs?

Caroline shuts the balcony door and draws the curtains. 'I'm dead tired, my sweetheart, and a little sad, because of Marc and Nina – and a little happy, because of Marc and Jens. What a mess! I hope I can sort all this out. What do you think? Well, for now I'll just go to bed. I won't solve the problem today anyway. Good night, Hercules!'

I run to my basket and curl up in my cuddly blanket. I'm tired too, but at the same time my head is buzzing. First Daniel, then Jens. Or maybe Dr Wagner? How could it be possible that just a couple of weeks ago, there was no one in the running for the position of my future master, and now there are three all at once? And I didn't pick out a single one of them, even though I had such a great plan.

A sobering realization is making its way through my weary canine brain: young women and little dachshunds have vastly different tastes in men.

chapter twenty-one 🐾

When we walk through the doorway, Willi sits up in bed with a look of astonishment.

'Wow, you're visiting me! That's great!'

'Well, I hope it's not too exhausting for you, but the nurse thought it would be all right.'

'No, I'm delighted. I hadn't expected this at all. You're the woman with the violin workshop, aren't you?'

'Yes. My name is Caroline Neumann.' She holds out her hand to Willi, who shakes it.

'Pleased to meet you. I'm Wilhelm Schamoni, but everyone calls me Willi. And what's the name of your little friend down there?' He points to me.

'That is Hercules.'

Caroline pulls over a chair next to Willi's bed, sits down, and puts me on her lap. Willi reaches out his arm and strokes me. Phew! I guess he's not annoyed with me. I'm relieved.

'You're quite the sweet one! And now you've even saved

Willi's life, huh?'

Caroline raises her eyebrows. 'How in the world did you know that? Did you see Hercules arrive with Dr Wagner?'

'No,' a voice rings out behind us, 'I just told Willi about it.'

Caroline's head whips round. Marc Wagner is leaning on the doorframe and grinning at us. 'I see we had the same idea. Like you, I thought a little company would be just the thing for Willi.'

'Oh, hello, Marc.'

It's strange. Caroline doesn't sound especially happy. I thought she liked him. Whatever the case, I myself try to spread good cheer by wagging my tail.

'Well, are you happy to see me?' Marc pats my head. 'You're our little canine hero, aren't you?'

Well, *canine hero* is laying it on a bit thick. I'll be happy if Willi doesn't think I'm to blame for everything that happened. But Willi smiles, and it's obvious that he's still in a good mood.

'Yesterday was a crazy day – Hercules and I seem to have rescued each other. Before I had the heart attack, I freed Hercules from a rabbit burrow. He was stuck and couldn't get out. But the only reason I knew that was that all of a sudden, the fat cat turned up next to my park bench. At first I wondered whether I was starting to lose my mind; after all, this is the second time that I thought the cat wanted to take me somewhere. But it was true. Great, isn't it? I mean, the way animals help each other out. They seem to be real buddies.'

Wagner nods. 'Yes, many people underestimate animals.

And I admit that I was surprised myself yesterday. It was almost like an episode of *Lassie*.'

Lassie? Who or what is that? Caroline and Marc laugh, and even Willi giggles weakly, but cheerfully. It must be funny.

The door opens, and a woman in a white coat comes in.

'Well, Mr Schamoni, I have to ask your visitors to wait outside. I will need to examine you again soon, and besides, you need a lot of rest.' She turns to us – and she trains her stern glance on me. 'Animals are not allowed here! Please do not bring the dog with you again.'

Caroline has a guilty look on her face. 'Oh, I'm sorry; we'll go right now. But Hercules was the one who found Mr Schamoni yesterday, so I thought that just this once …'

The woman shakes her head. 'No, there are no exceptions. You are welcome to come again tomorrow, but without the dog.'

Caroline puts me down on the floor and stands up. ' So, Willi, here's wishing you a speedy recovery! Perhaps I'll stop by again.'

'Yes, that would make me so happy!' He shakes Caroline's hand again as he says goodbye.

Wagner shakes his hand too. 'Bye, Willi; get well soon!'

'Thanks again for your visit, and I hope to see you some time.'

Willi gives a quick wave, and then we're back in the hospital corridor.

'Shall we go and get some coffee?'

Caroline hesitates. 'Hmm, I don't know; they don't really like dogs in the hospital grounds.'

'Then let's go out the main entrance. There's a café two streets away.'

And that's how, just a short while later, the two of them find themselves seated at a cosy wooden table, while I curl up under the bench next to it. At first they chat about unimportant things, but then Caroline's voice takes on a strangely grim tone.

'Marc, I would like to call off our trip to the concert on Wednesday.'

Oh no! That is surely not a good sign – and just when I'm starting to get used to the vet! Damn. Marc doesn't seem too pleased by this turn of events.

'But why? I thought you were looking forward to it.'

'Yes, I was.'

'It's because of Nina, isn't it?'

'No. Well, maybe a little. Actually, the answer is yes.'

Marc shakes his head. 'I thought something like this might happen after the way she acted in the park yesterday, although I didn't entirely understand it, since there was nothing at all between Nina and me. Yes, we went out a couple of times, but that was it.'

'Nina evidently sees it differently.'

'I noticed, though I can't work out why. To be honest, the last time we got together was rather a disaster, and I never heard from her again.' Marc reaches for Caroline's hand. 'Please don't call it off. I'd like to get to know you properly, not just when some emergency brings us together. I really like you, and I promise to behave in an exemplary manner and like a gentleman.

I will give no cause for complaint.' He raises a hand. 'Scout's honour!'

Caroline smiles, but pulls her hand out of his. 'Really, Marc. I was delighted by your invitation, but my life has been quite stressful and complicated lately, and I don't want to drift right into the next problem. Nina is my best friend, and she was there for me when I was in bad shape – which wasn't all that long ago. I like you too, but maybe now is not the right time for us to get to know each other better.'

Ahh! That stupid Nina! It's not as though there aren't plenty of other men to choose from in this city. And Mr Beck knows that up to now Nina has never had problems meeting a whole lot of them. So why does she have to get in the way here? Marc obviously has the same take on this situation. He has such a pained look on his face that you'd think old von Eschersbach had just given him a good lashing with the dog whip.

'And there's nothing I can do? Maybe I could talk it over with Nina.'

Caroline shakes her head vehemently. 'No, please don't. It's not only about Nina. I didn't sleep a wink last night. I had so many thoughts swirling around in my head. And then, at about four in the morning, I realized that I have to have more peace and quiet in my life, and find out what is important to me. I need to find out who I really am. Please don't be angry with me; I can't do it any other way.'

Marc looks sad, but he doesn't say anything else. The two of them sit next to each other in silence for a while, then Caroline says goodbye, and we leave poor Wagner sitting all alone in the café.

●

'She says she needs to find out who she really is. Can you make any sense of that?' Once I'm back home, I get to pour out my heart to Mr Beck.

'Have you ever heard such nonsense? She's Caroline Neumann – who else? She surely has some kind of family tree, and she can find out everything she needs there, I mean all the names and whatever else. Or don't humans have that?'

I'm really bewildered. I never would have thought that Caroline of all people wouldn't know who she is.

'Come on, calm down, little guy. You took that wrong. Of course Caroline knows what her name is.'

Clearly, he thinks I'm stupid. I know what I heard!

'No, no, no! She said these exact words: "I need to find out who I really am." These exact words, Mr Beck, these exact words! It's not as though I'm deaf.'

Then I suddenly get a new idea. Maybe poor Caroline is in the same boat as me – somehow not as pedigreed as she'd thought. Or whatever you call it when humans don't know who their fathers are. If that's the case, it stands to reason that she would be extremely cautious when it comes to picking out a mate, seeing as how she can't know exactly who would be especially well suited to her. But when I explain this new theory to Beck, he rolls on the floor with laughter.

'Hercules, you're one of a kind! It's high time you realized that there are a couple of fundamental differences between humans and dogs. Humans are thinking beings!'

Well, thanks a lot! I suppose that means I'm unable to think? I growl a little.

'I should have known that you would take that the wrong way again and get insulted. Of course we think too. But humans – or maybe I should say *some* humans – are self-reflective, which means that they're constantly thinking about themselves. Who am I? Where do I come from? Where am I going?'

'Well, I have to tell you that what you're saying doesn't sound all that special.'

'I'm speaking figuratively! Caroline wants to know what is special about her as a human being. What distinguishes her from other humans. What is important to her. Things along those lines.'

Jeez, I keep coming back to my original theory, namely that walking upright is not good for the brain.

'What a pity that I can't talk to humans. If I could, I would just tell Caroline what is special about her, and she wouldn't have to spend any more time pondering the subject. It's pretty clear that she's a good person. She cares about the people around her, about Nina and Daniel, and even about Marc. And she also cares about animals. If she didn't, she wouldn't have brought me home from the animal shelter. Well, I think that's plenty. You don't need to know more about yourself to feel good. Now all she needs is the right man, and all will be well. On the other hand, if she keeps going like this, we'll have lost all our current candidates and will have to start all over again. But this time I'll have to come up with another ploy.'

Mr Beck sighs. 'Nah, believe me, Hercules – as long as Caroline feels as though she has to find herself, there's no point in having even the greatest guys in tow. Apparently, some people can only feel all right in a couple if they also feel all right alone. And Caroline probably really does need some time for that. So let's just be patient.'

'I hope you're wrong for once. But there is one more option: Jens. At least our outing to the river was wonderful, so maybe something will come of it for the two of them.'

'Yeah, maybe.' Mr Beck nods thoughtfully – but the look on his face tells me that he doesn't really think so.

chapter twenty-two 🐾

'C an you give me one good reason why you didn't tell me that?' Daniel sounds angry. 'I don't understand you, Caroline. We sat right here not too long ago, and I was quite open with you, so I might have expected the same on your part, don't you think?' He is *really* angry.

And yet the day had started perfectly well. When we came downstairs to the workshop, there was a big bouquet of flowers on Caroline's workbench. Caroline was delighted – that is, until she saw Daniel standing at his own table with a sullen look on his face. And from there things went downhill very quickly, because it turned out that the bouquet was from Jens, and that Daniel was jealous – truly jealous.

'I just didn't want to hurt you.'

'Well, congratulations. That was a terrific idea. But in case you're interested, now you've really hurt me. If you had told me right away that you were interested in someone else, it would have been much easier for me. But now I feel like a complete fool.'

Caroline swallows hard. 'But why? I just …'

'Because I kept on insisting *maybe it's not a good idea for us* and *maybe it's better this way*. I played the understanding guy. Man, am I an idiot! I can't even think about it without feeling sick to my stomach.'

'Now calm down, would you? It wasn't really like that. I enjoyed our cooking too. And the fact that I can't imagine it going any further has absolutely nothing to do with Jens. I've only seen him once. What could I have told you? There wasn't anything to tell.'

'Who are you trying to kid? You know exactly what I mean. I didn't stand a chance. And I would have liked to know that. I thought we were friends.'

Little red spots appear on Caroline's cheeks. 'Of course we're friends! And I can imagine that the situation is difficult for you. But it is for me as well, and I don't think I'm the bad guy here!'

'I didn't say you were.'

'Didn't you? I think you did.'

'Oh, what bullshit!' Daniel bangs his fist on the table so loudly that I bound under the workbench, then he runs out of the room and slams the door behind him.

Caroline and I stay behind. She bends down to me and pulls me out from under the workbench.

'That was nice and loud, wasn't it?' She strokes me. 'Well, it looks as though one after the other, all my friends are getting furious with me. It's a good thing I still have you.'

I look at Caroline wide-eyed. I'm honoured, of course, that

I'm just as important a friend to her as Daniel and Nina. Even so, I hope that everything gets straightened out fast. I have rather a liking for harmony. Caroline seems to be able to read my thoughts.

'Don't you worry. I promise that we'll all get on again. And to make that happen as quickly as possible, I'm going to call Nina right now and arrange to see her. What do you think – is that a good plan?' I wag my tail. 'Ah, so you think so. Well then, that's how I'll do it.'

I guess Nina feels an urgent need to talk to Caroline as well, because the minute Caroline is finished speaking to her on the phone, we head out to our usual café round the corner. When we arrive, Nina is already there, and she waves to us in a very friendly way, or so it seems to me.

'Hello, Nina! How nice that this worked out so spontaneously,' Caroline says to her as she sits down.

'Yes, what a lucky concidence. Two of my patients had just cancelled on me. And then when you called, I thought about how fate wanted us to talk to each other again at long last.'

Both of them laugh. Well, this certainly seems like a reconciliation. The waitress comes to our table.

'I don't know how you're feeling, but I think this calls for two glasses of champagne!'

Nina nods. 'Exactly. Special situations require special measures. Can you please bring us two glasses?'

Bring me one too, would you? That's what I'd like to say to them. If that's something special, I wouldn't mind trying it as well. But the only choice I have is heading over to the dog bowl of water, which this café is kind enough to provide right at the door.

Two glasses with a light-coloured liquid arrive, and the ladies reach for them eagerly.

'So, my dear – to us!' Nina declares to Caroline.

'Yes – to us!'

The two of them take a big sip.

'Honestly, I'm glad you finally called. It was starting to get weird. But by tomorrow I would have rung you myself. I still can't believe that we got into a fight over a guy. Tsk, tsk.' She shakes her head.

Caroline smiles. 'Yes, but the part I'm sorriest about is that I really have been bending your ear with my doom and gloom all the time these days. You're absolutely right, and I feel terrible about that. I'll do better!' She raises her right hand. 'I promise!'

'Well, now that I think back on it, I have to say that I was also pretty uptight about it. After all, I really did tell you that Marc isn't the one for me. I don't know why I flipped in the park like that. I expect it was partly my wounded pride.'

'Seriously, Nina, if I had known that Marc still means so much to you, I'd have steered clear of the whole thing anyway. And in case this makes you feel better, I called off the date with him.'

'Oh!' Nina sounds rather shocked. 'But you shouldn't have! At least not on my account. I admit I was angry, but if you two really clicked, I can live with that. It means there's a higher force at work.'

'No, you're not the reason – or at least not the only one. Of course I thought about Marc quite a bit after the fight with you, and then all of a sudden, I felt as though it was all too much for me, and that I first have to settle down after the chaos of the past few weeks. A new man really has no place in my life at the moment. Even a great guy like Marc.'

What can I say; Mr Beck has got the knack. It's positively alarming how well that fat cat can size up the situation again and again.

Nina looks thoughtful. 'Normally, I would say you're right on this, but maybe you should mull it over again. The streets are not exactly plastered with wonderful men, let me tell you. They are in really short supply.'

'At the moment I have more like the opposite problem: too many wonderful men, which is why I want to take a break now until I know what I really want.'

'Ah. Interesting concept. What if they're all gone by then? And who are the others? OK, Jens. He's really hot. But who else?'

'You know that evening when I wanted to cook with Daniel – that was actually planned as a romantic evening. I've never told you about that because I thought you would laugh at me. But for a while there were some sparks flying between Daniel and me, so I decided I ought to try it out.'

Nina is staring at her wide-eyed. 'You wanted to start up something with Daniel?'

'Well, the idea isn't *that* absurd. Daniel is an attractive man. He's witty, fun and tender…'

'And you've known him for something like a hundred years! Nah, that's not on the cards for you. And imagine what would happen if things went wrong.'

Caroline nods. 'Yeah, I had a little taste of that today. Daniel found out that I went out with Jens. Actually, I told him myself when Jens sent me roses at the workshop. Daniel was not exactly pleased.'

Ah! Now I understand. This morning I was a little confused, but I expect delivering presents like sausage for dogs or large numbers of flowers for humans is part of the human mating ritual.

'That doesn't surprise me. I already knew that Daniel was in love with you. But the idea that you were seriously thinking about it ... no way! Let's be honest – Daniel is simply far too nice!'

One thing's for sure: if Mr Beck should ever need a new master or mistress, Nina would be the perfect woman for him. I've rarely seen any human and animal be of one mind as often as the two of them. The only problem is that Nina can't be seriously called an animal lover, so I suppose nothing will come of that dream team.

'You're mean. Poor Daniel.'

'That's ridiculous. Daniel has to get his act together, otherwise he won't get anywhere with other women either. But here's what I find much more fascinating: are you going to get together with Jens again now – or does he also fall under the rubric of your self-discovery?'

Caroline sighs. 'Well, I have a date with him tonight, then I'll probably tell him that I don't want to see him again.'

Nina gasps. 'Are you insane? That gorgeous guy? After your romantic day at the Elbe? Someone should take your pulse; something's got to be wrong with you.'

'Why? I told you what the problem is. Of course our little outing was lovely, and it was also quite romantic and exciting. But the main thing I enjoyed was the setting. I don't know whether I could seriously fall in love with Jens.'

Nina shakes her head. 'In that case, if you give him the bad news today, at least give him my number. I could put it to good use.' The two of them laugh.

'Speaking of which, one thing does interest me.' Caroline studies Nina over the rim of her glass. 'What was the problem you had with Marc?'

'Oh, it's really silly. I admit that I botched it up.' Nina takes a deep breath. 'Well, by the second time I went out with Marc, I had started to notice that while he was charming and fun to be with, there were no real sparks flying. I found that pretty frustrating. Oh, and on our last date we also had a bit of a falling out after a stupid comment I made.'

'Really? You didn't tell me about that.'

'I wanted to that evening when we cooked with Daniel, but then Daniel was out with the dog for such a short time that we didn't have enough of a "running start". The subject is still a bit unpleasant for me.'

'That sounds rather mysterious. Come on, out with it!'

'We were spending the day at the Elbe too. The weather was beautiful, so we decided to go to the Strandperle – you know, that snack bar right at the water.'

Caroline nods. 'Of course; everyone knows that place.'

'Well, anyway, I was already in a so-so mood, because our last date had not gone the way I'd imagined. I was unsure of where things stood. And when I feel like that, I have this tendency to get a little nasty.'

'Yes, I'm well aware of that. I've known you for a day or two.'

'Well, what can I say? We were sitting on our blanket, and Marc had bought some sausages and potato salad for us at the snack bar. Then a family sat down right next to us, with two snotty little brats. One was a baby that didn't stop crying, and the other was a little rugrat, maybe two or three years old, who kept running back and forth between all the people there and whirling up a ton of sand everywhere he went. A real dream come true!'

Caroline laughs. 'I have an inkling where this is heading. I know how much you love children.'

'Yes, that's where you and I differ. I know you like kids. But not everyone goes into raptures at the sight of two little monsters. I mean, the baby was so loud that we could hardly carry on a conversation. And the other kid tripped and got loads of sand all over my potato salad. Then I came right out with it and told those crummy parents exactly what I thought of their children. I admit that I may have been on the loud side, but my nerves were pretty frayed.'

'And Marc was not entirely on board with your reaction, I take it?'

Nina nods. 'You can say that again. He was really shocked. He hauled me over the coals and told me to calm down, reminding me that these were small children and they hadn't meant any harm. He told me off in front of the parents. I was really hurt. I got up and just left Marc with all the sandy potato salad. And I took the first bus that came along the street. So there you have it – that's basically the whole story. After that I didn't hear another word from Marc until he phoned me the other night looking for you.'

'Oh no! That is really an awful story! And he didn't get back to you at all?'

Nina shakes her head. 'No. And I didn't get in touch with him either. OK, maybe it was up to me to do so, but I couldn't. And then I meet up with him again and it turns out that he's made plans to go out with you. That was a bit much for me.'

'I can see why, and I'm sorry. I had absolutely no idea.'

The waitress comes back to our table. 'Anything else you'd like?'

Caroline and Nina look at each other and giggle. Then the two of them answer in chorus: 'Yes, two more glasses of champagne, please!'

chapter twenty-three 🐾

I'm not sure whether it's possible to have this feeling if you're a dog, BUT, on the off-chance that it's not restricted to two-legged creatures, I have to say that I'm frustrated. Totally!

I'm lying in my favourite spot in the garden, the weather is lovely, and the birds are chirping. I just had something yummy to eat, and Caroline has already taken me for a walk today. There's also a reasonable amount of harmony in the workshop; at any rate, Daniel and Caroline are back on speaking terms. But all the same, I feel like howling – so I go ahead and do so. Startled by all the noise I'm making, Mr Beck comes over and keeps me company.

'What's wrong with you?' he asks. 'Are you in pain?'

'Yes. Emotional pain.'

'Why?'

'Nothing is working out. I went to such great lengths to find a man for Caroline, and she's ruining everything. Now she's going to give Jens the brush-off too. Then we're back where we started.'

Mr Beck sits down next to me. 'How about you look at it this way? You wanted a man for Caroline because she was so unhappy single, but now she has come up with the idea of trying to go it alone, which means she's no longer unhappy. And you don't have to look any more. It works out well.'

'No! It doesn't work out at all, because *I'm* unhappy. I want a master. You know, the day at the Elbe with Jens and Caroline was unbelievably beautiful. That's the way it needs to be; I want to be a dog with a happy couple. And since I've come to realize that, I just hoped that Caroline would really fall in love – and soon. It doesn't have to be Jens, but it can be. You know, I think I want a real family. A pack of humans to call my own.'

Mr Beck sighs. 'You dogs will never learn! Why do you always set your hearts on humans? That will bring you nothing but aggravation! A human can never be your family, Hercules. That is nonsense; get it through your head once and for all!'

'But that's what I want!'

'Then go on being frustrated. It won't be your last frustrating experience with humans; I can guarantee you that.' With these words, Mr Beck turns round and goes off again.

Let him go. He was no great comfort anyway.

I sit down and decide simply to ignore Mr Beck's words of wisdom. Of course a dog can be part of a human family. In fact, I'm even quite certain that a cat can be as well, as long as it wants to. Which brings me back to my original point: how do I find a family for myself? Well, perhaps it's not too late for Jens and Caroline. After all, they're going to have a date tonight. Maybe I can somehow make sure that they have a good time. Caroline herself said that she thought the day with Jens was great. No matter what, I somehow have to wangle my way into this date, so I spend the rest of the afternoon lying in wait to make sure Caroline doesn't leave the house without me.

Sure enough, she's finishing off earlier than usual today and going up to change her clothes. I stay glued to her heels and don't leave her side even when she goes to the bathroom for the umpteenth time.

'Hey, Hercules! What's going on with you today? You're so clingy.' She shoos me away from the bathroom door and closes it.

Well, all right then, when she comes back out, she'll have to get past me unless she climbs out of the window.

And she doesn't do that, of course. After quite a while, she reappears in the short black dress we already discussed not too long ago. Also, she's piled her hair into a little mountain on top of her head. My hope is restored. If Caroline puts so much effort into her appearance, maybe she is rethinking the thing with Jens.

The bell rings, and Jens is standing at our door. Caroline gives him a little kiss on the cheek, then she bends down to me.

'Well, Hercules, today you stay here, so be good and make sure not to jump down from the balcony again!'

No way! I don't want to stay here. I run over to Jens and sit up and beg. He laughs in amusement.

'It seems as though your buddy is determined to come with us. I guess I won him over with the sausage ploy.'

'That is out of the question. He will stay here like a good dog.'

Ugh! How heartless of her! But I'm not going to let her get away with that so easily. When Caroline opens the apartment door, I just race out past her to the staircase. Once I get downstairs, I'm in luck: ol' lady Meyer, who owns the parakeet, is just coming into the house, and I can whiz by her and get outside. The car without a roof is right there, smiling at me invitingly. If my legs weren't so short, I could jump right in, but as it is, I have to wait for Jens and Caroline.

'Listen, you naughty dog!' Caroline comes up to me and scolds me. 'If I say you stay here, then you stay here!'

She reaches for me, but before she can grab my collar, I run to Jens and rub against his legs with my tail wagging. While doing so, I try to bark in the friendliest way I know how. Jens bends over and lifts me up.

'Well, old chap, I would take you along, but your mistress is really strict today. I'm almost a little afraid of her.'

Caroline laughs. 'I don't think I'll be able to hold my ground against two men with a united front. So, fine – bring him along with us.'

'You see, buddy, you're in luck. Let's get this show on the road.'

He puts me onto the floor on the passenger side, then both of them get in, and off we go. Persistence pays off!

When we arrive at the restaurant, I find myself wondering why Caroline didn't want to take me along. It turns out to be an outdoor restaurant, and my very first glance reveals two dogs lying under other tables. One is an old boxer, and the other is a very attractive lady retriever, who nods at me graciously as we take our seats at the table next to hers. I pick a spot to lie down that gives me a good view of her. Maybe I shouldn't always be thinking about Caroline's heart and think about my own for a change. On the other hand, I have to prick up my ears today more than ever if I want to hear what Caroline is saying. After all, I have to intervene if she starts her 'I need to find myself' nonsense.

But for now, the conversation is still focused on choosing dishes and drinks. Caroline orders sparkling water, and Jens laughs.

'I was actually thinking that to celebrate the beautiful evening we could order something bubbly – and I'm not referring to the fizz in your sparkling water.'

'You won't believe this, but this morning I already drank two glasses of champagne with Nina. Sort of a rite of reconciliation; there was a bit of tension between us. So that's why I'll stick to non-alcoholic drinks for the moment.'

'Whatever you say. I don't want to talk you into anything. Why were you two fighting?'

'Oh, it's a silly story. Kind of by accident, I had made a date with someone she really likes. She was not pleased.'

'Kind of by accident? That sounds interesting. How do you manage that?'

'Well, it wasn't really planned as a date. It was more like … oh, I don't know either. In any case, Nina was annoyed.'

'I see, an unplanned date. I knew right from the start that you are a woman who is very much in demand.'

He laughs and reaches for Caroline's hand. She hesitates, but before she gets the chance to pull her hand away, I jump up and start barking. Caroline leans over to me.

'Hey, Hercules, what's the matter?'

'Maybe it's another dog?'

'Hmm, Hercules isn't really a yelper. Something must have frightened him.'

Of course something frightened me, namely the prospect of Caroline frightening off the next man in her life. Still, I've circumvented this situation forcefully and effectively. I hope this is not going to go on the whole evening.

It *does* go on the whole evening. Whenever I get the feeling that Caroline is steering towards the wrong topic, I get restless. This pattern repeats itself about once every ten minutes. Caroline is really on edge by this point.

'Say, what's wrong?' she hisses at me. 'I wanted you to stay at home, and that would have been much better. You're unbelievably naughty! If you keep this up, we'll lock you in the car.'

OK, that'd be bad. Maybe I need to take my foot off the accelerator for a bit. I lie down obediently under Caroline's chair. The retriever at the next table is checking me out.

'Hey, little guy, do you have a weak bladder?'

'Who, me? No. Why do you ask?'

'Because you've been fidgeting the whole time.'

How embarrassing. This lovely lady thinks I'm incontinent.

Naturally, I can't just let that go by.

'Well, the reason I'm so fidgety is that I'm trying to keep my mistress from making a big mistake.'

'You mean with that guy? He doesn't look so bad. He has a nice voice.'

'I think so too. But we have the opposite problem. I'm afraid she wants to dump him.'

'I see. Well, she probably has her reasons.'

'I don't see it that way. She likes him, but she wants to find herself first. That's totally nuts, isn't it?'

'Little guy, can I give you some advice?'

'Sure.'

I'm expecting an excellent suggestion from an attractive lady in a matter such as this. She's probably been in the same situation as Caroline.

'Stay out of human affairs. All it does is stir up trouble. And the scene you're making now also looks pretty silly.'

Bam. That hit home. You almost get the feeling that the lady has been briefed by Mr Beck. Feeling insulted, I retreat back under Caroline's chair. So I won't play my part! You can all do what you want. Just don't tell me afterwards that I didn't warn you.

I spend the rest of the evening virtually silent under Caroline's chair. Then again, Caroline isn't making any more attempts to tell Jens the bad news. I wonder if she's had second thoughts about it. When the two of them finally get up to leave, Jens makes a suggestion that I really like.

'What do you think about us taking a little walk with Hercules? Last time we were at the Elbe, and now we can show him the Alster. Does that sound good? After all, he's been remarkably quiet this past hour. That lecture you gave him seems to have done the trick. We should reward that. You know, use what they call "positive reinforcement". What do you think?'

My heart beats faster. I'm now pretty sure that Caroline has rethought the whole matter, otherwise she would have turned him down politely.

The lake known as the Alster is right next to the restaurant. We stroll along the wide path at the edge of the water. Normally, I would just run off and explore the area, but of course I also want to hear what the two of them are talking about, so I stay there for the time being. And then – Jens puts his arm around Caroline! I'm so excited that my heart is starting to race. How will Caroline react?

At first, she doesn't do anything. That's a good sign. The two of them keep on strolling, with me right behind.

'You know…' Caroline is about to say something, but then she falls silent again. Uh-oh! Not such a good sign after all.

'What?' Jens stands still. The two of them are now looking right at each other, and he takes her hands.

'You know, I think you're very nice, Jens, but I feel I'm not ready, and I'm afraid to give you false hope.'

'How do you mean?'

'Well, we had a very romantic day at the Elbe, and tonight was also quite lovely – aside from Hercules's little fits. But I think you may be hoping for more than I can give at the moment, and I don't want to disappoint you, so I think it's better for me to be honest with you right away. I feel as though I'm not ready to fall in love now. Before I think about starting a relationship again, I first have to find out a few things about myself.'

Jens lets go of her hands. 'I see.'

That's all he says. Oh my. I find the situation so unpleasant that I wish I could go and hide under some bush.

'Are you angry with me now?'

'No. I'm just astonished.'

'Yes, I can imagine you would be. I should have said something sooner.'

'No, that's not what I mean. I'm astonished that you have seriously given thought to a relationship between us and were concerned that I want one.'

'Well, don't you?'

Jens laughs. 'No, of course not. After all, I do already have a girlfriend.'

WHAT WAS THAT? We're obviously looking at Thomas no. 2 here.

'Yes … but … I didn't know that.' Caroline sounds totally bewildered. Rightly so.

'Well, come on, girl, don't you ever read *Gala* or any of the other women's magazines?'

'No, I have to admit that I don't.'

'All right,' Jens says patronizingly, 'then you don't. But if you were to read them, you would know that for the past four years

I've been with Alexa von Schöning, a very successful model.'

'Yes, but … in that case, what did you want from me? Why did you go out with me at all?'

'Because I find you really cute, and I like to have some fun. Alexa knows that, and it's all right with her. Naturally, I thought you knew that too.'

It's a good thing I can't speak, because I'm at a loss for words. He's even worse than Thomas! He doesn't even have a guilty conscience. Caroline is also speechless.

'You're not saying anything. I mean, now that you know that I am in a steady relationship, there's no reason not to have a little fun, is there? You don't have to worry about my wanting something serious. That ought to work out quite well for you.'

Caroline is silent; she is just staring at him.

'Hey, Caroline, how about a laugh?' Jens gives her a nudge.

I growl at him. Take your hands off this woman – now!

'Oh boy, this mutt is really starting to get on my nerves. What's wrong with him today? I thought he liked me.'

'Yes,' Caroline says almost inaudibly, 'I thought I liked you too. Just goes to show how you can be fooled. I'd like to go home now.'

'OK, let's do that – even though I don't know why you're insulted. I mean, nothing at all has happened. Which is a pity, by the way.' Jens grins, and Caroline glares at him.

We get back into the car without a roof. My ears blow in the wind, which is a nice feeling, but apart from that, nothing at all feels good. I feel like a complete idiot. I wanted to pair off

Caroline with this man. Incredible! It seems I have no insight into human nature at all. Not that Caroline does either, but that's cold comfort.

Jens stops in front of the house. Just as Caroline starts to say goodbye, Jens leans forward and gets really close to her.

'Caroline, let's get real now. You and I have electricity. Let's at least try it out. Let me be quite honest with you – I really want you. The way you're holding back makes the whole thing even more interesting.'

Caroline doesn't say anything, and reaches for the door handle. Then all of a sudden, Jens grabs her, pushes her back onto her seat, and starts kissing her on the mouth. Caroline screams and tries to push him away, but Jens keeps a firm grip on her hands and goes on kissing her.

I'm totally shocked – this can't be happening!

But my fright doesn't last long. I jump up from the floor to the two of them and bite Jens on exactly the same spot that worked wonders last time. He yells and tries to hit me, and while this is going on, he has to let go of Caroline. She uses this moment to fling open the door, grab me, and jump out of the car. Caroline slams the passenger door shut and runs to the house, but then another idea comes to mind, and she turns back to the car.

'Best regards to Alexa,' she says. 'No need for her to worry. As far as I know, a tetanus shot lasts a good ten years.'

chapter twenty-four 🐾

'Ah, there's the heroic dog!' Nina comes up to me, bends over, and makes a grand gesture of giving me a piece of pork sausage. 'You did great, and I hope that Mr Uhland continues to think of you for a good long time to come. Well done!'

I have to admit that I find this reaction quite appropriate. And the fact that I was allowed to sleep in Caroline's bed last night strikes me as a suitable reward for a brave dachshund like me. I happily chew away at the sausage while Nina gets another blow-by-blow description of last night's events. Every once in a while, she throws in a comment ('Incredible!' or 'Hard to believe!'), and one or the other of them keeps petting me. I'm now lying on my back between Caroline and Nina on Caroline's couch with all my legs outstretched. Fabulous! I love having my belly rubbed! Life can be so beautiful. I guess we don't need a man after all.

'Have you told Daniel about this yet?'

'No, and I think I'm not going to. Although we're getting along well again, and he says everything is just fine, the atmosphere is still strained somehow, so I'm not going to bother him with a description of my marvellously catastrophic rendezvous.'

'Hmm, good point. But it will all straighten itself out again; there's no doubt about that.'

At that moment, the doorbell rings.

'Are you expecting a visitor?'

'No, you're the only one I invited over. That's odd.'

'Maybe the florist, with a bouquet of flowers from Mr Uhland to apologize?'

'At nine in the evening? Pretty unlikely. Besides, that guy certainly doesn't have any sense of wrongdoing.'

The bell rings again. Caroline stands up and goes to the special telephone that tells you who is standing downstairs in front of the house.

'Hello?'

Now there's knocking too.

'It's me, Daniel. I'm at your door.'

Nina has come out into the hallway as well. Caroline gives her a quizzical look, then she opens the door. Sure enough, it's Daniel – although he doesn't look like his usual self. He looks sad, somehow, yet determined.

'Hello, Caroline. Sorry for disturbing you so late in the evening, but I have to talk to you.'

Now he notices Nina for the first time. 'Oh, hello!'

'Hi, Daniel! Everything OK with you?'

'Yes, of course. But I have something important to discuss with Caroline. Would you mind leaving us alone? I know that's not exactly polite, but it's really important.'

I feel the hair on my neck starting to rise. The tone of Daniel's voice tells me that nothing good is going to come of this. Nina seems to be thinking something along the same lines. She looks at Caroline questioningly.

'It's OK, Nina.'

'Well, then, I'll clear out of here. Bye, you two; see you soon.'

Once she's gone, Daniel hangs his jacket in the closet and sits down on the couch. Caroline follows him, but sits down in the easy chair across from him.

'What's going on that's so important?' she asks.

'I'll come right to the point. Next month I'm going to go away, and I'll be gone for three months.'

'What?'

'Yes. Aurora asked me quite a while ago whether I would go with her on her concert tour. While I'm there, I'd also be able to check out any violins she is offered.'

'You want to travel with Aurora for three months? You can't be serious!'

'Yes, I am. I have to get out of here. You know, I thought I'd be able to sort out this thing with you and me, but I was wrong. I can't do it; it's too painful for me to see you every day, which is why I need some distance.'

Caroline swallows. 'I'm sorry. I didn't know it was so bad.'

'You don't need to be sorry. I didn't know it either. Besides, you can't help it that you're not as in love with me as I am with you. That's just the way it is.'

'Will you come back? I mean, after the three months?'

'Quite honestly, I don't know at this point. But I don't want to think about that now. Of course, I'll continue to pay for my portion of the workshop; don't worry about that.'

Caroline gets up and sits down next to Daniel. Then she takes his hand and squeezes it tight. 'Daniel, that is really the last thing on my mind. I'm sad that it's turning out this way. You are my closest friend.'

'I know. But right now it's really hard for me to be your buddy.'

•

I'm fast asleep, when all of a sudden, someone starts shaking my basket. I look up. It's the old von Eschersbach, glaring down at me!

'Come on, get up, you good-for-nothing! You've had it good and comfortable here for quite enough time. I've decided that Caroline needs her distance from you – for at least three months. So take your dog bone and get out of here!'

My heart begins to race. I want to hide – but where? Von Eschersbach is grabbing me, and there's no escaping him. I howl in terror and try to duck under my cuddly blanket, but he's already nabbed me. Oh no! I'm going to wind up back in the animal shelter!

'Hercules, wake up! You're dreaming!'

I glance up fearfully – and find that I'm staring into the eyes of Caroline, who's looking at me in surprise. 'My goodness, you're making such a racket. Are you dreaming about hunting rabbits again?'

Hunting rabbits? If she only knew. I hop out of my basket and huddle close to her.

'You're trembling, you poor thing. I guess it was more like a nightmare, wasn't it? But if it's any consolation, I can't really sleep either. The thing with Daniel has hit me pretty hard. Why does everything always have to be so complicated?' She sighs, and so do I. I've also come to realize that when it comes to humans, absolutely everything is complicated. To make her feel better, I lick her bare toes. She giggles. 'That tickles, Hercules!'

Grabbing me under my belly, she takes me in her arms. 'I have a very good idea how we can both spend the rest of the night a little more peacefully. You can sleep in my bed again tonight. I don't feel like being alone either. I'm probably totally spoiling you, but I don't care a fig about that!'

Hmm … I wonder if figs taste good.

Once I'm in Caroline's bed, I cuddle up on one of the pillows right away. Caroline also lies back down and strokes me.

'You know, maybe all that stuff about finding myself was actually nonsense. I mean, it felt good for about a day, but now I'm no longer so sure that it was right. I admit that Jens was a complete disaster. But now Daniel is going away for a while. Was that the wrong thing – I mean, letting him go? I wish you could talk, Hercules. I would love to know what you're thinking. On the other hand, what else could I have done? The way Daniel wants things to turn out is just not going to happen. I'm not in love with him. I had hoped I could be, but I can't.'

She's quiet for a while, so I think she's fallen asleep. But then she goes on talking.

'And I suppose I have no business contacting Marc at this point. Oh man, I think I totally messed up. The fact is that I found him rather fascinating. Why in the world did I tell him that I don't want to see him any more?'

Yes, indeed: why? Not a clever move. I said it right from the start – or I *would* have said it if I could talk. But no human listens to me anyway.

'Marc *is* nice, isn't he?' I lick her cheek in confirmation. 'Eww, Hercules! I believe you that you like him even without all that licking. I like him too. To be perfectly honest, the thing with Nina was what really disturbed me. After all, she's my best friend. And the feeling that she was still infatuated with him wasn't all that great. Do you understand that?'

All of a sudden I'm gaining new hope for my plan for a happy family life. Maybe we'll get to that goal after all. How we'll do so is still a mystery to me, but that's not the important thing right now. In any case, it can't hurt to position myself as someone who understands women. If I do, maybe Caroline will tell me a little more about Marc, so I try to give Caroline my most loyal look.

'Wow, look at those big sad eyes. You think that what I did

with Marc was a mistake, right? Well, maybe it was, but he did overreact a little when he was with Nina. The poor woman. I admit she's not all that fond of children, but to tell her off in front of everyone? That's not all right either, is it?' I blink again and sniff her. 'That makes him seem rather unappealing somehow.'

No, not at all! I shake my head and growl a little.

'OK, then we have two different takes on this. I do think it makes him a little unappealing, so in that respect it may have been the right decision after all. I mean, after Thomas, I've had quite enough of hot-tempered men.'

Woof! What is she talking herself into this time? Who knows exactly what Marc said to Nina, and even more importantly, what Nina said to Marc? If I carefully review her options, Marc is far and away the one who suits us the best. So if I have anything to say about it, Caroline should call him up really fast and put that 'finding herself' thing on hold for the time being. She can always do that later. I nudge her again, but there's no reaction. Unbelievable. Caroline really has fallen asleep, right in the middle of our interesting conversation.

But not me: I can't fall asleep. Not yet. All kinds of ideas are rattling around in my head. What do the things I've learned about humans over the past few weeks tell me about Caroline and men? First, she thinks Marc is nice. Second, she doesn't want to speak to him even so, because she's uncomfortable about the conversation they had in the café. And third, that's why she's talking herself into the idea that nothing would have come of it in any case. Wait a minute – I know what has to be done! I have to get Marc to speak to her. But how? How am I going to pull that off?

chapter twenty-five 🐾

'So your theory is that Marc is the right man for Caroline after all, and that she just doesn't want to admit it, because if she did, she would have to get in touch with him, and she's ashamed to do so. And that's why she's come up with something that's supposedly unsuitable about him. Hmm.' Mr Beck is deep in thought. 'Wow! You've learned so much – and it's no wonder. After all, you've had an excellent teacher.'

'Yes, you're great. But what do you think I should do now? The matter is certainly very complicated. I can't just walk up to Marc and say "Hey, call her up, would you?" On the other hand, I'm afraid that if he doesn't turn up, nothing will ever come of the two of them.'

Mr Beck nods. 'Yeah. Complicated. Really.'

We sit there in silence. Then Beck starts up again. 'There's essentially only one thing you can do: head to Marc's surgery and hope that he sees this as a sign.'

'As a sign? Of what? Of a dachshund pursuing him?'

Mr Beck giggles. 'You see? There's still plenty you need to learn about humans. Here's how it works: when humans wish hard for something, they tend to see everything as a sign – even though most of the time it isn't. So, let's assume that a human would like to have children. In this case, he is sure to stumble over a pram soon, and regard it as a sign that his own offspring are imminent. In reality, of course, it's only a sign that someone put a pram in his way.'

'I see.'

Somehow I'm not quite getting what Mr Beck is telling me. What does a pram have to do with Marc and Caroline? Apparently, I look stumped, because Mr Beck shakes his head and turns condescending.

'It's really quite simple, Hercules. If Marc is pining for Caroline and then he sees you, he takes it as a sign that he should try to contact her.'

'Yes, but that's exactly what I'd mean. That would be my *actual* intention.'

Mr Beck snorts impatiently. 'Of course. But Marc doesn't know that. It would not occur to him that a dachshund has a plan. All he sees in you is a simple-minded animal, and so he will believe it's a sign. Do you get that?'

Frankly, no, but I don't dare to admit that.

'So I should run to Marc and hope that somehow he sees me?'

'Precisely. That's how you'll do it.'

•

Once I get to the surgery, I realize that our plan has a series of critical flaws. At this time of day, the street is pretty loud here, and Marc probably won't even hear the sound of a barking dog. Also, he's unlikely to be at home; he'll be working in the surgery. And even if I get inside the surgery, I'm hardly going to be able to slip past the receptionist. And without a dog owner accompanying me, she'll almost certainly throw me out. I'm not exactly in her good books after having chased those rabbits, Bobo and Snow White.

So I sit on the pavement in front of the entrance and think over my options. Do I go back home and get Beck to help out? No, my only alternative is to find my way into the waiting room and get Marc to notice me.

When a woman heads towards the entrance with a cat in her arms, I get ready to spring into action. She rings the doorbell, the door opens, and I slip in behind the two of them. The cat looks at me in amusement. 'So, little guy? You're going to the vet on the sly? Your mistress won't believe that you're sick?'

I shake my head. 'No, I'm here on a sort of secret mission. And the only sickness involved is that my mistress is heartsick. And so is the doctor.'

'Well, well. So he's in love. That news will really bomb in this surgery. I would guess that about half of the patients are dragged in here only because their mistresses enjoy the company of the vet. I, for example, have been getting dewormed much more often since Dr Wagner took over the practice from his father.'

That makes me happy, of course. After all, Caroline deserves only the best – the best man, that is. We don't want to wind up with a reject. But this also brings home the point that I have to act fast. The competition is already waiting in the wings.

The cat owner finally stops at the reception desk to sign in her little darling. The young woman behind the desk looks first at the cat, and then at me.

'Oh, you have a dog now too, Mrs Urbanczik?'

She shakes her head. 'No, why?'

'This little fellow came in with you.' She points at me.

'Oh, I didn't even notice him. He must have just run in behind me. But he's not my dog.'

The young woman in the white coat looks into the waiting room. 'Does this dog belong to someone?'

Three people are sitting in the row of plastic chairs, and they all shake their heads. So if Marc doesn't turn up soon, my plan is down the drain, because his assistant will certainly throw me out soon. I give her my most pitiful look.

'Hmm, somehow this dog looks familiar. But I can't place most of the animals without their owners.' She thinks it over. 'What are we going to do with you now? I don't want to just put you outside, but if you're really all alone here, maybe we should take you to the animal shelter until we can find your owner.'

WOOF! Animal shelter? No way! Damn, it looks as though I've just sealed my own doom. Oh dear, how do I get back out of here? And where is Marc, anyway? Just then, the door to the consulting room opens. Before I get a chance to thank the dachshund Lord, I see that a small girl comes out instead of Marc. Nothing at all is going the way it should today. The little girl looks at me. She has really big blue eyes, curly brown hair, and lots of tiny brown dots on her nose.

'So, are you next? What's your name?' she says to me.

'Well, I don't know what his name is. He seems just to have come in here,' the assistant explains to the girl. 'I'll be calling the animal shelter soon.'

'Oh no!' the girl insists. 'He's so sweet!' She bends over to me and scratches me behind the ears. 'Then I'll keep him. Wait, I'll ask Papa!'

The assistant smiles. 'But Luisa, it's not that simple. I'm certain that this dog already has an owner who will probably be missing him soon. The animal shelter just takes care of animals until their owners show up.'

The girl called Luisa makes a face and announces, 'He's so cute. I want to keep him!' Then she stomps out and heads into the consulting room. Through the half-open door, she can be heard talking to someone.

'Papa, there's a cute dog sitting outside who's all alone. Take a look; I think he needs our help. Can't we keep him? Mrs Warnke wants to send him to the animal shelter.'

Papa? Who is that child talking to?

The door to the consulting room now swings open all the way and Luisa comes out with Marc Wagner! Marc is 'Papa'? Does that mean he has a child? And if he does, does he also have a wife? Totally confused, I plop down on my behind.

'Hercules! What are you doing here?'

'You know this animal?'

'Yes, Mrs Warnke. This is Ms Neumann's dog. Is he really here all on his own?'

'Yes, he just came in when Mrs Urbanczik was bringing in her cat. I thought I would have to call the animal shelter, but if you know the dog, I can just call the owner.'

Marc thinks for a moment. 'Do nothing for just a minute. And you come in with me, Hercules.'

'I want to come too!' Luisa declares, and walks behind Marc. Once we're all in the consulting room, he closes the door behind us, then he lifts me onto the table and looks me up and down.

'Well, Hercules. Tell me what's going on. Is someone in trouble again?'

Luisa giggles. 'But Papa. Dogs can't talk.'

'You'd be surprised, my sweetheart. This one can!'

Exactly! To confirm what he's saying, I give a quick bark. Luisa's eyes open wide.

'So, does Caroline know you're here?'

I shake my head as well as I can. Then I gently take hold of Marc's coat sleeve with my teeth and tug at it.

'You want me to come with you? To Caroline?'

I yelp twice. Of course I have no way of telling whether I ought to be so straightforward – since I'm supposed to be a sign – but I'm hardly in a position to ask Mr Beck.

'Well, Hercules, I'm not sure if that's such a good idea.'

I get it. He does have a wife – that's probably it. I lower my head sadly.

'Aw, come on, don't be sad. I would love nothing better than to come with you, but your mistress told me unequivocally that she doesn't want to go out with me any more. Believe me, women don't like you going against that.'

So there isn't another woman? This is just a tactic? I'm a bit confused, but I decide not to be thrown off course. It's obvious that Marc is still interested in Caroline, and that should be enough for me to go on. Maybe there's a good explanation for everything.

'I have a much better idea. But in order for it to work, you have to be quite honest with me. Do you remember when I examined you recently after your seizure?'

How could I forget that? I try to nod again.

'Very good. Frankly, I had the impression back then that you were in perfect health. Is it conceivable that this seizure was an expression of your enormous theatrical talent?'

I've been found out. How embarrassing.

'Papa, now you've lost me altogether.'

'Hold on a second, Luisa. So, Hercules, come on: do the seizure!'

Huh? Is that a command?

'Do the seizure – get going!'

Fine; I'll do what he says. Here goes. I turn onto my left side, and start to twitch with my front and back paws at the same time. I writhe around, foam at the mouth, howl – all the while making sure I don't fall off the examination table. I think it's a pretty impressive performance. Luisa's eyes are even wider than before, and Marc is grinning.

'Holy Toledo! Our dachshund is a world-class actor. I knew it. OK, good dog! You can stop.'

I lie there quietly, and Luisa rubs my belly.

'That was like in the circus, Papa!'

'Right.'

'And what happens now?'

'Now dear Hercules should go home, and there, Hercules, you will perform this lovely seizure once again for your mistress. It would surprise me if she didn't react by phoning me, and then I'll show up like a knight in shining armour. Got it?'

Got it! A fabulous plan. You'd think Mr Beck and I had come up with it. I jump up again and give a short bark. Then Marc lifts me down from the table and takes me outside.

'So you know what you have to do. I'll be waiting for Caroline's call!'

•

I writhe in terrible spasms. This has to be my performance of a lifetime. As soon as Daniel left today, I threw myself directly in front of Caroline's feet right in the workshop. She seems to have believed that I was having a seizure, and she went quite pale with fear. I hope she reacts the way Marc predicted.

Sure enough – she's getting the telephone!

'This is Ms Neumann. May I speak to Dr Wagner? Thank

you.' She waits for a short while. 'Hi, Marc, it's Caroline. I'm sorry to bother you, but Hercules just had another really terrible seizure. Much worse than the last time. Yes? You'll come by right away? Thanks so much; that's really nice of you. We're in the workshop.'

Mission accomplished! So now I can start letting my seizure die down. I was getting a little tired of this act. I'm lying quietly on my back and playing the role of a very weary dog. Caroline sits next to me on the floor and strokes me.

'Poor Hercules. I feel so sorry for you. But Dr Wagner will be here any minute now, and then everything will be all right. You can be sure of that.'

Shortly afterwards, the doorbell rings. Marc must have dashed off immediately. He comes in and puts his medical bag down next to me. Then he examines me exactly the same way he did last time, saying *hmm, hmm* every once in a while, and then sits down next to Caroline.

'Well, I can no longer rule out the possibility of epilepsy, so I would make the following suggestion: tomorrow morning I have to go to Eschersbach Castle anyway, so how would you feel about my picking up both of you then and we'll go out there together? Once we're there, we can find out whether Hercules is really a member of the von Eschersbach family and whether this could be hereditary epilepsy.'

'Yes,' Caroline says in a soft voice, 'that sounds like a very good idea. I would like to come with you. Thanks so much.'

Eschersbach Castle? With Caroline and Marc? Sensational!

I'd love to jump for joy, but I decide not to. That wouldn't go along with my supposed exhaustion.

•

The sky is bright blue, exactly the way it has to be on such an important day. And this day is important – no doubt about that. I will see Eschersbach Castle and my family again. And if Marc's plan works out, there's still a chance for him and Caroline. I didn't understand the finer points of his scheme, but for the moment I'll rely on his having thought them through quite well. How did Mr Beck put it? A guy who needs a dog to win over a woman's heart is going to have a hard time of it ... so I will stay out of this now.

I wait impatiently for Marc to finally get here. Caroline seems to be nervous as well. She keeps looking at her watch. Then there is a knock on the window of the terrace door. It's Marc – and he's brought along Luisa.

Caroline opens the door.

'Hello! So, are you ready for our little outing?'

'Hello. Yes, I'm ready.' She looks at Luisa. Marc follows her gaze.

'I've brought someone with me today whom I'd like to introduce to you. This is Luisa, my daughter. Luisa, this is Caroline.'

I wonder if that was such a good idea. Female dachshunds certainly don't take well to others' offspring. I hope things are different with humans. One look at Caroline's face tells me that there are similar areas of tension in the world of humans.

'Your daughter? I don't quite understand…'

'I was once married. Luisa is my daughter. She usually lives with Sabine, her mother. But school's broken up, and Luisa always spends her summer holidays with me.' He takes a deep breath. He must have something quite significant left to say. 'Since you're both so important to me, I wanted the two of you to meet.'

'You have a daughter.' Caroline says it again as though she hasn't really grasped the fact.

'Yes, and a fantastic one at that.'

Luisa extends her hand to Caroline. 'Hello!'

Now Caroline is smiling. That's a pretty big load off my mind.

'Hi, Luisa. It's nice to meet you.'

'Can I go into the garden? I saw a swing there.'

'Of course you can.'

Once Luisa has left, the two of them stand there in silence. Then Marc clears his throat.

'Luisa is with me as often as possible. I don't want to be a weekend dad. I never wanted to. It's important that she suffers as little as possible from this break-up. Sabine and I are now thinking about having Luisa move in with me permanently soon. Sabine is an air stewardess and wants to step up her work schedule. I have to say I'm delighted at the prospect. It'll be more stressful, but I would like to share my child's everyday life. Children grow up so fast, and then the time is over, never to return.'

'Is that why you had the row with Nina – because she told you how annoying she finds children?'

Marc nods. 'That's one reason, but not the only one. By the time we went out on that second occasion, I had already realized that there was no real spark between us. But the scene she made at the beach was pretty outrageous. I hadn't told her about Luisa then, but I was actually about to. Well, you know the story. Children are very important to me, and it was clear to me right away that that made no sense.'

'Yes, I understand why that hit you so hard.'

'When you told me that you didn't want to see me any more, I wanted to tell you the whole story from my perspective, but you sounded so determined. Also, I didn't want to say anything nasty about your best friend.'

Caroline reaches for his hand and squeezes it. 'I'm glad you came. When I think about how I acted, I'm really annoyed with myself, because actually I quite enjoy being with you.'

Marc smiles. 'Well, then, there's a silver lining in the cloud of Hercules's ill health.' He gives me a wink.

'While we're on the subject of health, do you think it'll be a problem for Hercules to go there again? I mean, these people *did* take him to the animal shelter.'

'No, quite the opposite. He will now be able to make a grand entrance.'

'Is that so?'

'Well, after all, he may soon become the veterinarian's very own dog.'

Caroline looks at him. 'You think so?'

'Yes, perhaps.' He hesitates for a second. 'What am I saying?

I'm absolutely certain.'

Then he pulls Caroline close to him and kisses her gently on the nose. At this moment, Luisa comes back from the garden.

'Oh, Papa! You are so embarrassing!'

Marc lets go of Caroline. 'No I'm not – I'm in love!'

Caroline stands on tiptoe and whispers something in his ear. But my outstanding hearing makes it possible for me to catch what she's telling him: 'Me too.'

I poke my head out of the car window and let my ears blow in the wind. Today is a truly outstanding day. Carl-Leopold von Eschersbach can now return to Eschersbach Castle. Then I look deep within myself and change my mind. In fact, it's just the other way round: Hercules Neumann is honouring Eschersbach Castle with his visit. How delightful!

acknowledgements

Thanks to:

Bernd, Wiebke, Flora, Iris, Steffi, Sanne, Dagmar,
Bettina and Anja.
Schellong Osann Violin Makers in Hamburg.
And, of course, to Alex and Fiete.

More thanks to:

Shelley, for making Hercules bark English.
Sarah and Anthony, for giving Hercules a new kennel.
And Laura, for making him feel at home in the UK.